Target: NIMITZ

A novel by
Gary Carter

BookLocker

Published by BookLocker.com, Inc., St. Petersburg, Florida.

Printed on acid-free paper.

This is a work of fiction set in northern Virginia, Washington, D.C., and the Persian Gulf. The characters are a product of the author's imagination and do not represent any former or current persons. I have used actual ships, aircraft, and locations to add realism to the story. Historical events and related data are included to provide background and context.

BookLocker.com, Inc.
2019

First Edition

Library of Congress Cataloging in Publication Data
Carter, Gary
Target: NIMITZ by Gary Carter
FICTION / Thrillers / Military | FICTION / War & Military |
FICTION / Thrillers / Political
Library of Congress Control Number: 2019937215

Dedication

To my wife Debbie, for her love and support.

"It is natural that we always conduct training, drills, and exercises for confrontation with the operational goals we have, and the Americans and the entire world knows that one of the IRGC Navy's operational goals is to destroy America's Navy."

Islamic Revolutionary Guard Corps
Navy Commander
Rear Admiral Ali Fadavi

List of Characters

In Washington, D.C.

-Francis J. Warren, assistant to the Assistant Secretary of Defense for Readiness; Captain, U.S. Navy (ret); former commanding officer, S-3A squadron; former airline pilot; wife: Mary

-Rear Admiral Joseph Donaldson, U.S. Navy; N98, Navy Department, Pentagon; "Joe 2-star"; "Shooter"; wife: Karen

-Sharon Fleming, Assistant Secretary of Defense for International Security Affairs; husband: Ronald Fleming, Congressman, 12th District, Ohio

-William Stimson, staff member, House Armed Services Committee; Captain, U.S. Navy (ret); "Will Call"; former commanding officer, F/A-18 squadron

-Anthony Darnell, CIA analyst; friend of Will Stimson; Colonel, U.S. Army Reserves (ret); former Special Forces officer

-Edward Michael Sheppard, President of the United States

-Edward S. Scott, Under Secretary of Defense (Personnel and Readiness)

-Martha Wheatley, Secretary of State

-Lawfton Collier, Secretary of Defense

-Rand (Randal) Powers, Director of National Intelligence

-Grayson Harvey, Director, Central Intelligence Agency

-Lieutenant General Walter V. Townsend, U.S. Army; Director, Joint Staff, Joint Chiefs of Staff

-Darren Ballinger, National Security Council staff member

-Peter Sanders, President Sheppard's Chief of Staff

-Tom Worthington, Principal Deputy Under Secretary of Defense (Policy); Sharon Fleming's immediate supervisor

-Denisha (Denise) Emerson, staff assistant to Frank Warren; born Naghmeh Mitra Zargari

-Emmett Jensen, security guard, CIA Headquarters

In the Middle East
-Ayatollah Hamid Javad Ghorbani, Supreme Leader of the Islamic Republic of Iran

-Marzban Pedram Mazdaki, President of the Islamic Republic of Iran

-Amin Sasani, Secretary of the Supreme National Security Council

-Major General Ramin Basir Mokri, Chief of the Armed Forces General Staff

-Rear Admiral Bijan Hashemi, Islamic Revolutionary Guard Corps Navy Commander

-Achmed Farhad Ahmadi, Iranian arms dealer; bother of Ali Ahmadi

-Ali Karim Ahmadi, brother of Achmed; employed by the Port Authority of Bandar Abbas, Iran

-Michael and Shannon Wheeler, "legend" names of undercover CIA operatives

-Lieutenant Susan B. Anderson, U.S. Navy; "Tony"; Officer in Charge, USS *Bunker Hill* (CG-52) motor whaleboat

-Farzin Hassan, Officer in Charge, Iranian small boat

-Arman Kazem, Iranian small boat crewmember

On the USS Nimitz (CVN-68)
-Captain Charles S. Hathaway, U.S. Navy, Commanding Officer, USS *Nimitz* (CVN-68)

-Commander Josh Stoner, U.S. Navy, *Nimitz* Navigator

-Lieutenant Commander Alton "Husker" Cobb, F/A-18 Flight Lead

-Lieutenant Pete "Preacher" Johnson, F/A-18 pilot

-Lieutenant Jared "Swamp" Marsh, F/A-18 pilot

-Lieutenant Michael "Hoss" Cartwright, F/A-18 pilot and squadron duty officer

In Diego Garcia
-Major Wesley Barnes, U.S. Air Force, B-52 aircraft commander

-Captain William Robert Washington, III, U.S. Air Force, B-52 co-pilot; "Buff 1"

Others
-General Karl W. Alexander, U.S. Army; Commander, U.S. Central Command

-Lieutenant Robert "Stogie" Hickman, U.S. Navy; Radm Donaldson's former radar intercept officer; wife: Karen

-Thomas Middleton, Delta Air Lines Captain

<u>Glossary</u>

AFB-Air Force Base
AfCent-U.S. Air Forces, Central Command
AK-47-7.62x39mm assault rifle, developed by Russian Mikhail Kalashnikov
ASCM-Anti-ship cruise missile
ASD-Assistant Secretary of Defense
AWACS-Airborne Warning and Control System

BUFF-Big, Ugly, Fat, Fellow (or other choice word). B-52 Stratofortress

CarGru-Carrier group
CDCM-Coastal Defense Cruise Missile
CentCom-Central Command
CIA-Central Intelligence Agency
CIWS-Close-in weapons system (R2D2)
CJCS-Chairman, Joint Chiefs of Staff
ComFifthFlt-Commander, Fifth Fleet
CNO-Chief of Naval Operations
CO-Commanding Officer
C2BM-Command and control battle management
Combat plot-The tactical picture maintained in a ship's combat information center
CoTac-Co-pilot/tactical coordinator, S-3 Viking naval flight officer crewmember

DCI-Director, Central Intelligence
DIW-Dead in the water
DoD-Department of Defense
DNI-Director of National Intelligence

DSP-U.S. Defense Support Program
D-GAR-Diego Garcia, British Indian Ocean Territory
EOOW-Engineering Officer of the Watch
EEOB-Eisenhower Executive Office Building

GCC-Gulf Cooperation Council
GDP-Gross Domestic Product
GMT-Greenwich Mean Time
GPS-Global Positioning System

ICAF-Industrial College of the Armed Forces
ICCS-Integrated Catapult Control Station
I-HAWK-Improved Homing All the Way Killer
IMINT-Imagery intelligence
IOC-Initial Operating Capability
IQD-Iraqi dinar
IRGCN-Iranian Revolutionary Guard Corps Navy
ISA-International Security Affairs
ISR-Intelligence, Surveillance, and Reconnaissance

JO-Junior officer
JSTARS-Joint Surveillance and Target Attack Radar System

LOS-Line of Sight
LRE-Launch and Recovery Element (RQ-4 Global Hawk)
LSO-Landing Signal Officer

Mach-Mach number, an aircraft's speed through the air divided by the speed of sound
MCE-Mission Control Element (RQ-4 Global Hawk)
MTI-Moving Target Indicator (RQ-4 Global Hawk)
NATO-North Atlantic Treaty Organization

NATOPS-Naval Air Training and Operating Procedures Standardization
NavCent-U.S. Naval Forces, Central Command; Commander, Fifth Fleet
NDU-National Defense University
NFO-Naval Flight Officer
NOBLE PROPHET-Iranian naval exercise
NSC-National Security Council

OEOB-Old Executive Office Building
OIC-Officer in Charge
OPEC-Organization of Petroleum Exporting Countries
OSD-Office of the Secretary of Defense

PCL-Pocket Check List
PDB-President's Daily Brief or President's Daily Briefing
PDUSD(P)-Principle Deputy Under Secretary of Defense for Policy

RPG-Rocket Propelled Grenade

SAM-Surface to Air Missile
SAR-Search and Rescue
SCRAM-The sudden shutting down of a nuclear reactor, usually by the rapid insertion or fall of control rods, either automatically or manually. Also known as a "reactor trip."
SEALs-Sea, Air and Land teams, the Navy's primary special operations force
SecDef-Secretary of Defense
SES-Senior Executive Service
SIGINT-Signals Intelligence
SNSC-Supreme National Security Council

Trap-Aircraft carrier arrested landing

UAE-United Arab Emirates
UAV-Unmanned Aerial Vehicle
UHF-Ultra High Frequency
USD(P)-Under Secretary of Defense for Policy
USPaCom-U.S. Pacific Command
UTC-Universal Time Coordinated

VHF-Very High Frequency
VSI-Vertical Speed Indicator

XO-Executive Officer

Arabic Expressions

As-Salaam Alaikum "Peace be unto you"

Insha'Allah "If Allah wills it"; "God willing"; "if God's will"

Masha 'Allah "God has willed" or "as God willing"; expresses joy, praise, or thankfulness for an event or person that was just mentioned.

Ma'a as-salaama "Goodbye"

PROLOGUE

Accept the things to which fate binds you,
and love the people with whom fate brings
you together, but do so with all your heart.
                              -Marcus Aurelius

Spring, 2006

Tehran, Iran

The meeting took place in the House of Leadership, where the Supreme Leader of the Islamic Republic of Iran conducted state business. Ten people—all men—gathered around a well-worn wooden table in a tastefully appointed room. Four men to a side, one at each end, facing each other. Some smoked, some sipped tea; all wore beards, many tinged with touches of gray as was the hair of those who didn't wear a turban. The group comprised the Supreme Council for National Security (SCNS)[1], Iran's highest national security body, charged with preserving the Islamic Revolution, territorial integrity, and the national sovereignty of Iran. Outside, a cold, rainy spring day enveloped Tehran's roughly nine million people, practically all unaware of the meeting. Inside, Iran's senior leadership enjoyed comfortable, well-lighted comfort.

Ayatollah Hamid Javad Ghorbani, Iran's Supreme Leader, sat at one end of the table and presided over the meeting. Selected by Iran's 88-seat Assembly of Experts[2] to be the Supreme Leader, he faced the other nine men, five of whom he appointed to this prestigious body. One of those appointees was Amin Sasani, secretary of the SCNS, a close confidant of the Supreme Leader. Marzban Pedram Mazdaki, the elected president of the Islamic Republic of Iran, sat opposite Ghorbani. The members of the SCNS gave the Supreme Leader their full attention as he spoke.

"I am tired of the Islamic Republic of Iran being the depository of the ceaseless sewage of ridicule and condemnation flowing from the mouth of our perpetual tormentor," claimed the Ayatollah.

All nine members around the table mumbled affirming views and energetically nodded their heads in support of the Supreme Leader's statement.

President Mazdaki spoke above the din of voices. "Supreme Leader, do you have some action in mind we might take against the incessant scourging from the West?"

Mazdaki's stock had started to rise in the minds of many Iranians when he addressed the United Nations—twice within a year's timeframe. He was held in high regard by many; no one's opinion of his standing and importance, however, exceeded his own. The discussions subsided as all heads turned toward the Ayatollah, who spoke slowly in a grave tone, conveying the seriousness of the moment. "I want to strike the imperial aggressors and make them bleed from their filthy nostrils. I want to blacken their eyes, scar their faces, and make them wince in pain and embarrassment. Our actions must be bold, swift, and severe, minimizing our exposure while maximizing our impact, and causing great discomfort, conflict, and confusion among the infidel's evil forces. We must show the imperialists, and the world, we will not be manipulated, threatened, or coerced by other nations, no matter their might. The will of our people and of our great country is undeniable and unyielding. It is time for direct, forceful action.

"Let me hear your thoughts about how to accomplish this righteous objective."

The group erupted into a cacophony of voices, each member convinced of the invincibility and superiority of his plan or idea. This greatly pleased Ghorbani, who, as the commander in chief of the armed forces, was the sole individual within the Islamic Republic of Iran who could declare war or peace, and who served as the final approval authority for all military plans and operations. By addressing his SCNS, he empowered each of them by appearing to solicit their suggestions of possible courses of actions. It was an effective leadership tactic, to be sure, but an unnecessary one. He had a plan in mind. Now he subtly herded his advisors toward his solution, so they would ultimately feel ownership in a plan they thought to have conceived themselves.

After nearly ninety minutes of spirited debate, the SCNS settled on enhanced "swarming" tactics by the Iranian navy, maneuvers previously practiced on a smaller scale. This was Ghorbani's desired concept all along. The Supreme Leader ordered his chief of the Armed Forces General Staff, Major General Ramin Basir Mokri, to be in overall charge of executing the plan, and appointed Rear Admiral Bijan Hashemi, the Islamic Revolutionary Guard Corps Navy commander, based in Bandar Abbas, as the officer in tactical command.

Ayatollah Ghorbani issued one specific order to the SCNS. "The primary target of the operation must be the zealot's aircraft carrier *Nimitz*. The infidels launched their helicopters from the *Nimitz*, which landed on *our* soil, during their pitiful rescue attempt of American embassy spies[3] after the November Revolution. Their pathetic plan ended in flames; the burnt and rusted carcasses of their helicopters and planes remain a potent reminder to us all of the depths of depravity the Zionist-loving people will stoop to in their continual attempts to denigrate and vilify our country and our people. Discover when *Nimitz* will next be in our waters and plan accordingly."

Major General Mokri stood and replied, "It will be as you say, Supreme Leader, *Insha'Allah*" (God willing). Rear Admiral Hashemi nodded grimly in agreement.

*****

Washington, D.C., United States

"Good morning, Sharon." U.S. Navy Rear Admiral Joseph Donaldson greeted Sharon Fleming, his former war college colleague, as they approached one another, coffees in hand, in one of the numerous corridors of the defense department's main headquarters, the Pentagon.

"Hey, Joe, good morning. How're things going this morning?"

Rear Admiral Donaldson oversaw the apportioning of naval aviation's slice of the annual budgetary pie, which included the development of the navy's latest fighter aircraft, the F-35. Sharon Fleming worked in the secretary of defense's policy division. The two first met years earlier at a White House social function when Joe Donaldson was a senior lieutenant and Sharon Fleming's husband, Ronald, was a freshman congressman from Ohio. Their careers later crossed paths again while students at the National Defense University, a military war college located at Fort McNair in Washington, D.C. Now both had jobs in the Pentagon.

"As usual, I suppose. I need more money, everyone wants more money, and there isn't more money. There's hardly enough money for day-to-day flight operations in the fleet. The development of the F-35 Lightning has become a proverbial and perpetual sucking chest wound which we treat with costly band aids instead of the major surgery the program requires. Other than that, not much is happening. What's up in your world?"

"Besides all the issues in Iraq," Sharon replied, "Iran is making noise again; the dust never seems to settle over there." Sharon moved a little closer and lowered her voice, nearly whispering, suggesting the following words were sensitive, perhaps even classified. "I read today about a major Iranian naval exercise being planned; it's uncertain when it'll happen. Sources suggest that every seaworthy Iranian vessel based in Bandar Abbas will be ordered to get under way—simultaneously. Every unit will target their favorite whipping boy, the bastards of the West—us. I think we're mutual pains in each other's rear end; not sure who has the edge in that comparison."

"So, ops normal in your world, just like mine. You know the Iranians: always up to something. Well, I have a meeting I'm almost late for. Nice to see you again, Sharon. See ya around the fort."

"Take care, Joe. Keep that aviation checkbook balanced." They smiled at each other with a slight shaking of their heads as they went their separate ways.

*****

In the air near Reagan National Airport, Washington, D.C.

The day's flying route was Atlanta to Washington Reagan, back to Atlanta, then to Los Angeles (LAX). It was like any other day in the cockpit. But as we know, how we play life's cards determines our fate, our future.

"Delta Seven One Four, Potomac Approach, turn right, heading one one five, maintain 3,000 feet and report the river in sight." The air traffic controller's voice came in clearly through the pilots' headphones.

Delta Air Lines Captain Thomas Middleton could see the Potomac River out his left side window and straight ahead as his co-pilot, First Officer Francis J. Warren, complying with the directive from Air Traffic Control, slowly turned the 757 to a 115-degree magnetic heading and descended through 3,500 feet toward the assigned altitude of 3,000 feet. It was a perfect flying day: sharp spring skies, light winds at Reagan National out of the south at seven knots, a temperature of 65 degrees. The outlines of the busy airport were visible through the right-side window as an aircraft approached on short final for runway one nine.

Twenty-five miles to the west lay Washington Dulles Airport, the area's primary international arrival and departure location. Some thirty miles north BWI, Baltimore-Washington International Thurgood Marshall Airport, also handled long-haul flights in addition to U.S. traffic. Reagan National was designed for, and catered to, domestic air travel. With its closeness to the capital, it was the ideal destination airport for everyone connected to the government. Delta knew this and, like all other airlines serving DCA, charged higher fares on flights into and out of this convenient location.

Frank Warren was flying this leg of the trip. A former navy pilot, he had spent a career on active duty—25 years—before retiring at age 47. After flying for a regional airline based at Dulles and working as a flight instructor in off-hours, Delta had hired him a few months before his 49th birthday, giving him 11 years to fly before the mandatory retirement age for airline pilots of 60 years old.[4]

Frank glanced at his captain when Approach Control called and gave him an affirmative head nod and a thumb's up indicating he had the river in sight. Both pilots had visually acquired the Potomac River. Captain Middleton keyed his mic: "Delta Seven One Four has the river in sight," performing one of his pilot monitoring duties, while his co-pilot was controlling the aircraft.

Frank leveled off at 3,000 feet, 180 knots, flaps at 5, heading 115 degrees. He felt one with his airplane, his hands moving on their own as he made small, minute changes to the throttles and control yoke. Pressure flying, Frank used to tell his Cessna 152 students, involved scanning the instruments, listening to the airplane, thinking the corrections you want to make, and with tiny amounts of pressure you'd achieve the desired result.

"TRAFFIC, TRAFFIC." The unexpected voice from the TCAS (Traffic Alert and Collision Avoidance System) interrupted the tranquil atmosphere of the cockpit, alerting both pilots to search for the unknown aircraft that had entered a system-generated conflict area in front of the 757. The advisory alert required no action by the crew and produced a small, moving amber circle on each pilot's VSI (vertical speed indicator) and the radar display. Referencing the relative position of the airborne contact, they scanned outside, searching for the other airplane. Even in the pristine weather, neither pilot could locate it.

"CLIMB, CLIMB!" The TCAS commanded immediate evasive action, without coordinating with the controller, to ensure safe separation between the two aircraft. A red, square traffic symbol replaced the small, amber circle on their displays. Frank immediately added power and climbed, the two powerful Pratt and Whitney engines instantly responding. He referenced his VSI where a TCAS-generated green arc was displayed, depicting the required rate of climb necessary for avoidance with the other aircraft. He kept his climb rate in the green and adjusted his power to maintain a safe flying speed. The two planes' transponders were "talking" to each other, instructing their pilots to take different actions which would result in increased altitude separation between the two aircraft—

provided both pilots responded as directed. Apparently, only one of them did.

"DESCEND, DESCEND NOW!" For the first time in his career—either in an airplane or the simulator—Frank heard the TCAS change its mind and command an opposite action. The green arc on his VSI relocated to the descent area. Frank reduced power and firmly "pressured" the yoke forward, causing the cockpit crew and 180 passengers to rise against their seatbelts. The big Boeing's nose eased below the horizon as the VSI needle swung to a descent indication.

Captain Middleton transmitted, "Delta Seven One Four is complying with Resolution Advisory commands."

Approach Control responded, "Roger, Delta, we had a pop-up target for a moment in your general vicinity, and it went away. Did you get a visual on the guy?"

With Frank shaking his head "no," the captain replied, "No, sir, we never saw him."

"Roger that, Delta. Well, we show you clear of all traffic, and you're now cleared for the River Visual approach to runway one nine. Keep your speed at 180 knots or greater until 5 miles from the airport due to following traffic. You can contact the tower now—good day."

Captain Middleton replied, "Delta Seven One Four, roger, cleared for the River Visual, switching to tower—good day." He flipped the switch to the tower frequency and put ground control in the standby window. On the other radio, he selected Delta's Reagan Operations frequency which they would use to confirm their gate assignment once on the ground.

Frank banked the airplane to the right and flew toward the David Taylor Research Lab located just east of the Potomac River, about ten miles northwest of the airport, an oft-used landmark for commencing the River Visual. He called for flaps 15, both pilots confirming the selection by viewing the flap indicator needles.

Captain Middleton announced, "Frank, I'll be off the radios for a moment to talk to the passengers." Frank nodded, as his captain selected the aircraft's cabin announcing system. Middleton calmly reviewed the preceding incident and the reasons for the maneuvers, stressing that passenger safety was never in question. This was, for the most part, true.

The River Visual to runway 19 at DCA offers passengers some magnificent views of the DC area, especially for those seated on the left side of the aircraft. Today's perfect weather made for excellent sight-seeing. Frank snaked his way down the Potomac River toward Reagan National, monitoring his descent rate, airspeed, distance from the airport, and alignment over the river. To veer a little left toward the Lincoln Memorial and the National Mall, in the direction of the White House, would bring a number of unfriendly voices on the radio. Nothing good can come from being a little left or east of the river. It makes too many people uneasy since 9/11. But nothing bad happens if you cheat a little right, to the west, as you fly south down the river. Frank's approach briefing noted he preferred the right side of the Potomac so the captain, in the left seat, could almost see the western side of the river.

Frank dirtied up (extended the landing gear and flaps) at six miles and began slowing from 180 knots to approach speed at five miles. He called for the landing checklist and maneuvered for landing on one nine. Reagan Tower cleared Delta 714 to land as the gleaming jet flew over folks playing soccer at Gravelly Point, located immediately north of the airport.

The 01/19 runway at DCA is only 6,800 feet long (the shortest runway at Dulles measures 9,400 feet). The target landing spot is 1,000 feet down the runway, leaving 5,800 feet of runway for the 757 to land and stop comfortably.

Frank landed the plane with a thump, put the engines into reverse thrust, and gradually applied the brakes. Captain Middleton took over, using the tiller (connected to the nosewheel) to steer the plane onto the yellow taxi line. First Officer duties after a landing are always the same: clean up the aircraft (retract the spoilers and flaps), handle radio communications, silently complete the after-landing checklist, but verbally announce its completion, and monitor the aircraft's movements.

At Gate 19, Captain Middleton stated, "Let 'em up, shut 'em down."

Frank turned off the fasten seatbelt sign, then moved each engine's fuel control switch to the "cutoff" position, positively stopping all fuel from getting to the engines.

The two pilots completed the shutdown checklist, and before they removed their headsets, Reagan Ground Control called. "Delta Seven One Four, are you still on frequency?"

Frank exchanged a surprised glance with his captain and replied, "Delta Seven One Four is here."

Ground Control continued, "Ah, Seven One Four, I wanted to let you know the intruder aircraft that caused your TCAS to activate is now on the ground at Leesburg. The pilot is currently engaged in a conversation with the FAA and the Secret Service. F-16 interceptors launched out of Andrews Air Force Base and escorted the twin aircraft to Leesburg. Just wanted to let you know."

Frank acknowledged, "Thank you, Ground, we appreciate the follow-up. Delta out."

The pilots removed their headsets and unbuckled their seatbelts and shoulder harnesses. They sat, motionless, reflecting on the past few minutes, each knowing that the area surrounding the nation's capital is the most highly controlled and regulated airspace in the United States; it nearly takes a note from the Pope for a private pilot to get clearance to fly there.

Captain Middleton looked at his FO and asked, "You ever see him?"

"Nope—never did."

"Me, neither."

"Oh, well ..."

Middleton added, "Well, excellent maneuvering, Frank." Grinning, he continued, "Now let's see if you made anyone sick!"

Frank stood near the aircraft's open exit door, thanking the deplaning passengers for flying with Delta and apologizing for the Six Flags experience. Captain Middleton's stomach was growling, so he scooted up the jetway toward the food court, through a sea of humanity, and past passengers lining up to board their flight to Atlanta, the crews' next leg.

This flight to Atlanta would be followed by their last leg back to LAX and the completion of their four-day trip. In Atlanta, their schedule called for a three-hour "rest and recovery" period before launching for LAX. Most pilots would prefer to keep going, particularly on the last day of a rotation. Such was not the case for this Delta crew.

First Officer Warren thanked the last departing passenger for choosing to fly Delta and received a compliment on his landing—both passenger and pilot cordially smiled at each other, each knowing full well the landing had not qualified for any positive comment. Frank completed the external walk-around inspection of the aircraft for the flight to Atlanta, then strolled up the jetway toward the gate area. A Delta gate agent opened the door to the jetway and asked him if she could commence boarding for the Atlanta flight. Frank knew the cabin cleaners were still readying the aircraft, so he replied, "I'll take the flight plan and see if the flight attendants are ready for boarding." Frank and the gate agent stepped toward the counter where she retrieved the flight plan to Atlanta. She handed the papers to Frank and, with an on-time departure foremost in her mind, asked him to *please* let her know when boarding could commence. He said he'd be right back after verifying the cabin status. The whole event took less than 30 seconds. That was long enough.

In line, waiting to board the flight to Atlanta, was a tall, lean gentleman—nicely attired, unassuming, computer bag slung over one shoulder, carry-on roller bag next to him. His hair was slightly thinning and graying—like Frank's. Quiet and reserved, his face broke into an ever-widening grin as he chuckled to himself. Mr. William Stimson, known as Will to his friends and "Will Call" to his former navy buddies, caught a brief glimpse of his former close friend and fellow commanding officer (CO). Will Call was Captain William Stimson, U.S. Navy (retired), now working on Capitol Hill in his second career as a member of the House Armed Services Committee permanent staff. Will Call loved the political environment and thrived in the energetic atmosphere that surrounded the legislative branch of government.

Years before, he and Frank Warren served as CO's in the same air wing and developed a deep, abiding friendship. While not unheard of, and certainly not unique, friendships between F/A-18 Hornet drivers and S-3 Viking pilots weren't all that common. Tactically the two aircraft had vastly dissimilar roles and missions; certainly, the "lawn dart," the F/A-18, was the far more prestigious and, in the minds of many, more career enhancing. There was, however, that one common bond: the F/A-18 burned a lot of gas on its missions, relative to the fuel-efficient S-3, which also served as an airborne tanker. The Vikings usually had lots of fuel to give to their thirsty Hornet brethren, and that link sometimes acted as a common thread between the two communities. Throughout their 15-month command tours, served nearly simultaneously, Frank and Will Call established an informal, friendly association which now, after many years, consisted mainly of annual Christmas cards. *But that may change*, thought Will Call Stimson, *that may change.*

After an uneventful flight to Atlanta, Will Stimson shuffled up the single-aisle of the parked 757, nodded at Captain Middleton and said: "Nice flight, Captain, thanks for the ride." The captain thanked him, and Will Call asked, "Your FO still around?"

Tom Middleton turned toward the flight deck and saw Frank getting their rollerboards out of the cockpit. "Yeah, he's right there. You know Frank?"

"He's a former navy buddy—we were CO's together in Air Wing 11. Mind if I say hello?"

Captain Tom Middleton, who, over the years, learned much about military friendships established by those who had served on active duty, stepped aside to allow Will to get by and greet his former fellow commanding officer. Frank instantly recognized his navy friend and greeted him with a strong handshake and admiring eyes. As cabin cleaners scurried around them, the two former naval officers gathered their bags and proceeded up the jetway, exchanging pleasantries about kids, grandkids, work, their wives, and the current political environment. Will asked Frank how long he had before his next flight; then he asked if there was some place quiet where they could talk privately. They walked a few minutes in the concourse and found some seats at an empty gate.

After getting settled, Will looked Frank in the eye and said, "There's an opening in the Personnel and Readiness directorate at the Pentagon and they're—quietly—soliciting names of candidates to fill it. When I saw you today at Reagan, I thought you'd be perfect for the job. I'd like to get your name in the mix—see what shakes out—see who your competition is. I know a lot of people at DoD, Frank; I could call in a few markers if needed. But I probably wouldn't have to. I know who your immediate boss would be and the folks up the chain of command to SecDef (the Secretary of Defense). It would be a good entry-level job for someone with your experience, and there's obvious upside potential. So, my friend, what are your immediate thoughts?!"

Frank looked out the window, collecting his thoughts, as people do when they get surprising news. The implications of Will's comments were profound. Still processing, he replied, "Will, thank you for thinking of me, but I have a job—a damn good job—one that is highly competitive to get and tremendously satisfying. It pays well, has excellent benefits, I work with great people, and I'm getting paid to do the very thing I like to do: fly airplanes. I get to operate well-maintained aircraft and I'm with a well-established company that is competitive in the marketplace; I'm in a good place."

Will courteously listened to his friend's argument but held firm. "Let me e-mail you everything I know about the job—duties, responsibilities, who you would work for and who would work for you. I'll provide a detailed chain of command up to SecDef with background material on each individual; bios of the staff, folks you'd be working with and anything else I can think of. You and Mary can review the material and talk things over. By the way, don't your in-laws live west of DC? That'd be nice, particularly for Mary. You'll have it all on your computer before you land at LAX. Look at the data, and let Mary read it, too; discuss the transition and changes involved, and then we'll talk again."

Will pressed on with his pitch as Frank continued to process what he was hearing. "I know this is a huge step to take, especially at this stage of your career—and life. Frank, I know you—I know the passion and the patriotism you have. My guess is you'd still be in the navy if they'd let you serve until you were 70 years old. We both left active duty about the same time and made our career choices. I know how great a job you have and that you're very good at it. But I also know this about you: you care—deeply—about your country. I know you inquired about coming back on active duty after 9/11—even said you'd serve at a lower rank if they'd take you back. I sense the call you heard to serve others still resides in your head; indeed, it's in your soul. When I saw you today, there was no decision to make regarding this discussion—you are the right person for the job. Done. Easy. So here I am. Look over the material—talk with Mary. And, so you don't feel pressured or anything, I'll need to hear from you inside of 48 hours! The train's moving kind of fast on this one!"

Frank was stunned but tried not to show it. How did Will know about his attempt to return to active duty following 9/11? His wife knew, of course—but no one else. Will knew?

"Will, thanks again for thinking of me for this incredible opportunity. I am truly honored—and amazed. So, here's what I'll do: I'll look over the information you send me, and I'll review it with Mary when I get back home. I'll let you know if I'm interested in throwing away a perfectly superb job and career in exchange for a lesser-paying, much more stressful, time-consuming job with longer work hours, more headaches, greater tension and little to no job security. To say nothing of the pure joy of getting to and from work every day in the DC area traffic!"

"And the opportunity to make a difference," Will added, "to inspire others—to work with similarly motivated individuals—and to answer the call to service that I know you hear."

"Yes, that, too," Frank admitted. "Hey, let's get our stuff and start heading toward your departure gate, which, conveniently, will take us past the food court, where I'll break off. Chick-fil-A awaits my arrival."

Off they went, back in the comfortable conversation of good friends, thoughts in alignment with each other, enjoying the kinship that previous service together brings. Following one more hearty handshake and a man-hug, they bid each other goodbye. Frank ordered the deluxe chicken sandwich and a chocolate chip cookie but didn't taste a thing as he thought about the opportunity just presented.

*****

After a trip Frank Warren used to face a two-hour southbound drive from LAX to San Diego on the 405 and 5 freeways to get home; now it was a one-hour flight to Sacramento followed by a 90-minute drive. Frank and Mary had moved to northern California and Frank willingly tolerated the inconveniences of the new commute to be near their grandchildren. At the end of his flying career when he walked out the door—out of the cockpit—for the last time, he and Mary would already be right where they wanted to be. That was the plan—until today.

On this occasion, the best option to Sacramento was a Southwest Airlines flight and Frank was now on the road, driving in darkness with the speaker activated on his cell phone. Mary Warren had read Will Call's e-mail and she knew a lengthy discussion was forthcoming. An essential element of their marriage was their ability to honestly talk things through, each firmly believing the other's ideas, plans, and desires were equally important as their own.

They talked during his drive home and continued their discussion late into the night. They listed on paper the pros and cons of another change of careers and assigned point values for each. Tallied up, the lopsided count favored staying right where they were, both with Frank's job and where they lived. But what number does one assign to a definite and persistent call of duty and service? He'd had it since grade school, when he read through some files located in the basement of his house that contained Coast Guard correspondence about his father's attempt to remain on active duty following the end of the Korean War. The Coast Guard was reducing its officer ranks following the war and his dad was let go—against his desires. Frank had wanted to fulfill his dad's desires. Now, Will Call Stimson presented him an opportunity to serve once again

34

when he'd always thought that once he left active duty, that was it, as had happened with his father. What would his dad think about this? Frank admitted he'd have stayed in the navy to at least 60 years of age (not 70, like Will Call had suggested) if he'd been allowed to serve that long. However, as an 0-6 (with no realistic chance at promotion to admiral), he was limited to 30 years of service, an up-or-out policy he understood and supported, but didn't like.

Mary knew her husband well and suggested he apply for the DoD position, to see if he was even competitive for the job. If selected for an interview, he could then make a more informed assessment of what the assignment offered—and demanded. The interview went well, and Frank accepted DoD's offer of employment, never knowing if Will Call had any influence in the selection process. With the decision made, it was all ahead flank as he and Mary returned to the Washington, D.C. area and the familiar environment they had previously known when Frank was on active duty.

Midway through their first January back east, Frank Warren, late on a Friday evening, told his wife he needed a few hours at work the next morning to tie up some loose ends. "This is a holiday weekend," she replied. "You're going in on Saturday?"

"Just this one Saturday, Mary," he assured her.

1

Written in Chinese, the word crisis, is composed of two characters. One represents danger and the other represents opportunity.
-John F. Kennedy

Saturday
January 13, 2007

The Washington cold always finds its way through the layers of clothing arranged to thwart its assault. Ohio native Frank Warren, softened by numerous San Diego winters, bristled in the early morning breeze, head bowed, gloved hands thrust deep into the pockets of his overcoat, trudging toward his bus stop over hardened snow in the shadowy glow of occasional streetlights. Perhaps it felt colder since it was a Saturday, a three-day holiday weekend (Dr. Martin Luther King, Jr.'s birthday was on Monday), and his presence at work was his own doing, a voluntary effort rather than his expected appearance on a normal work day.

There was an odd appeal to the prospect of uninterrupted work and quiet solitude, an atmosphere he expected this morning at the puzzle palace—the Pentagon. Mary had nodded knowingly when he'd informed her of his plans for this morning. She understood—and quietly admired—the ever-present determination to serve that drove, even possessed, her husband. Temperatures that would cause the Michelin Man to shiver and the possibility of a snowstorm were minor inconveniences that failed to deter his drive.

The darkness and raw, threatening conditions could dampen the spirits of the most ardent of government employees. Frank's current mood and perspective were similarly impacted, as his thoughts drifted to Hawaiian beaches on a January layover, ankles deep in the warm sand of gently swirling Pacific waves rather than cold, icy snow and toes quickly losing their sensation.

The usual routine was to bus to the Vienna Metro station and ride the train to the Pentagon. It could take 45-55 minutes to get to work, including a change at the Rosslyn station from the Orange line to the Blue line. Driving to work was a non-starter; far too many type-A personalities lived in this area, all trying to cover too many miles in too many cars. They say your commute defines your life and lifestyle in the Washington, D.C. area; whoever "they" are, they are correct. Frank thought the DC area would be a wonderful place to reside if one could live wherever one wanted. The problem, of course, was most people could easily exceed their financial means with each step closer to Capitol Hill; the closer "in" one lives, the higher the cost of real estate. Since one's commute is so important, a common first subject when introduced to someone is where you live, and how you get to work. You'd think this was classified information the way people harbored the details of their commute to work. They believe the word will get out and "their" route will get saturated with more cars. Once the word "Metro" gets mentioned, there's no threat to them, and they revert to normal, polite conversation. But you must get the commute thing settled first.

On this dark, cold, holiday Saturday, the usual commuters were at the Vienna station but in fewer numbers, which meant getting a seat should be no problem. All had the DC stare—a version of a zombie look—the government worker trudging off to the "salt mines." The look reflected the routine of going to and from their government job, of filling a role within the hierarchy of the massive government machine. It could be seen in everyone—from GS-5s and -7s (General Schedule, the predominant pay scale for federal employees) all the way through the SESers (Senior Executive Service, equivalent to a general or admiral) to the political appointees and even the elected officials on Capitol Hill. They stand on the station platform waiting for the Metro train to arrive; when it does, the doors open, and there's a great flourish of activity as all board and quickly scout out their favorite seat, which for Frank, is any seat. Then it's off to the next station where the process repeats itself. When you arrive at your destination or a change station like Rosslyn, you're a part of a mass movement as you head toward the next segment of your commuting experience. It's the same every day: keep up, move with the flow, stay to the right on the escalators, maintain your game face, and be ready at the ticket scanner. You will be the subject of universal ire and disdain if your card fails at the scanner and the barriers do not open. Everyone is in a hurry, and these are influential people who have prominent issues to resolve. Keep your commuter face on and physical mannerisms under control: the burdens of keeping our free, democratic society operating smoothly weighs on each and everyone. Cubicles await with emails, faxes, reports, to-do lists, all needing attention and resolution. Even on a Saturday, in January, on a three-day weekend.

WTOP is a Washington, D.C. area news and traffic talk radio station that usually ranks either number one or two among the most listened-to radio stations in the metro area. It competes with local easy listening stations but is the go-to station when traffic updates are a must. This morning, like most, Frank had his earbuds in and his iPod tuned to the station. The news updates included domestic and international events with traffic reports given every 10 minutes. Frank found that once at work, the traffic reports often provided a common topic of discussion with the staff and co-workers, easing the transition into the challenging issues of the day. Today, he pondered what the president faced each morning when he arrived at work, starting with the PDB, the President's Daily Briefing, prepared and personally delivered by the office of the Director of National Intelligence.[5] Talk about issues to consider! On the other hand, there's someone with a great commute.

Among the news stories that morning, one grabbed Frank's attention. He listened carefully:

> Reports from numerous sources indicate unusual activity by Iranian naval forces has been observed in the vicinity of the Strait of Hormuz in the Persian Gulf. Intelligence reports state several patrol boats and an Iranian submarine stationed at Bandar Abbas, on the southern coast of Iran, left early Friday morning, and are apparently headed to an area

west of the Strait. Additionally, the U.S. Navy's nuclear-powered aircraft carrier USS *Nimitz,* currently operating in the eastern portion of the Persian Gulf following a recent port visit to Jebel Ali in the United Arab Emirates, is scheduled to transit the Strait of Hormuz sometime today or tomorrow, according to a navy source at the Pentagon. We'll have more updates on this situation as events unfold. Now with traffic on the 8's, here's WTOP's Jamie Anderson with your morning commute.

Frank switched off the iPod to consider what he'd just heard. He wondered what SecDef and the chiefs (members of the Joint Chiefs of Staff) would think about this little development. As this thought crossed his mind, a familiar figure boarded the car.

Ah, yes—Joe 2-star. Frank had mixed feelings toward this naval officer, resplendent in his Navy Blues, adorned in his bridge coat with an admiral's gold shoulder boards, white scarf, admiral's hat situated squarely atop his perfectly groomed hair and shoes gleaming (most likely corfams; wipe them off with a moist cloth, and you're good to go). He possessed excellent posture, square shoulders, and that ever-present look of self-importance combined with natural grace and command. The whole package transmitted a clear message of ease and confidence with the problems and challenges of the world, which told everyone: you can relax—I'm here, I am in control, everything will be okay.

Rear Admiral Joseph Donaldson, United States Navy, former F-14 Tomcat squadron commanding officer, Air Wing 11 commander, and Battle Group commander. He was now the navy's director of air warfare, known in navy parlance as OPNAV N98, an unquestionably excellent job in the DC/Pentagon arena due to its important responsibilities and visibility. N98 bore responsibility for "resourcing the current vision for the future of naval aviation while also sustaining near-term readiness, modernizing the current aviation force while simultaneously advancing naval aviation's future capabilities" (per the navy's job description). In layman's terms, this naval officer scours the budgetary process for as large a share of the monetary pie as possible and then helps to decide where, in naval aviation, that money goes. There is never, ever, enough money to go around; no department ever has enough and never gets all it requests. It seems budgetary battles are always being fought in government—a part of daily life in the five-sided wonderland known as the Pentagon. How do you budget for a new aircraft—say, the F-35 Lightning—that takes years (approximately 20 years for the Lightning) from concept to IOC (initial operating capability) when your portion of the defense budget will be different each year? N98 is one of those positions that requires skill, knowledge, tact, experience, and the right disposition. One must have the ability to work through endless challenges, setbacks, funding shortfalls, and performance irregularities as new systems are developed and tested. Understating, it is a tough job.

Rear Admiral Joseph Donaldson was well suited for it. The guy was good, very good. He deserved his rank and current assignment; he'd earned them both. His call sign—

many pilots have one—coming up through the ranks, started with "Shooter." While training in the F-14, Donaldson had a particularly good day in a 2-vs-1 dogfight. An ensign at the time, Donaldson "shot down" two aggressor aircraft during a syllabus event and subsequently earned that moniker. Later, however, while in the fleet, some thought his call sign should be changed to "2 chutes" after his second trip up the rails, when he ejected out of his Tomcat during a mission in his fleet squadron. Stories, some critical, circulated in naval aviation circles about those two ejections, but there was no hard evidence to back up the rumors. Donaldson, as far as Frank knew, was still called "Shooter" by his closest associates. Warren, while on active duty, had had his own personal associations with Joe 2-star.

Frank was the commanding officer of Air Anti-Submarine Squadron 29 (VS-29) when his initial experience with Donaldson occurred. They were on cruise in the Persian Gulf as part of Air Wing 11 embarked aboard USS *Abraham Lincoln* (CVN-72), *Lincoln's* first full deployment following her commissioning. Donaldson was, by that time, a lieutenant and a seasoned F-14 junior officer (JO) with one previous cruise under his belt. Warren was the pilot and aircraft commander of an S-3A Viking flying as the night recovery tanker during what turned out to be an eventful ten-plane recovery. Not only did the weather and sea state adversely affect flight operations that night, but the ship also had to contend with multiple surface vessels in the vicinity.

An aircraft carrier is not easy to identify at night by other ships due to its unusual shape and the location of its navigation lights. Carriers display international signals during flight operations—shapes (day) or lights (night)—

to indicate they are restricted in their ability to maneuver. The aircraft carrier steers the required course and plows through the water at the appropriate speed that produces approximately 25 knots of wind down its angled deck. Mother Nature, therefore, plays a significant role in the direction and speed of a carrier when conducting flight ops. The nighttime aircraft holding pattern—called the marshal pattern—can be established anywhere the ship desires, irrespective of the ship's course and speed, but the last 20 miles of the approach are aligned with the ship's angled deck. If the ship changes course, usually due to surface traffic but also if the natural winds change, aircraft on the straight-in final approach must adjust accordingly.

On this night, the factors that influence carrier flight operations—weather, sea state, and surface traffic—were all in play. A broken-to-overcast ceiling existed at 800 feet with cloud tops at about 3,500 feet; not that bad—more a nuisance and a distraction. The ship, however, had to make several course changes due to uncooperative surface traffic. That night other vessels were either confused by what they saw, or they chose not to give way when the rules of the road dictated they should. There were several wave-offs, or go-arounds, issued by the LSO's (landing signal officer) because some aircraft couldn't realign themselves in time with the changing final bearing (the magnetic alignment of the angled landing area). Everyone understood the drill—the safety of the ship always comes first. No aircraft carrier bridge team ever changes course when a plane is nearing for landing—unless it must. When that happens, it often leads to a wave-off commanded by the LSO. The pilot adds power, climbs, levels off at 1,200 feet, flies straight ahead of the ship and gets vectored around for another approach. The plane flies upwind, then crosswind, downwind, and base leg, and is then vectored to the final bearing for another try, all of which consumes fuel.

Flying at 1,200 feet, in and out of thick clouds over the Persian Gulf, on the last recovery of the night, with multiple go-arounds, an occasional bolter (where the aircraft's arresting hook misses all the arresting wires) and an always-decreasing fuel state, a pilot might notice a slight involuntary flexing of the sphincter muscle and an ever-increasing grip on the control stick. Topping it off, someone "shits" in the wires, meaning a pilot fails to promptly clear the landing area following his "trap," or arrested landing. That pilot fusses about, trying to follow the directions of the yellow-shirted flight deck director frantically giving hand signals to raise the tailhook, now lower it to get free from the arresting wire, stay off your brakes, now raise the tailhook again, fold your wings, come straight ahead, turn slightly to the right, add some power, add some more power (indicated by the stomping of a foot) for a faster taxi speed. Then everyone on the radio hears the command: "Wave off, wave off," and the taxi director resumes a controlled, methodical manner, because there's no longer any need to expedite clearing the landing area. The plane about to land screams over the flight deck at full power in compliance with the LSO's wave off command. In this case, that aircraft, an F-14 Tomcat, was piloted by Lt. Donaldson.

Donaldson's was the last aircraft, other than Warren's, to be recovered, and due to his low fuel state, Warren was ordered to "hawk" the next approach: to maneuver the S-3 Viking, the airborne fuel tanker, to be in a position, relative to the F-14, that if a wave off or bolter occurred, the pilot (Lt. Donaldson) should be able to look up to his right—to about the 2 o'clock position—and see the tanker to join on. The idea was to create a situation where a join up could be accomplished quickly, and in-flight refueling could begin immediately. It works like a champ in clear, daylight conditions. It's more challenging at night and in marginal weather conditions. Time is never your friend in these situations.

In this case, they caught a break as the ship sailed into a small clearing; the ship claimed it was intentional, but the pilots knew better. Warren hawked the Tomcat during his approach but it was ordered to wave-off due to a course change by the ship. Lt. Donaldson added power, started to climb, raised his landing gear, looked up and to his right and saw the S-3. He cautiously joined up, and as they climbed, they immediately went into some clouds.

Warren radioed, "212, I'll keep climbing to angels 4 (4,000 feet); we should be in the clear up there."

Donaldson acknowledged, "Roger that."

Passing 3,500 feet, they were out of the clouds, and leveled off at 4,000 feet. The Tomcat stayed on the left side of Warren's plane, which extended the refueling hose out of the buddy store hanging under its left wing. All S-3s had been plumbed with the necessary fuel lines to become airborne tankers; the buddy store was the device which contained the hose and basket that the receiver aircraft plugged into to receive gas.

The ship confirmed with Warren how much "give" they had: how much fuel the S-3 could transfer and still have enough for its own safe landing, maintaining a reasonable reserve. The Viking had 2,000 pounds to give and was ordered to transfer that amount to the F-14. The Tomcat lined up behind the tanker, added power and plugged in on his first approach. Warren started a gentle left turn back toward the ship and fuel commenced flowing to the fighter.

Everything looked good; about 500 pounds had been transferred when, on the tanker's second radio, which had the squadron common frequency dialed in (not monitored by the ship), the call came, "Tanker, this is 212, you up?" The S-3's CoTac (copilot/tactical coordinator, a naval flight officer [NFO] strapped in the right seat) and Warren exchanged surprised looks with raised eyebrows. He replied, "We're up."

Tomcat 212 came back, "We're a little low on gas tonight; can you spare more than 2,000 pounds?" Shooter was asking for more gas than had been directed and was attempting to avoid any discussion on the topic, keeping the ship in the dark. More gas on board equals more options. Shooter had been waved off once and had boltered once (later, after a discussion with the LSO, changed to a hook skip, avoiding a negative input on his overall landing grades). Give him a few more pounds of gas? The tanker could oblige.

"We'll give you a little more–no problem." But that's where things got dicey. The S-3 planned to provide an extra 500 pounds of gas but miscalculated their fuel and gave Shooter 1,000 pounds of additional fuel—3,000 pounds total. Refueling complete, the controller vectored the Tomcat into the approach sequence, and the carrier's Air Ops requested an update of the tanker's fuel on board—and they fudged a bit, reporting more gas on board than actual. In the end, Shooter finally trapped aboard, following one more wave-off for what was leniently called a pitching deck (no adverse impact on his landing grades). The S-3 followed, by what most would say was more a coincidence than a landing. As the Viking started to cross over the arresting wires, the bow of the carrier pitched downward, the stern raised up, and the entire ship seemed to rise upward. The combination of forces raised the 4th and final arresting cable up just enough to snag the tailhook of the S-3 and pulled them back to the flight deck, averting what they thought was a sure-fire, ugly looking bolter.

The LSO called out on the radio, "Gotcha, Viking—welcome aboard!"

"Thanks, Paddles, it's good to be here!" Warren eked out, his heart pounding as he viewed the aircraft's fuel totalizer. It registered the lowest amount of fuel he'd ever landed with, on land or an aircraft carrier. His CoTac sat in disbelief and silence, having never experienced anything resembling an arrestment like that.

As it turned out, Shooter had misrepresented his fuel state that night. He landed with much more fuel on board than he reported, and around an aircraft carrier, that was the height of unprofessionalism.

Frank kept mum about Shooter whose career continued to blossom. Donaldson had a kind of Teflon exterior to him—negative things didn't stick. Something about that bugged Frank.

Frank felt the Metro train slowing for another stop as the first rays of sunrise fought their way through the overcast skies. The doors of the car opened and, along with a penetrating shot of icy air and, —snow flurries! —in walked Sharon Fleming, Assistant Secretary of Defense for International Security Affairs (ASD for ISA). Sharon reported to the under secretary of defense for policy (USD(P)) through the principal deputy under secretary of defense (policy) PDUSD(P). Her work focused on matters regarding international security strategy and policy issues related to the nations and international organizations of Europe (including NATO), the Middle East and Africa, and their governments and defense establishments. She also had oversight for security cooperation programs, including foreign military sales, in those regions. Her husband, Ronald Fleming, was a fifth-term congressman from Ohio's 12th district, located in the central part of this perennial swing state in presidential elections.

Sharon, from Worthington, Ohio, and Ron, from Newark (Ohio), met on the campus of The Ohio State University in Columbus, Ohio, while pursuing their master's degrees—she in international relations and he in political science. Both had obtained their undergraduate education from Ohio State and became acquainted while taking a common graduate course. Sharon was hard not to notice, with cover-girl looks, a friendly, engaging personality and a razor-sharp mind that could easily assess competing issues and then formulate clear, uncomplicated policies. Ron Fleming, for his part, enjoyed some notoriety peculiar to the state of Ohio. On a freezing, overcast, late November Saturday afternoon the visiting University of Michigan Wolverines football team was playing the Ohio State Buckeyes in Columbus. Late in the fourth quarter, Ohio State was marching toward a possible game-winning touchdown when they fumbled deep in Michigan territory. The Maize and Blue, ahead by a score of 20-14, recovered the ball on their own 22-yard line, and the chill in the Horseshoe suddenly became more severe. Michigan called two running plays to milk the clock, netting two yards. On the second play, an Ohio State defensive back twisted an ankle and was helped off the field. Journeyman and perpetual second string and special teams player Ron Fleming was dispatched to replace the injured Buckeye. The Michigan coaching staff, noting the substitution and inexperience of the replacement player, called a play-action pass play on third and eight from their own 24-yard line, a decision which fooled over 100,000 people in the stadium, millions more watching on TV, and especially Ron Fleming. However, the wide-open Michigan receiver turned his head a moment too soon and the tight spiral bounced off his chest into the waiting arms of the substitute defensive back. He scampered untouched into the end zone, the extra point kick was good, and Ron Fleming became the most well-known name in Ohio and throughout the sporting world. ESPN reruns of the play went on for days and included Fleming's after-game parade around the field on the shoulders of his ebullient teammates and adoring fans. After four years of near obscurity and one, single moment of glory—in a football game—Ron Fleming could have become governor of Ohio had an election occurred shortly after the win. The incumbent, along with the rest of the state, would have voted for him. In Ohio, if you shine in a victory over Michigan, you're each party's favorite person.

Sharon and Ron Fleming married after receiving their master's degrees, and Ron immediately ran for state senator and won. Sharon was also interested in politics, both at the state and federal level, with the Middle East a specific area of her concentration. Through her work on the Ohio governor's Economic Development staff, she sought to expand Ohio's reach into domestic and foreign markets. She traveled widely; several heads of state considered her a friend. When her husband won Ohio's 12th congressional district seat in Congress, Sharon continued to work on policy issues, first at the State Department and then at the White House. Staff associates were amazed when Benjamin Netanyahu, who'd been Israel's prime minister and was, at the time, the leader of the opposition in the Knesset, phoned Sharon directly to thank her for her insights at a recent Oval Office meeting with the president of the United States.

Congressman Fleming, a seasoned, knowledgeable, well-liked and respected gentleman, listened to people and left one convinced he was interested in your opinion and point of view. There were not many of his kind still around. His wife, on the other hand, outwardly warm and gracious, harbored a caustic, even egotistical drive to continually prove her policy successes were due to her abilities and insights, not because of her physical attractiveness or her congressman-husband's standing. She was her own woman and was continuously intent on proving it.

From the rear of the Metro car, Frank noticed that Sharon sat beside Joe Donaldson. Frank reflected on the peculiar and sometimes propitious social and professional dynamic that existed among the political and military spheres in Washington, D.C. Years earlier, freshman Congressman Fleming and his wife attended a White House social function held in honor of Great Britain's first sea lord and chief of naval staff. Guests included senior U.S. military officers, especially from the navy, plus selected members of Congress, including Congressman Fleming, one of the newest members of the House Armed Services Committee. Great Britain's ambassador to the United States and his wife desired to bring their single, mid-20s aged daughter to the event and asked the White House to provide an escort.

White House Military Social Aides, a cadre of 40-45 volunteer, single, male and female, mid-grade (0-2 through 0-4) officers, stationed locally, assist the president with diplomatic protocol at state and social events. As a lieutenant, Joseph Donaldson was assigned to the staff of the vice chief of naval operations and as a member of this prestigious and thoroughly vetted group, was selected to accompany the British ambassador's daughter. The pair immediately hit it off and mingled naturally among the many senior guests, especially with the new congressman from Ohio and his wife. Sharon Fleming and the ambassador's daughter exited the White House arm-in-arm at the conclusion of the evening followed by the congressman and the navy's rising star who were engaged in close conversation.

Years later, early in Frank's tenure as a civilian in the defense department, Sharon Fleming warmly greeted her former war college colleague when they ran into each other on the Metro en route to the Pentagon. They quickly reviewed their respective personal and professional activities during the intervening years since they'd last talked and discovered, due to their assignments, they'd occasionally see one another at work. A month or two later, a Pentagon Starbucks provided the setting where Frank and, now, Rear Admiral, Joe Donaldson renewed their acquaintance.

All three were headed to work, each with a similar objective in mind: in the (relative) quiet of a Saturday morning, make a dent in the never-ending parade of issues that required their attention. Frank assumed that neither Sharon Fleming nor Joe 2-star noticed his presence on the Metro that morning. He was wrong.

2

The Metro system in Washington, D.C., in service since 1976, encompasses nearly 120 miles of track, approximately 90 stations, and five color-coded lines: Blue, Green, Orange, Red, and Yellow[6]. During rush hour, over 40% of all riders are government employees, Frank Warren being one. Riding the Metro offered one time to read, mentally organize one's day, listen to a playlist, and avoid the clogged arteries of surface traffic migrating toward the capital from every direction.

The ride on the way to the District continued toward Rosslyn. Frank wouldn't enter the District of Columbia; the change to the Blue Line at Rosslyn going south would keep him within the borders of the Commonwealth of Virginia, the location of the Pentagon. Even for a Saturday, his metro car was nearly full, with many people standing. Before the Metro descended underground, Frank noticed the flurries mentioned earlier on WTOP had intensified into full-fledged snow. When it snows in the DC area or hints at it, the already tricky commute becomes nearly impossible. Frank had witnessed the significant impact of an impending snowfall on the workforce. The Pentagon, with over three times the floor space of the Empire State Building, over 17 miles of corridors, and some 25,000 military, civilian, and non-defense support personnel working under the same roof, can empty out amazingly fast when the weather threatens. Late afternoon meetings are always viewed with a critical eye, especially by those who carpool. If snow is forecast, it's considered an appropriate excuse for an early departure, regardless of one's personal schedule. Even on a weekend, with snow a possibility, taking the Metro today was an obvious choice.

The Orange Line train arrived at the Rosslyn station and most of the riders headed for the Blue Line to Franconia-Springfield, which would pass through Arlington Cemetery, the Pentagon, Pentagon City, Crystal City, Reagan National Airport, and others. Some commuters remained on the train for stops near the State Department and other places of work and interest in the heart of Washington, D.C. It always felt like everyone was going to the Pentagon and Crystal City, that area of underground shops and above ground office space seemingly leased in its entirety to the government. If Uncle Sam wasn't the tenant, some outfit doing business with the government—or more specifically, with the defense department—would be housed right where the action is. The United States Government, and particularly the Department of Defense, is big business: DoD is America's oldest and largest government agency. It is, in fact, the nation's largest employer with over 3,000,000 employees and an annual budget (in 2006-2007) of around $450-500 billion. On the Metro today were military and civilian employees assigned weekend responsibilities at various governmental agencies as the vast federal machine, including the Pentagon, is always in operation.

*****

The first stop on the Blue Line heading south from Rosslyn toward Franconia-Springfield is the above ground station at Arlington Cemetery, which consists of 624 acres and over 400,000 graves. This stop evoked a mixture of emotions within Frank Warren: thankfulness, inspiration, and pride along with lingering feelings of inadequacy. He was proud to have served his country on active duty, and now as a civilian, but he sometimes questioned how he measured up compared to those who had gone before him.

Frank had viewed the changing of the guard ceremony at the Tomb of the Unknowns many times—like most of the 4 million people who visited Arlington each year. Everything in a series of 21, alluding to a 21-gun salute, the highest military honor possible. 21 steps—21 seconds—all movements coordinated by mentally counting—then physically marching. The actual changing of the guard event: precision and discipline to perfection, as befits their duties as guards—watchmen over their fallen, unknown comrades. It is an emotional, moving, and unique ceremony.

3

"Next stop is the Pentagon. This is the Blue Line to Franconia-Springfield." The announcement jolted Frank back to the present. He turned his iPod off, removed the earbuds and put them in his pocket. By anyone's estimation, it was officially snowing—hard—in the DC area; the stop at Arlington Cemetery had confirmed that. He was pleased he'd taken the Metro to work even though Saturday traffic would have been much lighter than during the week. Add in the snow factor, however, and you have a recipe for a disastrous commute. At the Pentagon, Sharon Fleming and Rear Admiral Donaldson emptied out, heading for the fare machine and the escalators—some passengers opting to climb the steps as they ascended, thus the unwritten rule to stand to the right—then through a security check—usually a swipe of a security badge—and into the wonderment of the Pentagon. They say you're never more than a seven-minute walk from any one place to another in the building—an immense structure sitting on 29 acres of land comprised of 6.5 million square feet and six zip codes.

Frank emerged from the security area and watched Sharon and Joe veer off on different routes to their respective offices. Frank ambled along—no rush today—on his chosen path toward the working spaces of the Under Secretary of Defense for Personnel and Readiness, one of the five major "Unders" of the Secretary of Defense (SecDef) organizational structure. The other "Unders," as they're known, who work for the Secretary of Defense: USD for Acquisition, Technology, and Logistics; USD for

Policy (the Under that Sharon Fleming worked for); the USD for money—the Office of the Secretary of Defense's (OSD's) Comptroller and Chief Financial Officer. The fifth Under was the USD for Intelligence. Five critical areas: Force Readiness, Purchasing, Policy, Finance, and Intelligence, all working through the Deputy Secretary of Defense and ultimately to SecDef. There were many other directorates and subdivisions within the organization all contributing to the Defense effort within the Pentagon. One had to search far down the organization's wiring diagram to get to Frank. He hoped his current position would lead to an ASD job—Assistant Secretary of Defense—at some point. For now—he was pleased with his decision to leave the airlines and work in the OSD organization; he liked his assignment and the service-minded dedication of his fellow workers.

Rear Admiral Joe Donaldson, "Joe 2-star" having long ago replaced the call sign "Shooter" in Frank's mind, was, like Sharon Fleming, an extraordinary individual who excelled in everything he did. After one week in his Pentagon job, if you didn't know better, you'd swear the admiral had been there a year. Much like Sharon, Rear Adm. Donaldson could assimilate data, make assessments, devise courses of action, and execute the chosen option. His briefing capability was unparalleled. Listeners, usually senior officers and their civilian contemporaries, nodded in agreement as he spoke. Some were embarrassed when they couldn't pose a question or offer an opposing view at the end of a briefing. When 2-star finished, you felt further discussions were unnecessary, and were ready to hear: Execute!

Frank shared his reservations and misgivings about 2-star's past with Will Stimson, his fellow CO buddy and now congressional staffer. Will Call had heard stories, too, and was surprised by the admiral's selection for his plum assignments and his galloping, almost meteoric rise through the ranks. They both wondered who his "Sea Daddy" was—his cheerleader and protector who was pushing his protégé to the top using the carpool lane to get ahead of the main pack. Rear Adm. Donaldson was a superb naval officer, but his rapid accession to the navy's leadership ranks was the subject of much discussion, some admiration, and not a little skepticism.

Sharon Fleming was equally impressive—if not more so. She'd served in the White House as a Special Assistant to the President and as the Senior Director of Strategic Planning on the National Security Council. In the State Department, she worked as the Principal Deputy Director of the Secretary of State's Policy Planning Staff. Many thought she would be next in line for the Under Secretary of Defense for Policy job at OSD—an opinion she agreed with.

Most days at the Pentagon, Frank's work did not take him to an area where he could view the Pentagon Memorial, set on two acres of land just southwest of the Pentagon itself. It contains 184 memorial cantilevered benches, each with a lighted pool of flowing water, aligned along the flight path of American Airlines Flight 77. The memorials are arranged according to the victims' ages, from 3 to 71. Of the 184 people who lost their lives when Flight 77 crashed into the Pentagon at 9:37 am on 9/11, 59 were on board the aircraft, and within the Pentagon, 70 civilians and 55 military people perished. Many Pentagon employees and most Washington area residents do not see the Memorial in their daily routine, but its presence is transfixed in the minds of every Pentagon worker and millions of American citizens everywhere. It is a quiet, sobering setting and serves not only as a fitting tribute to those who died there but also as a reminder, if one is needed, about the importance—and honor—of service to your country, in whatever capacity one chooses.

4

Frank approached his desk with grand expectations of being able to complete the work that awaited his attention and then be on his way. There were few people around and no one in his immediate work area. Good—no interruptions. Frank found the quiet odd and unusual—but pleasantly so. He looked over his work and thought it shouldn't take too long. This might be an appropriate time, he thought, to do more research on a special project he'd started soon after his arrival in the Pentagon. It was the continuation of a paper he'd written while on active duty as a student at the National Defense University in Washington, D.C. The paper's central focus was Iran, which, in Frank's mind, perfectly fit Winston Churchill's description of Russia: "… a riddle wrapped in a mystery inside an enigma." Frank sought broader knowledge of the Islamic Republic, not only for his personal understanding of the country but also as a possible competitive edge over others seeking positions within the OSD hierarchy to which he aspired. When he confided in Will Stimson about this pursuit he received enthusiastic encouragement, with Will stating his research might be useful in future policy discussions somewhere within OSD. Frank felt fortunate to have his current job, but viewed it as an initial step on the upward path he hoped to take.

He sent a text to Mary to let her know he was hard at work solving the nation's problems and promoting democracy throughout the world. Next, he checked the day's message traffic, most of which would be deleted as not applicable to his world as an assistant to the assistant secretary of defense (ASD) for readiness. He read, clicked, and deleted, message after message and couldn't help but enjoy the quiet serenity that surrounded him. He glanced around to convince himself of his good fortune when he noticed her. "Oh, hi, Denise."

"Denise" was the preferred form of address of Denisha Emerson, an African-American administrative assistant who worked in Frank's section of the defense department empire. An engaging and entirely pleasant-looking young lady, Denise was the daughter of an Iranian cardiologist father and an African American mother. Her father was born and raised in Tehran and attended Tehran University of Medical Sciences. He fled the country in mid-1979 due to the unrest and uncertainty associated with the Shah's ouster and the increasing influence of Ayatollah Khomeini. Dubai, UAE, offered him the opportunity to establish a medical practice, and he met Denise's mother when she applied for an administrative position. She'd become comfortable with the Middle East culture while touring with friends, and had decided to stay. They wed in 1980 and became the proud parents of a baby girl, their only child, on July 3, 1981. Denise later attended college in the U.S. and found work in the Pentagon.

Denise had been assigned to Frank, when he reported to the Pentagon, to educate him in the conventions, standardized formats, and protocols of internal communications used within their directorate. It was like learning a new language even though you already knew the words. Frank, a willing student, steadily absorbed the basics and soon could push paper with the best of them. Some observers, however, might have concluded that the teacher/student association during Frank's initial days at work had become a little too cordial and familiar, although each participant claimed otherwise. At lunch one day, though, they unwittingly crossed a threshold when they were seen eating together and having "too much fun." Back in their workspaces, Denise's supervisor, the senior administrative director, who'd been around a long time and had seen this movie before, quietly and professionally took Mr. Warren aside. Using an aviation analogy so the new guy could keep up, she advised that the weather forecast called for increasing turbulence and a rough ride, and he should consider altering his course, his altitude, and his airspeed to keep all his "passengers" happy and content. Frank understood. A head-nod from the seasoned, experienced, take-no-crap-from-anyone supervisor settled the issue, and Frank became more circumspect about his dealings with the support staff. He was, nonetheless, always pleased to see Denise at work.

"Good morning, Frank," Denise answered with her perfect, I'm-thrilled-to-see-you smile. "Catching up on a few things?"

Frank strove to be casual in Denise's company.

"Yeah, I figured I could get some work done this morning with no one around. I plan on being here for an hour, and then I'll be on my way." He shifted, and cleared his throat. "What brings you here on a holiday Saturday?"

"Oh, I left some reading material here yesterday," she said airily, "and, since I'm here, a friend asked if I would pick up a few files over in Policy's work area. So, nothing inspiring, like I'm sure you're dealing with!"

Denise had a certain way about her, a beguiling, almost suggestive manner. One of those women who rarely pays for a drink.

"Naw," he cleared his throat again, "this is routine, regular business stuff. I'm trying to take care of a few items, so Tuesday morning doesn't overwhelm me. If you're going over to Policy, say 'hi' to Sharon Fleming for me. I saw her on the Metro this morning coming in."

Denise Emerson had found whatever she had come for, and was on her way out of their work area. As she passed by, she patted him on the shoulder and said, "Now don't stay here too long, Frank. It'll all be waiting for you when you come back on Tuesday." She kept walking but turned part way around and waved back at him. He watched her stroll away, enjoying the view, knowing full well she knew he was doing precisely that.

A moment passed as Frank tried to refocus on the reason for coming to work that morning. What was it about Denise that intrigued him? Maybe it was her indefatigable pleasantness—almost *too* nice; her daily fashionable appearance; the expensive location where she lived, one stop from Rosslyn on the Orange line; all on a GS-9 salary. He'd mentioned his personal project to Denise when she noticed his constant studying of documents and analyses of Iran. He saw her eyes sharpen and her whole persona become more focused whenever they ventured onto this topic, which, fortunately, was rare. Was she just politely interested, or was it something else? Denise Emerson was a little too perfect—that's what bothered him.

A red light continued to blink on his phone, indicating a message was waiting. He noticed there were two messages. Ignoring the phone, Frank continued to review his messages, deleting most of them, when he came upon a classified message with the subject line: IRANIAN ACTIVITY. That one grabbed his attention:

CONFIDENTIAL

O 131300Z JAN 07
FM: JOINT STAFF
TO: DISTRIBUTION BRAVO
BT
C O N F I D E N T I A L/NOFORN [no foreign dissemination]
MSGID/JOINT STAFF WASHINGTON DC/JAN//
SUBJ/(U) IRANIAN ACTIVITY

   RMKS/1. (C) UNUSUAL IRANIAN NAVAL ACTIVITY HAS BEEN DETECTED OVER THE PAST TWELVE HOURS. POSSIBLY TWO KILO-CLASS SUBMARINES MAY BE PREPARING TO SORTIE FROM BANDAR ABBAS AND MULTIPLE SMALL CRAFT HAVE BEEN NOTED OPERATING WITHIN FIVE MILES OF THEIR BANDAR ABBAS BASE.

   2. (C) IT IS UNKNOWN IF THIS ACTIVITY IS ASSOCIATED WITH A PLANNED IRANIAN NAVAL EXERCISE OR IS A COORDINATED EVENT INTENDED FOR OTHER PURPOSES. PRESENTLY DETAILS REMAIN VAGUE BUT WILL BE FORWARDED WHEN KNOWN.

CONFIDENTIAL

Frank kept this message active and continued through the remainder of the mostly routine, unclassified traffic that had accumulated in his message files. His mind never completely left that one message from the Joint Staff—he had a nagging feeling and it finally hit him: WTOP, obviously with excellent Pentagon sources, had mentioned something about Iran this morning as he approached the Metro station. He'd given the comments little thought. Now his brain started wandering, and different thoughts crept in: the secretary of defense was in Hawaii, returning from a much-publicized meeting in Beijing with his Chinese counterpart. The deputy secretary of defense was somewhere in Europe, visiting NATO facilities. The under secretary of defense for policy, not in his chain of command but certainly a key figure in critical military decisions (and Sharon Fleming's boss, working through the principal deputy under for policy), was currently a patient at George Washington Hospital following an emergency operation to remove a burst appendix.

Frank's thoughts drifted between the message he'd read and the fact that some very senior Defense Department officials were not in town, and the president and his family were at Camp David this weekend.

Frank pushed a button to listen to his messages and activated the speakerphone feature. The first message was recorded at 0723 that morning. A familiar voice floated up from the phone:

"Hey, Frank, how's it going? This is Will Call. I called you at home and Mary said you were coming in this morning. I wanted to give you a heads-up on something that's brewing. There's some stuff going on around the Strait of Hormuz that's beginning ..." Frank, practically alone in his nearly empty surroundings, immediately picked up the handset, which disabled the speakerphone, and continued to listen. "... to get a lot of attention. I expect you've probably seen some message traffic on this already this morning and I suspect there will be more. Frank, I know you're interested in this sort of thing and that it's outside your purview, but I wanted to let you know anyway. Also, I talked with our friend from Atlanta who's in town and staying at his favorite Comfort Inn; just keeping you up to speed. He said he might give you a call—nice guy—you ought to talk to him. More later, buddy—bye."

Frank Warren sat in astonished silence as he placed the phone back in its cradle. The translation of this phone call, made on an unsecured line, was: All hell's about to break loose in the Persian Gulf near the Strait of Hormuz. "Our friend from Atlanta" and the "Comfort Inn" were code. Will Call was telling him he'd spoken with a mutual friend, Anthony Darnell. Mr. Darnell was a West Point graduate and a former Army special forces officer, who, after 12 years of service, left active duty but continued to serve in the army reserves and ultimately retired as an O-6, a full bird colonel, the equivalent rank to a navy captain, the retired rank of both Will Call and Frank. This former colonel was employed by a government organization headquartered northwest of the District: the Central Intelligence Agency. He worked in the Directorate of Analysis and his primary area of expertise and focus was the Middle East. "Atlanta" in the comment not only signified Anthony but also alluded to the "Agency." The "Comfort Inn" meant the letter "C" and the letter "I." Will Call had already talked to Anthony at the CIA. Frank again read the Joint Staff message and considered Anthony Darnell's area of concentration. He reached for the phone and listened to the second message.

Anthony's voice filled the handset: "Hi, Frank, it's Anthony. Hope you took the Metro in this morning because driving's getting quite sporty out there. I'm going to send you some items which you might find of interest. Will Call said you like to keep informed of things going on around the world, so I'll send you what I can. Might be good if we could talk in private if you have a few minutes to chat. Have a good one." That was it.

Anthony's message also contained code words. "Send you what I can" meant, due to Frank's clearance and the security level of his computer, Anthony was limited in what he could transmit electronically. "Talk in private" meant: call me on a secure line. Frank reviewed his message traffic again, and found there was more amplifying information about the Iranian submarines which had recently gotten under way from Bandar Abbas.

Frank checked his watch: 1030 (10:30 am). He tried to recall what ships were currently in the Persian Gulf. The USS *Nimitz* (CVN-68) was over there now. Probably also a CG or two (guided missile cruisers). How about submarines—do we have any in or near the Persian Gulf? Rarely did anyone—ANYONE—mention submarine activities.

The silent service was a well-earned descriptor for that branch of our military. Frank recalled when he served as navigator of *Nimitz* he had asked the submarine officer on the Admiral's staff how best to coordinate the battlegroup's movements and formations with the submarine(s) that may, or may not, be in the vicinity. As *Nimitz* navigator, he was, by default, also the Battle Group navigator. The reply to his inquiry was forthright and to-the-point: "Don't worry about the submarines; they are not your concern." Following an awkward moment between the two officers, eyes locked together, Frank said, "Roger that. Thank you." He didn't give the submarine issue another thought throughout the entire deployment.

*****

Earlier in their active duty careers, Will Stimson and Anthony Darnell were classmates, and seminar mates, attending the junior course at the Naval War College in Newport, R.I. Through ten months of intensive instruction, the two of them developed a deep respect for each other and each other's profession. Will Call found Anthony's childhood stories and adolescent experiences enlightening and sometimes quite sobering. His youthful days in the suburbs of Atlanta, his four years at West Point, and, of course, his exploits as an Army Ranger and as a member of the Army's elite Delta Force gave new meaning to the words "life skills." These experiences were described to him from the perspective of a man "of color" —an African American. If Will Call Stimson learned anything that year, he finally began to have an understanding—a fleeting glimpse—into the life of an American whose entire existence had been impacted—almost always negatively—because of the color of his skin. Will had thought he understood the plight of African Americans living in the United States, but he realized, talking with Anthony, that he was clueless; he didn't know anything, and most people of his skin color—white—didn't know anything, either.

Frank met Anthony Darnell through their mutual friendship with Will Stimson. Will Call had suggested that Frank join him for an adult beverage after work one Friday, and Anthony had somehow decided to do the same thing, at the same time, and at the same place. It appeared to be a fortunate coincidence but of course, with Will Call, it wasn't. Will Call and Anthony had developed a deep and sincere friendship, and if Will Stimson considered Frank Warren a friend, Anthony was sure he'd be a good guy to know. So, over drinks and light snacks, a robust, respectful friendship developed deeply rooted in the common bond of service to their country. Over time, Anthony learned of Frank's interest in—and knowledge of—Iran, and admired his depth of knowledge in Middle Eastern affairs. Their active duty military service, completed in two markedly different branches of the armed forces, provided a backdrop for their discussions and served as a basis for their developing association.

*****

Another thought was ricocheting around in Frank's head: his visit to the CIA, at the request, and as a guest, of Anthony Darnell. He'd mentioned he'd never been to Langley, the shorthand name for the CIA compound. Anthony suggested a tour of the facility, an invitation Frank gladly accepted. Langley is an impressive site, situated on nearly 260 acres of land, comprised of the Original Headquarters Building and the New Headquarters Building, an expansion completed in 1991. CIA headquarters is officially named the George Bush Center for Intelligence, named after President George H.W. Bush (Bush 41), the only person to serve as head of the CIA and as President of the United States. A Memorial Wall in the main lobby holds 83 stars[7], one for each member of the CIA who died in service to their country. The identity of some of the fallen is public knowledge; for many others, their names are known only inside the walls of the Agency.

What Frank recalled, with the phone still in his hand, was a situation that developed during his eagerly anticipated visit to the facility. Anthony appeared harried and preoccupied when he met Frank at the headquarters and signed him in. Just another day at the office, Anthony assured him when Frank inquired if they should postpone the visit. Anthony carried several folders with him as they began their tour, one clearly marked TOP SECRET in bold, one-inch letters. In another folder Anthony had placed some CIA documents containing readiness data of several foreign countries' militaries.

They huddled in a conference room to review the readiness file when the door opened, and a colleague of Anthony's asked if he could spare a moment. Anthony paused, then asked Frank to excuse him for a few minutes, suggesting Frank review the readiness file without him. Frank had a Top Secret security clearance issued by DoD, and his clearance data had been forwarded to the CIA for vetting prior to his visit.

Anthony stepped outside to confer with his associate, leaving the door partly open. Frank could hear the undertones of the two agents while he read the readiness data. He realized he'd seen similar information in other dispatches at the Pentagon that were not marked Top Secret. Frank knew the classification of a document is based not only on the actual information contained in it but also on the sources and methods used to obtain it. Nonetheless, some of the data was new and all of it pertinent.

He turned over the final page of the file and the back of the folder turned also. A clip on the readiness file caught a similar one on the next file and it opened, revealing two sets of papers, one on each side of the folder. One side had the picture of a man, presumably of Middle Eastern descent, who had been captured by undercover CIA operatives roughly eight months earlier—several months before Frank started work at the Pentagon. Frank viewed the page with caution and uncertainty. He read that this individual, whose first name appeared to be Achmed, was initially from Iran but had been apprehended in Baghdad,

Iraq. His capture was the result of a clandestine CIA sting operation. Achmed, an arms dealer, had been led to believe he was meeting with a buyer representing a fringe terrorist group who had ties to what ultimately would be known as ISIS, the Islamic State in Syria. The CIA's target was organizing a shipment of AK-47s and RPGs (rocket-propelled grenade launchers) from Iran to the terrorists presently located in Iraq's capital. Naturally, no sale took place at the meeting and Achmed was secretly transported to an undisclosed location in Europe.

The details in the file about their detainee, compiled by the CIA, were startling to Frank: arms dealer Achmed was an evil, ruthless, cold-blooded murderer. His chief personal characteristic seemed to be the complete lack of a conscience. Every interrogation, every question asked of Achmed, every word he had ever said had been recorded. In addition to the printouts of all conversations, there was a CD in the folder labeled "Achmed file" which contained every scrap of information about the entire case. Frank was both surprised and dumbfounded—this was interesting, even fascinating data. But he was also conflicted; it's one thing to hold a certain level of clearance—Top Secret, for example—but one must also have a need to know. Only if you had both, the appropriate security clearance and the need to know—the information was pertinent to your current position and related to your present work—were you permitted access to the specific classified material. Frank clearly had no need to know anything about a gentleman named Achmed. He looked up, suddenly, as Anthony came through the door to the briefing room, then retreated and closed the door as he began another conversation in the hallway. Frank continued to gaze over the questionable file until his heartbeat and blood pressure reached uncomfortably elevated levels and he closed the files. Anthony finally reappeared, announcing the tour was now over, and Frank would have to leave. Anthony's presence had been requested elsewhere—he didn't elaborate.

The two of them headed toward the main entrance where Frank turned in his visitor's badge prior to departing the complex. Anthony detoured briefly to place the Top Secret material in a safe located in his office. They walked toward the entrance, Frank twice attempting to tell his friend about the Achmed file, but Anthony cut him off—not abruptly but in a smooth, natural yet almost intentional manner. Frank wondered if their friendship clouded their professional relationship. Near the visitor processing area, a large, broad-shouldered, muscular African American gentleman, attired in a well-fitting uniform, approached. His presence screamed, "Security." Frank thought this guy was the posterchild—well, poster adult—for discipline, authority, regulation and law enforcement. He was an impressive and imposing figure: freshly pressed form-fitting uniform shirt with military creases, Windsor-knotted tie, positioned squarely in the middle of his collar (no clip-on for this gent), with recently pressed trousers. Anthony and the security officer greeted each other with a fist bump and asked how the other was doing. At 6'5" and 230 pounds, Anthony's friend commanded your attention and exuded an "I'm in charge" confidence similar to Joe 2-star. "Francis," Anthony stated by way of introduction, "I'd like you to meet a friend of mine, Emmett Jensen. Emmett," he continued, "meet Francis Warren. Francis works at OSD in the Pentagon and was former navy."

"Hi, Emmett, pleased to meet you." Frank extended his hand and saw it disappear into the grasp of the broadly smiling Emmett. "Nice to meet you, too, Francis," returned his new acquaintance, in a deep, Barry White-kind of baritone. Abruptly the tone turned official and direct. "All done with your tour of my grand facility?" With eyes like sharp nails and that overbearing physical presence, height advantage, perfect uniform and position of authority—all pretenses of warm cordiality evaporated instantly.

Their handshake concluded, Frank replied, "Yes, Emmett, Anthony was kind enough to show me around. I'd never been here before. Fascinating place."

"Well, good, glad you liked it." Then this high and inside pitch: "You got your cell phone with you?" Wow, thought Frank, this Emmett Jensen has a way of dispensing with all niceties and getting right in your face, figuratively if not actually.

Anthony stood motionless and expressionless. Frank dug into his pants pocket and retrieved his cell phone, handing it to Security Officer Jensen. He cradled it in his massive hands, punched a few buttons, and asked, in a sheepish voice, "So Francis, am I going to find any naked pictures of your wife in here?" Frank, stunned and nearly speechless by this off-the-wall question, replied feebly, "No, Emmett, we keep those on a website for all to see." Emmett and Anthony both chuckled, and the tension in the air dropped a bit. Emmett continued to click slowly and methodically through the photographs stored on the phone. He started with the latest and was slowly working through the remaining pictures.

He groped for an answer when Emmett launched another bombshell question, this one more of a statement, the tone less biting this time: "I'm not finding any naked pictures of you and your wife together." A broad smile crept onto to Emmett's Hollywood face as he finished his comment, handing the phone back to Frank. Barry White had returned to Emmett's voice after a brief hiatus.

"No," Frank replied. "We keep the naked pictures of us and others in a specific area of our website that requires a security code not even the people who work here have clearance for." After a few laughs all around, Mr. Emmett Jensen returned the phone and said goodbye, with an ill-hidden wink to Anthony.

Frank and Anthony endured a brief, strained silence and then Frank remarked, "Well, he's quite an impressive gentleman, isn't he? I didn't know if he was going to break my cell phone into small pieces or eat the thing whole. And I didn't know about security checks on the way out of this place; that surprised me."

"Yeah," Anthony noted, "Emmett likes to mix things up—keeps everyone more focused on their day-to-day security. He's a pleasant guy, though."

With that, they thanked each other for their time and went their separate ways, Anthony to his newly scheduled meeting, and Frank to the parking lot. Everything looked normal and routine. It wasn't. Frank opened his car door and sat, reflecting on the file he had just reviewed.

Questions pounded in his head: Was he guilty of a security violation? Was Anthony? What should he do? He removed an airline air sickness bag from the glove compartment he'd taken from a flight—his mother-in-law was prone to car sickness—and opened it, just in case. Sweat formed on his forehead, and he loosened his tie and unbuttoned the top button of his shirt. The car door was still open, and he took several deep breaths to regain his composure, drank from a water bottle, then spit on the tarmac.

After a few moments, Frank closed the car door, started up the engine and headed to nowhere in particular. The CIA visit occurred on a Saturday, so he drove in the direction of his house, completely lost in thoughts and questions. When he finally arrived home, he told his wife Mary about his visit. It was a long talk.

5

The full name of Frank's inadvertent discovery was Achmed Farhad Ahmadi, an individual who represented the vagaries and uncertainties of intelligence gathering. He had been under the surveillance of the Central Intelligence Agency for 18 months because of a fortunate, unanticipated coincidence, an occasional byproduct of intelligence gathering efforts.

Originally, a female CIA operative, following a tip from an unnamed source, was tailing a woman with whom she hoped to have a brief, unexpected, totally innocent verbal exchange of typical daily pleasantries; in undercover jargon, she was trying to "bump" the woman, to establish a rapport or relationship. It was to be step one, similar to many other leads the CIA was pursuing, in the quest for information about Iraq's weapons of mass destruction— the location and extent of which, to the near exasperation of the U.S. intelligence community, was still undetermined. The subject woman was, per the source, "friendly" with a former Saddam Hussein insider. Saddam, found hiding on December 13, 2003 in what was called a spider hole, was awaiting trial and was no longer a factor in Iraq. But members of his former inner circle were possible sources of information, and the CIA had an interest in one of them. CIA handlers decided to try to "develop" this woman as a potential informant, all the while ensuring she didn't know she was being "developed." Such were the unique skills of the female CIA operative.

The tail, this day, led to a café selling bread and pastries in addition to coffee and tea. The undercover CIA operative, in line waiting to make a purchase as her subject had done, overheard a few, brief comments—in Farsi, not Arabic, which caught her ear—made by a male patron on his cell phone as he sat at a nearby table. The words that piqued her interest were "boxes", the number "47", "arriving", and some number which, even with her excellent command of the Iranian language, she couldn't make out. She determined this final number might be the amount due for a shipment of AK-47s. It was a stretch to reach that conclusion, but she followed her instincts. She made her purchase and walked outside to see if her target was still in sight.

The café had outside seating, and her mark was sitting with another woman at a nearby table. This day *two* CIA undercover agents (instead of one) were tailing the target woman. The second agent, a male, was nonchalantly smoking a cigarette across the street, observing the café scene.

The female operative sat down at an empty table, took a small bite of her bread, and gave the male agent a sign, made with her hand as she adjusted her *hijab*. She followed with a series of signals meaning: new contact of interest, male, and that he was leaving soon.

A male customer stepped out of the café, turned to his left and passed in front of the female agent as he departed. She put down her teacup and tapped the table twice with her right index finger. Her male associate realized the new mark had started up the street and commenced the first surveillance of a new person of interest: Achmed Farhad Ahmadi.

This day served as a prime example of the hit-or-miss nature associated with intel gathering, especially human intelligence (HUMINT). The female CIA agent continued her efforts to innocently ingratiate herself into the female mark's circle of friends and acquaintances, and was somewhat successful. From her mark's relationship with Saddam Hussein's "close" associate, the CIA eventually concluded that, after evaluating the HUMINT and data from other classified sources, there were no so-called weapons of mass destruction.

The U.S. later discovered that Hussein, upon learning the U.S. thought he had such chemical weapons, played along, keeping the Iraqi people and those closest to him in the dark, stonewalling UN inspectors, and essentially deceiving practically everyone. Among the lessons learned from the U.S. invasion of Iraq, an already known lesson was relearned again: reliable, actionable intelligence is often a scarce commodity.

6

Frank went to a nearby office to use a secure phone line; he couldn't use the phone on his desk. The "Unders" had secure phone access in their offices; for others, it wasn't as convenient. He dialed Anthony Darnell's phone number at the CIA, and after a few transfers, he was in touch with his friend. They both selected "secure" and could now talk freely without concern about someone listening in. The device altered their voices, but they could still understand each other.

"Anthony, good morning. Thank you for your call earlier this morning, and for the information you forwarded to me. The unusual activity by the Iranians—any ideas about what's going on?"

Anthony was all business. "Frank, we're still gathering information from a variety of sources, but here's a summary of what we know: two of their three Kilo submarines have lit off their power plants and may soon be under way, if they aren't already. Their destinations are unknown. We estimate perhaps no less than 50 of their small boats, many with .50 caliber machine guns, are, or soon will be, under way. There's a slight chance this is another NOBLE PROPHET[8] exercise, like the one the Iranians conducted back in late March and early April last year. They also held one in November, which tells me this is too soon for this to be another one. Last year these two exercises were widely publicized, and there was extensive press coverage, both of which are absent now. Also, the long-standing issue between Iran and the UAE (United Arab Emirates) about those three islands—Abu Musa and the Greater and Lesser Tunbs—was reignited after some threatening talk the other day by the UAE at an economic forum held in Abu Dhabi. And finally, I've come across some intel about the Navy's nuclear aircraft carrier, the USS *Nimitz*."

This piqued Frank's interest even more.

"This is still preliminary," Anthony continued, "and you may want to check with the Navy on this, but what I can gather indicates the *Nimitz* completed a 4-day port visit to Dubai. More accurately, they were pierside in Jebel Ali, southwest of Dubai, and after getting under way and heading toward the Strait of Hormuz, they experienced a propulsion problem. Not sure about the particulars, but my take on the data suggests they may be—what do you Navy guys call it? Unable to make your way, or under way but not making way?"

Frank broke in, "You mean they're dead in the water (DIW)?"

"That's the phrase I'm looking for—that's it," Anthony replied. "Something has happened, and they're floating in the Persian Gulf. Apparently, they have some auxiliary power capability to keep some lights on, and they have limited communications, but they can't steer the ship or fly airplanes; I'm sure you know more about that than I do. And as a CIA guy, it pains me to say that, Frank.

"So, that's the news as I know it. We're monitoring the situation closely and as time allows and events warrant, maybe we can touch base again. I know you're interested in Iranian issues, so I thought I'd pass on what I know, even though these activities are probably outside your wheelhouse. Being a Saturday, I'm surprised you're even at work, Frank. It can't be all that bad visiting with Mary's parents, can it?"

Damn, what did Mary say this morning, Frank wondered. "No, I enjoy visiting with them—I do. They're good people. I thought I'd come in this morning, get a little work done in the quiet with no one around, and be on my way. And you're right, while I appreciate the info you've passed on, this sort of thing comes more under the Policy umbrella than Personnel and Readiness. But it's good to keep informed and stay in the loop on operational issues. By the way, as you mentioned, *Nimitz* does have several diesel-powered auxiliary motors to power essential equipment when both reactors are off-line, which I presume is their present situation. But are there any indications the Iranians know about *Nimitz* being dead in the water and is there a link to the activity you see and *Nimitz*'s condition?"

"That's the question of the hour, Frank," Anthony replied. "If this activity is directed at *Nimitz*, which means, of course, directed at the United States, this could be the beginning of some coordinated multi-prong offensive plan against us. We're not sure—but we're evaluating every possible scenario and utilizing all sources to figure out the intentions of the Iranians. And with that, my friend, I must get back to work. Talk to you again, Frank. Bye for now."

Frank returned the handset to its cradle. He sat, deep in thought. Both nuclear reactors off-line; that was not planned or intentional. That only happens while in port, tied up to the pier. Even then, the ship occasionally kept one or even both reactors operating; it often depended on the level of support the port facility could provide. Having served as the navigator for two years on that very carrier, Frank recalled a time when the ship did have both reactors off-line while at sea.

The incident happened in the middle of the night off the coast of San Diego. It was standard practice for the reactor department to conduct drills and perform routine maintenance on their equipment during non-flying, low tempo operations. Flight operations would usually conclude around midnight or 0100 and not commence again until, say, 1300 (1:00 pm) the next day. During this time, having one of the reactors off-line had little to no impact on ship activities. Maintenance and drills were usually concluded by 0800; then the reactor department brought the deactivated reactor back on-line. However, this night proved to be different. With one of the reactors secured, something happened: some indication, reading, readout, a status light, some report—something regarding the on-line reactor caused the EOOW, the Engineering Officer of the Watch, to SCRAM[9], or immediately shutdown, the operating reactor.

Reflecting back, he realized he never got the full story. *Nimitz*, without either reactor on-line, could not make steam, which turns the turbine blades and, through various reduction gears, turns the four propeller shafts. They were DIW: 95,000 tons of steel and aircraft, floating on the Pacific Ocean, subject to the local current. Luckily there was no surface traffic in the vicinity, but they had everyone on the bridge searching for any contacts that might come close. It was such an unnerving and uncomfortable feeling that night, Frank remembered, sitting in his chair on the right side of the bridge, in the dark of the night, helpless and vulnerable, knowing there was nothing one could do except wait. When the operating reactor was secured, the officer of the deck had immediately awakened the captain, in his at-sea cabin, and he quickly came to the bridge. As the commanding officer took his seat on the left side of the bridge, Frank had noticed he resisted what must have been overwhelming urges to pick up his phone and start making inquiries. But the captain knew his people were sorting things out and he'd get a report soon. Minutes later, the EOOW called and explained what compelled the actions he had taken, and what steps were forthcoming. The reactor officer, a nuclear-trained commander (0-5), called moments later, providing more background information, but mostly restating the EOOW's report. Then the captain picked up his phone, waited a few seconds, and calmly said to his embarked superior, "Good morning, Admiral, this is the captain. I think someone forgot to pay the electric bill." He followed with a brief review of the nuclear event. The situation didn't last long—maybe 20 to 30 minutes, at the most. After securing the suspect reactor, the EOOW brought the other reactor—the one initially shut down through standard procedures—back to life. Then they were back in business and could operate normally.

At his desk in the Pentagon, Frank smiled. *Nimitz* would figure things out soon enough. He considered the unusual Iranian naval activity and the now-vulnerable *Nimitz.* Was there a connection? Did the dispute between Iran and the UAE have any bearing on ship movements? What impact would these developments have on commercial shipping and the overall security of the Strait of Hormuz? None of these questions concerned him directly in his job in the Personnel and Readiness area of the OSD staff. However, Sharon Fleming's office and the entire Policy directorate would be intimately involved in this morning's developments and were, Frank was sure, working on recommendations that would likely end up in the White House. DoD's Joint Staff was undoubtedly crafting plans, too. Yet, he worried. *Nimitz,* the mighty fist of American power, sat near gathering Iranian forces, defenseless. Two close friends, Will Stimson and Anthony Darnell, had contacted him this morning, knowing Frank's lingering connection to his former ship but more importantly, his unabated quest to understand all things about Iran. It was nice to be kept informed, Frank thought, but professionally, the ball was in someone else's court.

7

Frank returned to his work area, glancing at his watch: 1145. He completed some routine correspondence in quiet solitude while his mind drifted to Sharon Fleming and the under secretary of defense for policy directorate. Not surprisingly, there was less "quiet solitude" surrounding Sharon's office. Earlier, a White House staffer had called requesting Policy's presence at a 1300 (1:00 pm) meeting with the president to discuss Iran's activities in the Persian Gulf. The caller, aware of the absence of SecDef and the deputy secretary of defense, did not know about the under for policy's in-patient status at George Washington Medical Center following an emergency appendectomy the day before. When informed, he told Sharon to invite anyone she desired to accompany her at the meeting. Sharon, the ASD for ISA (assistant secretary of defense for international security affairs) had been continuously on the phone coordinating policy inputs with her contacts at the State Department and the White House national security staff. Many of these calls went to home phone numbers due to the increasing intensity of the snowstorm covering Washington, D.C. The under for policy, in constant pain and varying degrees of lucidity, had a phone beside his hospital bed which rarely left his ear. Tom Worthington, the principal deputy for policy, who would normally be coordinating all inputs (including Sharon's) to his superior, was out of the loop—with his boss's blessing—attending a Baltimore Ravens playoff game, accompanied by a guest, Denise Emerson. (Local op-ed writers and talking heads later questioned Worthington's priorities that day, considering many senior Pentagon officials were out of town. The president, perhaps saving the PDUSD(P)'s job, offered this view: "Someone offered him tickets, and after checking with his boss that morning, who was recovering from an operation, he decided to go. I'd have done the same thing. Lucky guy." Many observed that, had it been a Washington Redskins playoff game [the Redskins were a miserable 5-11 that year], no questions would have surfaced. Such was the power and influence of the NFL's Washington Redskins on the local populace.)

Sharon Fleming contemplated individuals who could contribute to a discussion of the Persian Gulf /Iranian navy threat analysis and were reasonably available. Deep in thought, she saw someone in her peripheral vision walk by her deserted work area. Her interest aroused, she walked in the same direction and approached a young woman who was looking over Tom Worthington's desk. "Denise?" she asked, somewhat incredulously, as she tried to rationalize why Denise Emerson would be here, on a Saturday, in Policy's work spaces, moving papers around on the principal deputy's desk.

"Oh, hi, Sharon," Denise cheerfully replied, looking up, a warm, gracious smile forming on her face. "Boy, first I see Frank Warren at work, and now you, both keeping the United States safe from all enemies, foreign and domestic," brightly stating the well-known phrase from the uniformed services oath of office. "Didn't expect to see either one of you at work today. How ya doing?" Her upbeat, carefree manner masked her surprise at being discovered in her boyfriend's office.

Sharon spoke cautiously. "Can I help you with something?" Sharon had met Denise Emerson months before when she and Tom Worthington began a relationship; her presence in Policy's directorate was now common, on a normal work day.

"Oh, no thank you. Tom and I are going to the Raven's game today. He said his boss was okay with him going. Tom asked me to pick up some files for him when I told him I'd be at work this morning. We're leaving soon because of the crazy weather out there."

"Yes, my under told me about the game. Should be fun—stay warm."

"Anything in particular you're looking for?" Sharon didn't want to appear suspicious but there was no harm in asking.

"Yep. And it's right here. Perfect—I'm on my way." Denise placed a plain, unmarked file in her tote bag and turned to depart. "As I told Frank, don't stay too long—it'll all be here on Tuesday. Nice to see you again, Sharon. Enjoy." Denise confidently went on her way, walking out the door with authority and purpose.

Sharon called after her, "Nice to see you, too, Denise. Say 'hi' to Tom for me."

Denise gave a half wave and continued down the hallway.

Sharon stood a moment longer, feeling the encounter ended a little too abruptly. She glanced at Tom Worthington's desk, usually neat and tidy, now with several files scattered about. She thought, *He asked Denise to pick something up for him? Hmm—odd.*

Back in her office and back on point, Sharon decided to call her primary navy contact, Rear Admiral Joe Donaldson, her years-ago war college classmate, and requested his presence at the 1300 briefing. Admiral Donaldson noted that hers was the second call he'd received regarding the White House meeting, the first one having come from the

Chief of Naval Operations (CNO). The CNO said he'd attend but wanted Donaldson there, too. Joe 2-star had read of *Nimitz*'s troubles and had attempted an Inmarsat[10] call to the ship's commanding officer but found the system was temporarily inoperative, due, he was told, to the winter storm blanketing the D.C. area. Donaldson, somewhat down the ladder in the navy's hierarchy, informed those admirals above him in the chain of command about the CNO's call and his inclusion at the 1300 meeting.

Frank Warren, his intended tasks completed, started to place some unclassified files into his backpack when he again noticed the blinking light on his phone. He zipped up his bag, looked at the flashing light, and decided to ignore it and head home. He put on his overcoat, adjusted his scarf, checked that his gloves were still stuffed into one pocket, grabbed the backpack, and started on his way to the Metro stop, thinking he'd be home by 1300, easy. His body was headed toward home, but his mind was in the Persian Gulf. His brain would not shut down, or at least switch to another topic. Slowly he stopped walking. He stood for a moment, then turned back toward his desk. What if this call couldn't wait? He lifted the phone receiver and pushed the message button.

The caller spoke hurriedly, sounding almost out of breath: "Frank, this is Sharon Fleming. I had a call from the White House not long ago from a staffer on the NSC (National Security Council) regarding the situation in the Persian Gulf. I assume you know what I'm talking about. Please meet me at 1300 (1:00 pm) at the White House for a briefing. Admiral Donaldson will be there, too. Your clearance info has already been sent over; and could you please call back to my office to confirm you received this message? Thanks, Frank, I'll see you there."

The message recorded at 1130, about the time Frank was ending his secure call to Anthony Darnell. Questions filled his head: why would Sharon Fleming call him about a briefing at the White House? How did she know he was at work? —she must have seen him this morning on the Metro. A briefing at the White House—what the heck does that mean? And why is a guy working in Personnel and Readiness, being asked—ordered? —to attend?

Frank called Sharon's office to confirm he'd received the message and that he'd be at the White House. He assumed his presence at this meeting was Sharon's doing—who else would have requested he be there? Who is briefing, and who is being briefed? Sharon hadn't mentioned any specifics, but when you hear the words "White House" you automatically assume the president is involved. However, many senior people work at the White House, and more have offices in the Eisenhower Executive Office Building. A grand structure, the EEOB was built back in the late 1800's and was located immediately to the west of the White House. Formerly known as the Old Executive Office Building, it houses the Office of the Vice President, the Office of Management and Budget, and the National Security Council. But Sharon only said the White House, the seat of the Executive Branch.

Frank sent his wife a short message saying he'd be a little late and he didn't know when he'd be home. Mary would understand; she'd received similar texts in the past.

Frank paused to think and reflect before heading to the White House: what did he know about Iran's naval capabilities, about *Nimitz*'s situation, and the roughly 35-year-old dispute between the UAE and Iran over those three islands Anthony mentioned? Years before, while on active duty, he'd participated in a war game while a student at the National Defense University (NDU) located at Ft. McNair in Washington, D.C. He'd received orders to attend the National War College, but preferred the curriculum at the Industrial College of the Armed Forces, or ICAF.[11] These two schools, known as war colleges, bestow master's degrees upon their graduates after about ten months of intensive study. The schools are housed in two old, beautiful buildings situated a couple of hundred feet from each other and constitute the two primary academic institutions (along with several others) that comprise the NDU.

When he reported aboard for duty, a couple of days before classes began, Frank sought out the head of academics at the National War College and told him about his desire to be at ICAF instead of National, and why that would be a better fit for him.

"Interesting timing," was the reply. Frank had no way to decipher that comment. The president of NDU, an air force lieutenant general (3-star), had, moments before, gathered the heads of the two schools and informed them he'd received a call that morning from a Congressman Ronald Fleming of the 12th district of Ohio. The subject on the congressman's mind was the placement of a student, his wife, Sharon Fleming, formerly an assistant in the White House, and now an incoming student at NDU, specifically, ICAF. Sharon, however, preferred the National War College over ICAF. Was it possible, the congressman had inquired, to accommodate this desire? That question had been posed not 30 minutes before Frank Warren appeared at National with the same, but opposite request. Thus, following one quick call by National's head of academics to NDU's president, Sharon and Frank traded places, avoiding a political flap.

Frank Warren and Sharon Fleming were informed their requests to change schools were approved, but neither knew of the other's involvement in the switch. That is, until later, during the academic year, when the two schools scheduled a combined three-day war game where, as it happens, they became team members. Frank and Sharon discovered the role each had played in the granting of their requests for the other school prior to the start of classes and developed a cordial and respectful professional relationship over the course of the game, even as Sharon's sometimes abrupt personality and sharp, cutting comments began to surface.

On the opposing team was one young-looking navy captain by the name of Joseph Donaldson. Captain Donaldson's team selected him to be their primary spokesperson, and Frank saw for the first time the almost extraordinary briefing and presenting ability of Joe Donaldson. He was "frocked" to 0-6, meaning he was still in the pay grade of an 0-5, a navy commander, but was authorized to wear the four stripes of a captain.

Most participants and war game evaluators thought young Captain Donaldson and his team had developed a strategy and employed their assets in an inferior manner when compared to Frank and Sharon's side. When Captain Donaldson completed his game-ending wrap-up summary, however, there were many positive head nods and approving glances between the observers suggesting his team had done quite well.

Frank recalled thinking: this guy is good, very good.

Through discussions with his National War College teammates, Frank picked up some history on Donaldson since their refueling incident years before. Donaldson was the youngest captain he'd ever seen. He was picked early for lieutenant commander, was an early selectee for aviation command, and was picked early (again) for the rank of commander. In the aviation community, an officer selected for command of a squadron first serves as the unit's No. 2 officer, known as the executive officer, or XO. Later he or she takes command of the same squadron during a Change of Command ceremony, relieving their former boss and becoming the commanding officer. In Joe Donaldson's case, soon after the command board met and published their selection results, an F-14 fleet squadron XO became ill with an unusually fast developing case of lung cancer and had to be replaced. Joe was ordered to fill the void. Six months later his CO received orders for a new assignment, and Joe Donaldson became a commanding officer before anyone else on the same command screen[12] list had even started their XO tour.

The navy had to figure out what to do with their young superstar when his commanding officer tour ended, since his career path was anything but normal. So, they sent him to the National War College as a one-year filler, a prestigious assignment for anyone, including a fast-tracker like Joe Donaldson.

During the academic year, then-Commander Donaldson was selected (early) for the rank of captain, continuing his unprecedented rise through the ranks. After the war game concluded, another aviation selection board—the Aviation Major Command Board—convened and reported their results: Captain (select) Joe Donaldson was a selectee for air wing commander.

Frank's thoughts returned to the present: the three islands and *Nimitz*. Is this a religious issue between Sunni and Shia? What time is it over there? What is the weather like in the Persian Gulf? Who gives the orders in the

Iranian political/military hierarchy? What is their objective? Another NOBLE PROPHET exercise?

The fact that Sharon Fleming had directed him to be at the White House made him uneasy. What the heck is going on?

While Frank was at ICAF the Iran-UAE dispute over three Persian Gulf islands had been a topic of discussion, and he'd written a paper on the subject. That was around fifteen years earlier, and the issue was still not resolved. He tried to recall all he could about those tiny specks of land: Abu Musa, Greater Tunb, and Lesser Tunb. Together, the three small islands amounted to about 11.5 square miles of land. Their location, however, near the shipping lanes to the west of the Strait of Hormuz, gave them their critical strategic importance.

An Arab family by the name of Qasimi ruled over the islands for at least two centuries; in the 1920's Great Britain assumed control of the properties. Later, in 1968, Britain announced its intention of withdrawing from the Gulf region by the end of 1971. Considering the extensive history of Arab oversight of the islands, Britain proclaimed the islands would be handed over to Sharjah, an emirate slated to join and help form the origination of the United Arab Emirates. Iran disputed this decision, citing its historical rights to the islands. The Iranians argued the islands of Abu Musa and the Greater and Lesser Tunbs had belonged to Persia since pre-Islamic times. They acknowledged that the Arab Qasimi tribe ruled over the islands, but it did so, according to the Iranians, from the Iranian port city of Lengheh, about 120 miles from Bandar Abbas, under the authority of the Persian Qajar dynasty. Thus, they claimed, the islands belonged to them. Ultimately, Great Britain arranged for Iran and Sharjah to share joint control of Abu Musa and possess equal shares of any future oil reserves. The agreement did not include the two Tunb islands, only Abu Musa. British forces departed the region on November 29, 1971.

The very next day, November 30, 1971—two days before the United Arab Emirates became an official federation—Iranian military units moved in and forcefully took control of all three islands. The takeover, Iran claimed, was, first and foremost, a follow-on action to the end of British colonial rule over the Iranian territories and was not intended as a hostile act toward the newly forming UAE.

Iran has occupied the lands ever since, despite many UAE and Gulf Cooperation Council (GCC) statements of protest to Iran and the international community. These requests for justice, made over 35 years, had been unsuccessful. Why, then, would Iran get two of their three Russian-built Kilo submarines under way along with a slew of their small patrol boats—Anthony Darnell estimated no fewer than 50 of them—all heading in a south to southwest direction toward the island of Abu Musa? Nearby, a national asset of the United States, the USS *Nimitz*, was adrift in the Persian Gulf.

Additionally, during the recent GCC meeting, some unusually sharp rhetoric emerged regarding Iran's continuing desire to expand its "sphere of influence" in the region. The GCC, established in 1981 in Riyadh, Saudi Arabia, and comprised of six Arab nations—Saudi Arabia, Bahrain, Kuwait, Qatar, Oman, and the UAE—affirmed their full support of the UAE in the event of foreign "aggression" in the Gulf. Iran's response was typical—boastful, extreme, and excessive: "We will not allow any country to carry out an invasion of our sovereign territory and we are willing to demonstrate the power of our military forces toward any offender." Iran asserted that diplomacy is the right avenue toward peaceful solutions, if, of course, everyone sees the world through their eyes. Clearly, the UAE had eyes of their own regarding the three strategic islands.

The one individual claiming center stage in Frank's thinking was Iranian President Marzban Pedram Mazdaki. Mazdaki's relationship with Iran's supreme leader, Ayatollah Hamid Ghorbani, had been the subject of several different messages Frank had read suggesting some friction and uneasiness between the two Iranian leaders. Did President Mazdaki order the submarines and patrol boats to get under way as a show of force and strength to the Iranian people and the supreme leader? Maybe the orders came from Ghorbani himself? Perhaps the Iranian admiral based in Bandar Abbas was responsible. When word of *Nimitz*'s propulsion problem filtered up to him (assuming an intelligence structure capable of providing such intel), he may have seized on the possibility of landing a sucker punch on the chin of the Great Satan by striking at one of the West's most visible and prized symbols, the infidel's mighty aircraft carrier.

Frank slung his backpack over his shoulder and headed for a quick meal stop at the Pentagon McDonald's. A northbound Blue Line train arrived as he forced the last part of his cheeseburger into his mouth. No food or drink is allowed on the Metro, but he fished his water bottle out of his carry-on and somewhat surreptitiously washed down the last of his meal.

8

A white, virgin expanse concealed the National Mall between the Lincoln Memorial and the U.S. Capitol Building with the Washington Monument standing proudly in defiance of the weather's onslaught. From the Metro Center station, Frank trudged over partially swept streets and sidewalks toward the White House, awed by the deserted landscape and hushed, muted sounds of the blanketed city.

Snow continued to fall from a vast, gray sky. There won't be any weekend flyers out today, Frank thought. He wondered which way Reagan National was operating, to the north or south? With reduced visibility and hardly any wind, he guessed they were in a northerly flow to runway 1. Occasionally he missed his former occupation. Stomping through the snow in the cold on a Saturday was one of those times.

Frank approached the northwest appointment gate to gain admittance to the White House grounds. The guards looked through his backpack while verifying he was on their list and, his identity confirmed, pointed him toward the west wing of the White House. Frank checked his watch: 1250—technically not late, but hardly early. He entered the official home of the president of the United States and was directed by several people, all pointing the way to the Situation Room. There was more screening, checking, verifying, and finally, he was issued a lanyarded badge, so it was always visible. Lastly, he was directed to place any personal communication devices into a lead-lined cabinet. None are allowed in the Situation Room. He was about to enter the Sit Room, or "the woodshed" as White House veterans called it, when he thought he heard a muffled sound in the distance, gradually becoming more pronounced—a helicopter?

*****

The White House Situation Room, officially the John F. Kennedy Conference Room, is comprised of three conference rooms, totaling well over 5,000 square feet. Recently upgraded, the renovations—started in August of 2006—were not quite finished.

The main conference room appeared complete, with lush carpet, sedate wood-paneled walls, a large dark mahogany table, with executive seating for 13, six chairs on each side, and one chair at the head, for the president. Chairs along the walls provided seating for assistants, the support staff—whose work enabled their principal, who sat at the table, to shine. Indeed, if you were seated anywhere in the Situation Room, you were at the pinnacle of the U.S. government.

But one need not be physically present to be in attendance. Six flat screen TVs arrayed around the room and a huge screen positioned opposite the president's chair provided video conferencing and live video feeds. Additionally, numerous digital time panels adorned the walls. These indicated the time in three places: 1) local time in Washington, D.C.; 2) wherever the President is; and 3) Zulu time, or Greenwich Mean Time (GMT), or UTC, which stands for Universal Time Coordinated but is said: coordinated universal time. Zulu time (Z), used throughout the military, avoids confusion when organizing or planning activities with people and assets in different time zones around the world.[13]

As Frank entered this inner sanctum, he found several people standing around the conference table, engaged in quiet conversation: Secretary of State Martha Wheatley; Lieutenant General Walter V. Townsend, U.S. Army, Director of the Joint Staff; Darren Ballinger, a National Security Council staff member; Sharon Fleming; and Rear Admiral Joseph Donaldson.

It was 12:59 local time, or 1759Z. The middle time of the three displayed also said 12:59, meaning the president was somewhere in the eastern time zone. Not knowing where or if he should sit, Frank stood along the wall.

Sharon Fleming was discussing something of importance with the secretary of state and the NSC staffer. Frank noticed Sharon's index finger point in his direction and surmised she was explaining his identity. The two uniformed senior officers were conversing together. Frank shifted his weight onto his other foot—it was now 1303 local and he wondered what time the 1300 meeting was to start. As if in answer, a door at the head of the room opened, and everyone—simultaneously—stopped talking and assumed the civilian version of the military's "Attention on deck."

Entering through the door, looking relaxed and confident, was the President of the United States, Edward Michael Sheppard. At 6'2", fit, with a slight stoop, hair still thick with a touch of gray, dressed in pullover sweater and sharply creased slacks, the president was an impressive presence. He was an enigma on the political scene: highly respected by both sides of the aisle. A veteran of both the House and the Senate, he had forged many friendships and alliances throughout Congress and was consistent in his political persuasions and ideology. A discussion—as opposed to debate—of different sides on an issue was more important to him than trying to impose his views on others. He listened to his opponents and when he said he'd look for consensus on legislative proposals, he meant it.

Practically everyone liked him, politically opposed lawmakers spoke respectfully of him, and there was a friendlier tone and more welcoming atmosphere in Washington than there had been for some time. The prospects for Congress to really "get things done" were quite high. When a member of the Supremes—a Supreme Court Justice—announced his retirement a year ago, President Sheppard's nominee to fill the vacancy didn't sail unfettered through the judiciary committee and win over the full Senate, but in the end, the 82-18 vote was both supportive and convincing.

The president greeted National Security Council staffer Darren Ballinger, and then his secretary of state, Martha Wheatley, joking he was surprised and yet pleased she somehow navigated her way through the snow to the White House. The president's chief of staff, Peter Sanders, followed his boss into the room and first shook hands with Rear Admiral Donaldson, and then Sharon Fleming, who received the cordial, slight cheek kiss and minor hug, common among friends and acquaintances in lofty circles. The army 3-star general shook the president's hand and the chief of staff's. Then, led by the president, everyone sat down, adjusted their chairs, organized the papers they had in front of them, then looked—expectantly—at their president.

In the moments while everyone was getting settled, Sharon quietly turned toward Frank. "Thanks for being here, Frank. I know it was on short notice. Both Joe and I thought you could offer some useful insights to today's discussion. Oh, Denise Emerson stopped by; that was nice."

"Yes, she said she had to pick something up for a friend over in your area. By the way, where's the principal deputy? With your Under in the hospital, I thought he'd be here today."

"Well," replied Sharon, still whispering. "That's why Denise was there this morning—to get some materials for Tom. They're going to the Raven's game today; they left a while ago. That's why I'm here."

"I see."

Sharon read his expressionless face and offered, "They've been seeing each other for about six months or so."

The president, pausing briefly to scan his own notes, began. "Thank you all for being here on such short notice and in this crazy weather. I wasn't sure I'd be able to make it myself. We repositioned the helo back up to Camp David early this morning as details of this situation in the Persian Gulf began to trickle in, and I'm sure glad we did. After I decided on this meeting, I told the pilots I needed to get down here today, but if they thought it was unsafe, we shouldn't try it. I couldn't see a thing outside during the trip here, but somehow, we made it. Others, understandably, weren't so fortunate. The vice president, jogging this morning before the blinding snowfall began, slipped and fell as he was returning to his quarters at the Naval Observatory. He landed on his lower back and is in some pain but is resting now—and will probably watch the Ravens' game."

Smiles greeted this last comment, which was followed by, "Anyone hear what the score is before we get started? I think it was a 12-noon start."

The answer would be forthcoming, as the Situation Room had watch teams that manned the facility 24 hours a day, every day of the year. If anyone could find out a football score, they could.

The president continued, "The secretary of defense and the chairman (of the Joint Chiefs of Staff) are traveling and will be joining us by video from the United States Pacific Command (USPaCom) headquarters in Hawaii." He then thanked Lieutenant General Townsend, the director of the Joint Staff, for being able to attend in person. "CIA and DNI (Director, National Intelligence) will also join us shortly, by video. The Chief of Naval Operations will be delayed. There's been some minor incident at the gate of the Washington Navy Yard," (the location of the CNO's quarters).

"Also, I should mention the vice chairman of the Joint Chiefs is stuck in upstate New York, at the Syracuse Airport. He was visiting family nearby, and his flight back to D.C. got delayed because the airport is currently closed." He said this last remark as he looked to his chief of staff for a confirming nod.

Peter Sanders offered the explanation. "During landing rollout an aircraft's main landing gear collapsed while swerving to avoid a service vehicle that unexpectantly crossed in front of them, resulting in an evacuation. Once the aircraft is moved, the airport will reopen."

"Finally," the president continued, "CentCom will soon join us, via video."

*****

CentCom, the U.S. Central Command, located at MacDill Air Force Base in Tampa, Florida, is one of eight unified combatant commands in the Department of Defense.[14] All are commanded by 4-star officers. Five are arranged geographically and are responsible for specific delineated locations around the world. The other three combatant commands are functional, operating worldwide across geographic boundaries. All combatant commands, CentCom included, have no permanently assigned military units. CentCom works with component commands, one for each of the U.S. armed services. Its naval component, for issues within the Persian Gulf, is the U.S. Naval Forces Central Command, or NavCent, located in Manama, Bahrain. The navy has several numbered fleets associated with specific areas around the world, and the forces operating in the Persian Gulf comprise the navy's 5th fleet. NavCent is ComFifthFlt, or Commander, Fifth Fleet. If a situation develops in the Persian Gulf and there is a need for military action, the president and the secretary of defense, together known as the National Command Authority, will task CentCom (the Persian Gulf is in CentCom's AOR or Area of Responsibility) to take action. If naval forces are required, CentCom will task NavCent to execute the orders that are in effect. If air force assets are needed, then AfCent—U.S. Air Forces Central Command, headquartered at Shaw AFB in South Carolina, with forward deployed headquarters in Qatar—will be tasked/ordered to provide them. These geographically dispersed commands illustrate the necessity of using Zulu time when coordinating military forces located around the planet.

*****

The president stopped briefly, looked around the table, a reassuring smile on his face, and he continued, "That's a brief rundown on why you're here, and others are not. I think we're all familiar with each other," he said, as he glanced around the room, and then he stopped, momentarily looking at Frank Warren, now seated in a chair along the wall. The president looked at Sharon Fleming, who quickly said, "Mr. President, may I introduce Frank Warren from DoD, the gentleman I spoke of earlier."

"Right, Sharon, I remember; thank you."

"Frank, please have a seat at the table. Sharon asked that you be included today, so welcome to the White House. I'm glad you're here."

This seemingly small directive— "have a seat at the table" —spoke volumes, and its significance could not be overlooked nor understated. Meetings at the White House, *especially* those in the Situation Room with the president, commonly involve high ranking people whose credentials, reputations, and résumés are well-established and widely known. Frank Warren—in stark contrast to the others in the Sit Room—was figuratively naked among these high-level attendees. With the president's invitation, he had been promoted to an equal. Whatever misgivings they may have had toward him, a member of the "club" —Sharon Fleming—had invited him, and the president, who enjoyed their utmost respect, had "blessed" him. Frank was like a minor league baseball player called up to the majors, soon to be sent back down. In the competitive environment of Washington, D.C., those gathered at the table were silently taking his measure.

The president continued. "She tells me you work for Ed Scott, the under for Personnel and Readiness, is that right?" Frank rose from his chair along the wall. "Yes, Mr. President, I'm on Mr. Scott's staff. I work as an assistant to the ASD for Readiness." He pulled out a chair from the table, and, clumsily, joined the group.

"Very good. Let's get started," the president said, giving a quick sign to his chief of staff, who rose to tell the Sit

Room watchstanders to bring up the video screens. The secretary of defense and the chairman of the Joint Chiefs, plus the director of the CIA (referred to as the director of Central Intelligence or DCI), and the director of National Intelligence, who had joined the DCI at Langley[15]—all were to be appearing on the secure video conference screens.

Introductions completed, President Sheppard said, "Let's start with an overview of what we know. Darren, please provide everyone with a summary of the activity in the Gulf."

Mr. Darren Ballinger was an NSC staff veteran who focused primarily on issues related to the Middle East. He and the president had become well acquainted. Unpretentious and unassuming by nature, with a serious demeanor, Darren possessed a vast knowledge of the intricate relationships between the Persian Gulf area states and the competing private interests within each country. He could name the rulers and presidents of all the countries in the region and each of their cabinet members. He spouted Middle East data like others recite sports statistics. Possessing limited knowledge of things military, he would be hard pressed to distinguish a private from a general. However, he could provide history, context, background, nuance, and insight into the complex forces and factions of the Middle East. And the president knew it.

While listening to the NSC staffer, Frank sensed the gaze of the president.

"Yesterday, overhead imagery indicated the Iranians had energized, or lit off, the power plants on two of their three Kilo submarines based at Bandar Abbas." Ballinger was all business. "Today we have confirmed that both submarines are under way and are operating on the surface near the southeastern coastline of Qeshm Island.

Additionally, a large number of patrol vessels and small boats are at sea or preparing to get under way. Indications are that as many as 50 of their patrol boats—many with .50 caliber machine guns—may become active.

"Also, the USS *Nimitz*, as I'm sure you all know, has suffered some propulsion failure and is, per the latest intel, not able to maneuver or conduct flight operations. She was most recently in Dubai, UAE—specifically, Jebel Ali, southwest of Dubai—and had to delay getting under way this morning because several trucks with food provisions, scheduled for a 0700 delivery, went to the wrong location in Dubai. By the time they got to Jebel Ali, the port services people who operate the pierside cranes had left the *Nimitz* and were working a container ship offload. *Nimitz* delayed its underway time from 0900 until 1300. She later conducted limited flight operations, which concluded around 2000 (8:00 pm) local, Dubai time—11:00 am here today. Shortly after that, something happened." Ballinger gestured toward the table. "Admiral Donaldson has some details about the *Nimitz*."

The admiral's delivery was crisp and to the point. "The reports I've received, sir, state that, following the last launch of the day, the reactor department commenced the standard process of securing one of their two reactors for routine, planned maintenance. There was still the one recovery to complete, but no more launches were scheduled. The last cycle of the day—the time between the start of one launch of aircraft and the subsequent one—was short, only 30 to 40 minutes long, so the recovery started soon after the last launch or cat shot. I assume the primary purpose of that last event was for night currency concerns in the air wing."

Glancing briefly around the room, Donaldson saw only blank, questioning stares from everyone, the president included, except Frank Warren. "Let me explain," Donaldson said. "A pilot needs a night landing every seven days to remain night current. If he or she goes beyond that, say, between 8 and 14 days since their last night arrested landing, they need a day cat and day landing, either a touch and go or a trap, and then a second flight that day that ends with a night trap. Then the 7-day clock gets reset. Exceeding 14 days since a pilot's last night trap requires even more day work before the next night landing. Keeping an entire air wing night current can sometimes be quite challenging, considering port visits, weather conditions, mission requirements, and aircraft availability. So, *Nimitz* conducting flight operations the same day she left port seems reasonable and routine. The fact that they concluded flight ops relatively early suggests the air wing is in fairly decent shape regarding night currency."

Darren Ballinger was paying close attention. He was thinking, processing, analyzing. "Well, that speaks to night landings. You said nothing about landings in the daytime."

Donaldson paused, considered his answer, looked briefly at Frank, then back to Darren, and replied, "Day landing currency is rarely an issue for an air wing. I think the requirement is for a day landing every month—no, every 29 days. A pilot needs a day landing every 29 days. A night trap resets the day counter in addition to restarting the night clock. I can't recall day currency ever being a factor, in all my experience on carriers."

Darren wasn't finished, even though they were far from the central issue before them. "And how many times have you landed on an aircraft carrier, uh, Admiral?"

To Frank, it felt like Darren couldn't remember Donaldson's appropriate form of address.

"I have 931 traps recorded in my log book."

Darren nodded as if the number meant something to him.

It certainly meant a lot to Frank Warren, whose career total of 620 traps felt far inferior to Donaldson's total.

Darren had one more inquiry for the admiral. "Do all pilots know exactly how many times they have landed on a boat?"

In a kind, ever so slightly condescending tone, Donaldson replied, "Yes, Darren, we know."

Frank nodded in agreement.

"The reports I have read indicate *Nimitz* completed the planned shutdown of one of the reactors," Donaldson said, "reactor #1 I believe, as the recovery helo landed after all the fixed-wing aircraft had trapped aboard. *Nimitz* was now operating solely on the #2 reactor, a normal, safe, routine configuration. The ship turned on course to begin its short transit to an area south of the western traffic separation scheme and all appeared normal and routine. Then around 2030 (8:30 pm) Dubai time, 11:30 our time, this morning—about two hours ago—the EOOW (Engineering Officer of the Watch) SCRAMed the #2 reactor."

"What does that mean?" the president asked. "And why would this watch officer shut down the operating reactor, knowing the other reactor was already secured?"

"Well, sir, Frank may have a better perspective on this than I have. In my experience on our nuclear carriers, if an indicator, a gauge, a light—whatever it may be—if protocol and procedure call for a particular action—in this case, a SCRAM, that is, a sudden, accelerated shutdown of a nuclear reactor—they complete the required steps and go from there." The admiral gestured for Frank to respond.

"You are correct, Admiral," Frank stated, suddenly very much aware everyone was now looking at him. "For the nukes, there is little, if any, gray area; they operate in a right or wrong, black and white world. The gauge, readout, or indicator says what it says, and the watchstander acts accordingly—there is no room for interpretation. I would add that this strict adherence to exacting standards and procedures is precisely the discipline we want in the people that operate our nuclear carriers and submarines. Something happened which required the watch officer to act, and the fact that the #1 reactor was offline probably had no bearing whatsoever on the decision to SCRAM the #2 reactor."

Darren could not contain himself. "Admiral, you're a, uh, well, you're an admiral—why do you say Mr., uh, ..."

"Warren."

"Yes, thank you, Mr. Warren. Uh, Admiral, you know all things navy—why would Mr. Warren have a, uh, 'better perspective,' I think you said."

"Darren, I don't know 'all things navy' —no one does. Frank Warren served in squadrons on several nuclear carriers in his navy career and had a tour as the navigator on one of them—which one, Frank?"

Frank replied, looking first at Darren and then at the president, "The *Nimitz.*"

After a quiet moment, Darren, in a perplexed voice, said, "You did time on the *Nimitz*?"

Frank, chuckling, said, "That's one way of putting it. But yes, I served two years as the ship's navigator."

"On the *Nimitz*—this same ship—the one we're talking about?"

"Yes—the same ship."

"And obviously you went to sea, right?"

"Yes, many at-sea periods and a deployment—to the Western Pacific, the Indian Ocean, and to the Persian Gulf."

Darren was incredulous. "You were in the Persian Gulf, on the *Nimitz*, as its navigator, where the *Nimitz* is now?"

"Yes, sir. That is correct."

Chief of staff Peter Sanders jumped into the conversation. "In your time on the *Nimitz*, did you ever experience a similar problem, like the one they have now—with both reactors offline while under way?"

Frank Warren relayed his story and emphasized how quiet, lonely and vulnerable he had felt while the reactor department worked on the problem.

A moment or two passed before Sharon Fleming spoke for the first time, in an attempt to refocus the discussion on the central issue at hand. "Frank, do you recall the traffic separation schemes in the Persian Gulf—their locations and what their purposes are?"

Frank Warren, recently a back-seat observer and now a fledgling participant in a world-impacting discussion, was feeling increasingly confident about his place at the table but also had a growing feeling that they were talking around the central, pertinent issues. Maybe he, similar to Sharon's attempt, could nudge the group back on point.

"There are two traffic separation schemes in the Persian Gulf area. One is in the Strait of Hormuz, and the other is just inside the Persian Gulf, at its eastern end. These are similar to others throughout the world—for example, the Dover Strait, separating Great Britain from Europe; the Straits of Gibraltar; and the Malacca Strait. They are all designed with one primary goal: safe navigation in busy, confined waterways. In the Strait of

Hormuz, the two shipping lanes, one inbound and the other outbound, are each two miles wide, with a two-mile buffer zone between them, and they are 25 miles long. In the other shipping lanes, called the western traffic separation scheme, each lane is three miles wide, and the buffer zone between them is eight miles wide. Here, the lanes are 50 miles in length. In both schemes, the inbound lane is to the north of the outbound lanes. Crossing traffic is supposed to pass through the schemes at a 90-degree angle to the designated lane."

President Sheppard inquired, "What are the tactical implications of transiting through the Strait of Hormuz? It doesn't sound like there is much sailing room there."

The chief of staff had a watchstander bring up a map of the Persian Gulf on one of the flat-screen TVs.

Neither the secretary of defense nor the DCI was displayed on any monitor in the Sit Room, yet. "We're working on it," they told the president. However, the commander of the U.S. Central Command and several members of his staff were now visible on one of the screens.

Frank, now the expert on navigation in the Strait, stood by the monitor with the map and used it for reference. "Solely as a navigation issue, the Strait is not overly challenging; the western traffic separation scheme is even less so. The Strait, at its narrowest point, is about 21 miles wide, between Oman and Iran. The world's largest crude-oil tankers—some in the vicinity of 150,000 tons, or more—routinely transit through the Strait. For comparison, the *Nimitz* displaces about 95,000 tons. Inbound traffic is slightly different in that the tankers are usually empty, so they can maneuver easily and may transit at higher speeds. With GPS, it is easy to stay in line and stay within the confines of your lane. Also, the water in the Strait, shallow by open-ocean depth standards, is sufficiently deep, between 80 to 130 feet, if I remember correctly. The *Nimitz*, fully loaded, would typically draw around 43 feet of water, leaving over 30 feet between the keel and the shallowest area of the Gulf, the Strait. On average, 14 to 15 tankers transit in each direction each day. So, the tanker traffic is continual yet not excessive. Numerous small fishing vessels regularly cross the traffic lanes, and many seem to have little interest in complying with the Rules of the Road, assuming they even know of them. There's also the fact that this area is very close to Iran, arguably in their territorial waters, principally when entering the Gulf, and that adds another dimension to the transit experience. Overall, as navigator, I felt comfortable dealing with the large tanker traffic. The many small patrol-boat-like craft and innumerable dhows (small fishing boats) can pose safety and maneuvering challenges for large ships like *Nimitz*. Their movements are often surprising, and not always in accordance with the maritime rules."

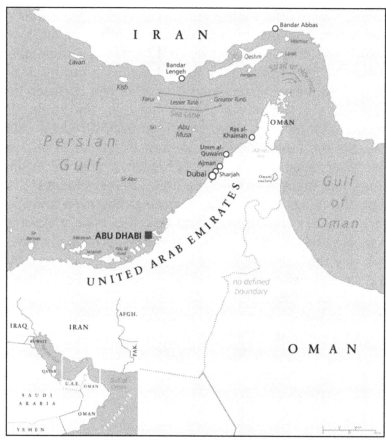

Copyright Peter Hermes Furian|Dreamstime.com

Frank remained standing by the map displayed on the TV monitor in case there were questions.

With none forthcoming, Sharon Fleming wanted to emphasize the issue of the three islands under dispute, but deferred to the secretary of state when she nodded at her and raised a finger.

"Mr. President," Martha Wheatley stated, "it is important to note that located in the western traffic separation scheme—in the buffer zone—are two of the islands, the Greater Tunb and Lessor Tunb, which are a part of the long-running feud between Iran and the UAE. South of the eastbound (outbound) lane is the third island Abu Musa, the largest of the three that Iran claims and occupies and probably the most important one. The Iranians have patrol boats, anti-ship missiles, and some coastal artillery assets based on these islands." Wheatly quickly reviewed the history of the islands and the territorial claims made by each side of the issue. She noted the regional impact of the unusually forthright and borderline caustic comments recently made by UAE representatives at the latest GCC meeting in Abu Dhabi. "I have restated to UAE officials our continuing full support of their position and our hope that the issue will soon be considered by the World Court in The Hague."

Two flat screen TVs simultaneously lit up, one with the secretary of defense, Lawfton Collier, along with the chairman of the Joint Chiefs, the other with the director of National Intelligence (DNI), Rand (Randal) Powers, and the director of the CIA, Grayson Harvey. The Situation Room watchstanders transferred all remote participants to quadrants on the giant screen that faced the President's chair, together with the map of the Strait of Hormuz. The symbol of an aircraft carrier was depicted on the Persian Gulf map about 20 miles east-southeast of Abu Musa island.

A watchstander stuck his head into the conference room and said *Nimitz* position bulletins had, moments ago, stopped changing. He reported the data indicated that the ship had "parked" itself. The ship was not indicating any movement. Frank remembered his previous experience with both reactors offline, drifting in water too deep to anchor in, and thought to himself as he took his seat, *"They've probably dropped the hook."*

Much to his surprise, he'd muttered this loud enough for everyone to hear.

Again comfortable, Darren Ballinger felt so at home among the giants of the U.S. government and military hierarchy that he blurted out, "What did *Nimitz* do? Something about a hook?"

Frank, recovering from his unintentional comment, explained, "The *Nimitz* has likely dropped its anchor, the 'hook,' until it gets one of its two reactors back online. It was probably starting to drift, and the captain thought it best to stay put until they get some power back to the screws—to the ship's propellers."

President Sheppard nodded in a way that suggested he didn't completely accept Frank's latest comments. He then welcomed Secretary Collier, the head of the United States defense establishment, to the meeting along with the most senior U.S. uniformed military officer, the chairman of the Joint Chiefs. He extended a welcome to the heads of the U.S. intelligence apparatus. All four gentlemen confirmed they had been able to hear the discussion so far, though the visual link had just been established. The video conferencing was now fully functional. As an example of how quickly, and widely, information gets reported and distributed, SecDef at USPaCom at Camp H.M. Smith in Hawaii, and the DCI at Langley, CIA headquarters, both confirmed that *Nimitz* had indeed anchored.

Darren Ballinger shook his head back and forth and kept repeating, "Anchored?" The question was on the mind of everyone in the Sit Room, including the president, and they all looked at Frank for an explanation.

"As far as bodies of water go, the Persian Gulf is comparatively shallow. I think the maximum depth of water in the Gulf is about 300 feet and the average depth is around 165 feet. It's practically a wading pool compared to the oceans of the world. The *Nimitz* has over 1,000 feet of anchor chain, so anchoring, considering water depth, would pose no problem."

Darren challenged, "And you don't need any power to drop the anchor, or the hook, as you call it?"

Frank replied, "The ship's backup emergency diesel generators power the anchor windlasses and allow the *Nimitz* to lower and raise the hook. Also, please understand that as the anchor drops, its primary purpose is to pull the chain out of the chain locker. The anchors each weigh 30 tons—60,000 pounds. Each chain link weighs 360 pounds. It's the weight of the chain that keeps the ship in place, not the anchor.

"As I stated, I am presuming the captain decided to keep his ship in one location while the reactor department addresses its issues as opposed to drifting with the currents, which can be substantial in the Persian Gulf, especially near the Strait of Hormuz."

9

It was now 1345 (1:45 pm) in Washington, D.C.; 1845Z, and 2245 (10:45 pm) in Dubai, UAE, the local time where *Nimitz* was currently anchored. Several moments of silence filled the Situation Room following Frank Warren's last comments.

The president, obviously processing what he had just heard, and thinking of his years of dealing with the Iranians and the overall complexity of the Persian Gulf area, had mentally devised several options in response to Iran's actions. The purpose of the meeting, however, was to consider the experiences and perspectives of the individuals participating via video conferencing and those gathered in the Situation Room before finalizing his decision. He suggested a framework of how to proceed. "I think our discussions going forward should focus on the following: we know what has happened, now I want us to consider what might happen over the next several hours, and perhaps over the next several days. As a part of that discussion, I want to hear your thoughts on Iranian motives and objectives, why the massive naval deployment, and what end they are striving to achieve. Some questions I have are:

"1. What are the Iranians doing?

"2. What are their full military capabilities?

"3. What do they hope to achieve?

"4. Are other actors—other nations—involved? If so, why?

"5. Are the Iranian actions being directed from Tehran? Is it possible this is some rogue operation?

"6. Is the U.S. clean? Do we have mud on our face—have we done something or said something to provoke the Iranians? Are we the target of their actions? Who is their target, if not us, assuming there is a target, and this is not merely a naval exercise?

"7. Lastly, of course, what do we do—militarily and diplomatically? I need several courses of action to consider with some pros and cons for each.

"Time is hardly our friend, so I want to put a clock on our discussions. Let's limit the discussion phase to 45 minutes until 1430 (2:30 pm; 1930Z). Then I am going to leave the room, and you can consult among yourselves and devise some strategies for me to consider. I want the secretary of state and SecDef to coordinate the discussion and recommendations. I'll come back around 1515 (3:15 pm; 2015Z), and we'll decide on a plan going forward. We have about 45 minutes for discussion, so, please, be brief and specific." The president looked around the room and looked directly at Sharon. "Your thoughts, Sharon, if you would start us out."

Thus began what Frank Warren considered, and would reflect upon later, as one of the most concise, informative, and insightful exchanges about U.S.-Iranian relations he'd ever witnessed.

Sharon began. "By way of review, in 1953, the United States, in a joint effort with Great Britain, participated in a plot that led to the ouster of Iran's democratically elected Prime Minister, Mohammed Mossadegh. The Eisenhower administration had been concerned about the Soviet Union's increasing influence on Iran and its prime minister. This action led to the restoration of a monarch, Shah Mohammad Reza Pahlavi. Not surprisingly, this coup is widely remembered by Iran as a sign of Western meddling and interference in Iranian affairs.

"Then in 1957, the United States helped start Iran's nuclear power program. We signed a civil nuclear cooperation deal with the Shah which provided technical assistance and the use of enriched uranium by Iran. And in 1975, a West German company began building a nuclear power plant in Bushehr.

"In 1976, the Ford administration indicated a willingness to participate in the Shah's plan to construct 23 nuclear power plants throughout Iran. The United States also agreed to sell Iran four *Spruance*-class destroyers."

Secretary of State Wheatley continued the summary. "During these decades, there was a growing undercurrent of political and religious unrest spreading across the country, primarily at the hand of Ayatollah Ruhollah Khomeini. He was the son and grandson of Shiite mullahs and wrote prolifically on Islamic philosophy, law, and ethics, and was an outspoken opponent of the Shah. Khomeini advocated for Islamic purity and denounced Western influences.

"Eventually, in November 1964, he was arrested and exiled from Iran. He first went to Bursa, Turkey, and then, less than a year later, settled in Al-Najaf in Iraq, a major Shiite theological center. In October 1978, then-Vice President Saddam Hussein of Iraq encouraged (some say forced) Khomeini to leave Iraq, which led him to a suburb of Paris. From there, his supporters relayed tape recorded messages which were aired to an ever-increasingly aroused and angry Iranian population.

"In late 1978, demonstrations, strikes, and overall civil unrest became widespread and led, ultimately, to the forced departure of the Shah of Iran on January 16, 1979.

Two weeks later, on February 1, 1979, Ayatollah Khomeini returned to Tehran and was hailed the religious leader of Iran's revolution. On February 11, 1979, Khomeini declared the country the Islamic Republic of Iran."

Everyone in the Sit Room was familiar with this general, recent history of U.S.-Iranian relations, but Secretary Wheatley's and Sharon Fleming's recall of specific dates and events was impressive.

The secretary continued. "As we all know, later that year, on November 4, 1979, Iranian militants seized control of the U.S. Embassy in Tehran, a plan Ayatollah Khomeini had prior knowledge of and sanctioned. Significantly, that date—November 4, 1979—continues to be celebrated in Iran as a national holiday. In early 1980, the U.S. severed diplomatic relations with Iran, and in April we attempted the embassy hostage rescue, which failed miserably. Also, in 1980, the Iran-Iraq war began, a conflict where the U.S. supported Iraq's Saddam Hussein, who had become president, by providing arms, money, and intelligence, and even tolerating (some claim, aiding) Saddam's chemical attacks on Iranian forces using sarin and mustard gas.

"In 1983, Iranian-supported factions, using suicide bombers, attacked U.S. personnel and facilities three times: two attacks took place in Beirut, Lebanon; the third, in Kuwait City, Kuwait. The first attack occurred on April 18th when a truck drove into the U.S. embassy and exploded, killing 63 people, including 17 Americans. The second attack was on October 23rd, when a suicide bomber targeted a U.S. Marine barracks resulting in the deaths of 241 service personnel.[16] An investigation found the Iran-backed Hezbollah terrorist group was responsible for both attacks. The third attack, in Kuwait City, occurred on

December 12th when Hezbollah and operatives of the Iranian-backed Iraqi Shiite group Da'Wa ("The Call") carried out a series of six coordinated bombings (a seventh was thwarted), killing six people (no Americans) and wounding nearly ninety more.[17] On January 23, 1984, George Shultz, then-secretary of state, named Iran a 'state sponsor of terrorism,' thus subjecting Iran to a host of U.S. and international sanctions."

Secretary Wheatley and Sharon Fleming seamlessly passed the briefing baton to each other. Secretary Wheatley continued. "1988 was a particularly challenging year for U.S.-Iran relations. First, on April 14, the USS *Samuel B. Roberts* (FFG-58), an *Oliver Hazard Perry*-class guided missile frigate, struck an Iranian mine in the Persian Gulf, suffering significant damages, with injuries to 10 sailors but no fatalities. The heroic actions of the ship's crew saved the ship from sinking. Four days later, the U.S. launched *Operation Praying Mantis* in retaliation, destroying two Iranian oil terminals, sinking the Iranian corvette *Sahand* and the missile patrol boat *Joshan*, and severely damaging a second corvette, the *Sabalan*.

"Then on July 3, the USS *Vincennes* (CG-49), a *Ticonderoga*-class guided missile cruiser with the Aegis combat weapons system, shot down an Iranian civilian airliner, an Airbus A-300. The aircraft, flying in international airspace above the Persian Gulf on the centerline of a published civilian airway, was on a flight from Bandar Abbas, Iran, to Dubai, UAE, a straight-line distance of about 150 miles. Earlier that same day a helicopter from the *Vincennes* had come under fire from Iranian patrol boats. The cruiser gave chase and, while in pursuit of the patrol boats, got a contact on its surface-to-air radar, misidentifying the airliner as an Iranian F-14

Tomcat on an attack profile. (The United States sold F-14's [approximately 80 aircraft] to only one foreign country: Iran.) After repeated attempts to establish radio contact with the erroneously designated threatening intruder, *Vincennes* fired two surface-to-air SM-2 (second generation standard missile) missiles which destroyed the airliner. All souls onboard, 274 passengers (including 66 children), and 16 crew members were killed, nearly all of them Iranian. The ship's calls on both UHF and VHF emergency frequencies went unanswered by the Iranian airliner."

Frank had never flown an Airbus and didn't know if they came equipped with UHF radios; he thought not, as they are more common to military aircraft. Boeing planes, which he flew at Delta, were not so equipped. Thus, calls to the Airbus on the UHF emergency frequency of 243.0 (called "guard") would not have been heard. The VHF emergency frequency of 121.5 (also "guard") is commonly monitored by civilian pilots worldwide. On a 30-minute flight across the Gulf, however, one could understand that listening to the guard frequency may not have been the pilots' top priority. Checklists and approach and arrival briefings could have easily consumed, even demanded, the crew's time and attention. With no response to its warnings and fearing an attack, *Vincennes* acted.[18]

Sharon Fleming noted that after the Iran Air Flight 655 incident and continuing into the latter part of the 1990's, the United States and Iran attempted to repair the diplomatic stalemate between their two countries. After the terrorist attacks on September 11, 2001, the two nations were able to work with each other against the Taliban in Afghanistan. Reports state some U.S. diplomats saw the possibility of reestablishing some form of cooperative relationship with Iran. Whatever was there—or might have potentially been a diplomatic opening to pursue—vanished with the January 2002, State of the Union address. That night, the president of the United States used the phrase "Axis of Evil" in describing Iraq, North Korea, and Iran. The Iranians, not surprisingly, were furious. The movement toward some degree of normalization with Iran was completely thwarted and has remained stalled, if not dead in its tracks, ever since. One senior U.S. diplomat reportedly lamented, "We were just that close."[19]

The discussion shifted to the Iranian military threat. As a former pilot of S-3 aircraft, the original primary mission of which was anti-submarine warfare, Frank was surprised to hear that the two Kilo subs were of little concern to anyone. Secretary Collier, the chairman of the Joint Chiefs, DCI Grayson Harvey, and DNI Rand Powers shrugged their shoulders at the presence of the two submarines. In fact, the intel duo was surprised that Iran got the subs under way—an eyebrow-raising event, in their minds, in and of itself. They said as a show of force, it was much more "show" than "force."

Russian-built Kilo submarines had been around since the early 1980s. Iran purchased three of the diesel-electric vessels from Russia between 1992 and 1996. The Kilo, one of the quietest diesel-electric submarines in the world, was expressly designed for anti-shipping and anti-submarine operations. It can carry a total of 18 torpedoes, or, in lieu of torpedoes, 24 mines or, eventually, submarine-launched anti-ship cruise missiles. How these two Kilos were fitted out was unknown, but the fact that neither had yet submerged suggested to the DCI and DNI that the condition of the two submarines was questionable and/or the Iranians were uncomfortable with the relatively shallow water surrounding the Strait (80-130 feet) with the preferred operating depth of the Kilo established at 150 feet.

10

The Situation Room participants thus placed the submarine threat below the more complicated and disconcerting challenge of Iran's many patrol and small boats. Everyone was familiar with Iran's self-proclaimed "swarming" strategy, used against the USS *Cole* in October of 2000[20], which involved numerous patrol boats approaching their target from several different directions, employing the principles of asymmetrical tactics and irregular warfare. It was an Iranian David against an adversarial Goliath scenario, straight out of the book of Samuel. The technique had been proven effective, and all Sit Room participants knew it.

The complicated and perplexing task before them was to determine the intentions of the 50 or so patrol and small boats, operated by the Iranian Revolutionary Guard Corps Navy (IRGCN). Overhead imagery indicated the boats were gathering in groups of between 5 and 20 units. Sharon Fleming, Rear Adm. Donaldson, and DCI Grayson Harvey discussed the issue and the threats posed by the "small boats."

These boats, less than 65 feet in length, with 1 to 10 crew members, were fast and maneuverable with speeds up to 60 miles per hour. Patrol boats, over 100 feet in length, were slower. Machine guns and rocket-propelled grenades were common on small boats, plus most could deploy mines, torpedoes, and anti-ship missiles. However, due to their relatively small size and their weapons load constraint, they could only employ small warhead, short-range munitions. Typically, boats of this length used the element of surprise to their advantage—contrary to the event currently unfolding. Their use in a suicide mission, as in the attack on the *Cole*, also presented a grave threat. A capital ship like the *Nimitz*, temporarily out of commission, might offer a target too tempting for some Iranian unit(s). Zealous sailors could try to be martyrs for their country by ramming and exploding their heavily burdened vessel(s) directly into the side of the *Nimitz*, the mighty symbol of the Great Satan. In their minds, what a glorious death that would be.

President Sheppard, continuing to process information, inquired about Iran's anti-ship missile capabilities. DCI Harvey estimated Iran possessed at least several hundred anti-ship cruise missiles (ASCM) and coastal defense cruise missiles (CDCM), plus several dozen mobile launch batteries. Many of the missiles had come from China or were based on Chinese designs, including the short range (5-25 miles) C-801 Sardine and its successor, the 75 mile, .9 Mach (690 miles per hour) C-802 Saccade. DNI Rand Powers noted that as many as 60 of an estimated arsenal of 75 C-802 ASCMs were installed on the island of Qeshm. Iran still possessed older CSS-N-2 Silkworm and CSS-N-3 Seersucker land-based anti-ship missiles with operational ranges of approximately 60 miles. Intelligence sources indicated the deployment of around 300 of these missiles near Bandar Abbas.

DNI Powers noted, "If ASCMs are loaded on some of the 10 French-made Kaman fast missile boats that Iran possesses, on their speedboats (with C-801s), or on some of the 10 Chinese-made Houdong fast missile boats (with C-802s), the problem is obvious: numerous ASCMs, many launch platforms, innumerable launch positions, and a limited operating area."

President Sheppard listened intently to the ongoing discussion. Much of what he was hearing was a review of what he and the others in the Sit Room were familiar with. Nonetheless, the data being presented helped the president to sharpen his focus on options he was considering in response to Iran's actions.

Rear Adm. Donaldson spoke of the tactical environment current in the Gulf. "*Nimitz* is in company with two escort ships, USS *Bunker Hill* (CG-52), a *Ticonderoga*-class guided missile cruiser (like *Vincennes*), and USS *Milius* (DDG-69), an *Arleigh Burke*-class guided missile destroyer. All three ships (including *Nimitz*) have defensive weapons systems to counter inbound cruise missiles, but the sheer volume of potential ASCMs suggests that some could possibly find their intended target. The three U.S. warships are each equipped with the Phalanx close-in weapons system (CIWS—pronounced sea-wiz) with an effective range of just over 2 miles. The system is nicknamed R2D2 from Star Wars because of its distinctive round, barrel-shaped radome. CIWS fires armor-piercing tungsten rounds at the rate of 75 rounds *per second* (4,500 rounds/minute); it is hard to assess the likelihood of an Iranian ASCM breaking through this defensive barrier of metal as it nears its target. By its design and name, CIWS is considered a last resort defensive system."

The admiral, an accomplished briefer, had everyone's attention. "Iranian ASCM launch platforms need initial target location data, even within the close confines of the Persian Gulf. Several types of radars provide that data, but by their nature, radars emit electronic signals. These emissions can be intercepted, interpreted, identified and correlated with specific weapons systems and their geographic location. The United States has several platforms—weapons systems—that can monitor, analyze, and assess enemy signals and then transmit this electronic data to an appropriate offensive asset which can, within minutes of initial detection, deliver a weapon and destroy the emitter. The electronic platforms include the RC-135 Rivet Joint aircraft, which can detect, identify, and geolocate signals, and then feed this data to JSTARS (Joint Surveillance Target and Attack Radar System) aircraft. JSTARS, with SAR (synthetic aperture radar), generates a map with likely radar locations and forwards that data to appropriate on-scene tactical aircraft."[21]

Admiral Donaldson, clearly in his element, continued his discussion, enjoying the attention of the president and the other participants. "An Iranian ASCM launch can also be detected by U.S. Defense Support Program (DSP) satellites, which have been operational since the early 1970s. The detection information is relayed to various ground stations, both fixed and mobile, and from there that data, using Link-16, is transmitted to ships and planes. The aircraft, the Air Force E-3 Sentry and the Navy's E-2 Hawkeye, both Airborne Warning and Control System (AWACS)[22] platforms, combine DSP data with altitude and direction of flight of an ASCM as it travels toward its target. The AWACS system can refine the estimated launch point of the missile. The combination of data from RC-135, JSTARS, DSP, and AWACS assets and the interoperability of these various systems enhances the U.S.'s capability to detect missile launches and determine the location of the launcher. With drones now entering the equation, specifically the Global Hawk unmanned aerial vehicle (UAV)[23] with its dual-mode radar, missile launch sites can be quickly determined and accurately targeted.

"An aggressor nation might consider the *Nimitz* to be the ultimate prize—the high-value unit—but an adversary who underestimates the impressive capabilities and total lethality of *Ticonderoga*-class cruisers and *Arleigh Burke*-class destroyers does so at extreme risk and their personal peril. The two warships joining *Nimitz* to form their battle group are each a potent force but are particularly effective when supported by their electronic partners."

Darren Ballinger was impressed by the admiral's comments and breadth of knowledge. As a former Battle Group commander, Donaldson was the primary speaker about battle group capabilities and characteristics and spoke glowingly of *Bunker Hill* and *Milius* and their impact on group tactics and offensive capabilities. Here was an aviator talking about "ship stuff" and battle group operations. Earlier, Donaldson said he didn't know "all things navy." Darren wasn't so sure that was true.

The president, checking the time, asked what some thought to be an unusual question: What about Iran's land-based air defense capabilities? Both the DNI and the DCI (and others) had concerned looks on their faces, each wondering if the president was thinking of sending aircraft into Iran on a bombing mission. Everyone tried to avoid looking surprised by the president's question, but failed.

Lt. Gen. Townsend, the director of the Joint Staff, fielded the president's question. "Between 12,000 to 15,000 personnel, out of Iran's 52,000-man air force, are assigned to its land-based air defense network. The SA-6 Gainful and SA-10 Grumble, both newer Russian-made surface-to-air missiles, are on order to update their aging defensive capabilities, but there is no evidence that Iran has received either system. Iran has over 150 I-HAWK (Improved Homing All the Way Killer) anti-air missile batteries which are all-weather capable and have a flight ceiling of 65,000 feet. Raytheon, headquartered in Waltham, Massachusetts, makes the I-HAWK. This is another example, like the F-14, of the United States selling a military system or aircraft to a country which later became adversarial. Iran has found it difficult, if not impossible, to procure spare parts for its I-HAWK batteries since November 1979 after the takeover of the U.S. embassy in Tehran. Now, approximately 28 years later, we question the operational status of those I-HAWKs. Also, since a U.S. company built and serviced the I-HAWK, (the predecessor to the Patriot missile system used by the U.S. Army), you'd think we'd be familiar with effective countermeasures to minimize its usefulness—which is true.

"The remainder of Iran's surface-to-air missile (SAM) defense consists of two systems which are old—nearly obsolete—and are subject to electronic countermeasures: the SA-2 Guideline (effective out to about 28 miles) and the SA-5 Gammon (with a range of approximately 35-155 miles). Both are Soviet-made systems, built in the 1950s, primarily to defend against large, non-maneuvering, high-altitude aircraft, such as our B-52 Stratofortress and U-2 Dragon Lady spy plane. Iran has placed the SA-2 around significant bases and cities, including Bandar Abbas. The SA-5, a longer-range missile compared to the SA-2, is deployed around oil facilities, major ports, and Tehran. The SA-5 is capable of speeds up to Mach 4 and is effective up to 100,000 feet while the SA-2 is a Mach 3.5 SAM and is lethal at altitudes from 60,000 to 80,000 feet. Operational since 1957, the SA-2 Guideline is the most widely deployed air defense system in history. By 1965, the Russians had over 1,000 SA-2's throughout their empire and their satellite locations, including many in what was then known as East Berlin. Now, fifty years after its initial installation (1957 to 2007), its capabilities still have to be considered."

"As many of you may know," Grayson Harvey noted, "the SA-2 Guideline enjoys some degree of notoriety in the world of SAM's: On May 1, 1960, a SA-2 missile shot down a U.S. U-2 spy plane piloted by Francis Gary Powers over the Russian city of Sverdlovsk (since 1991, renamed Yekaterinburg) in the Ural Mountains. The U-2's flight originated in Peshawar, Pakistan, and the planned route would traverse some 2,000 miles of Soviet territory en route to a military airfield in Bodo, Norway. Two SA-2's, from what we were able to determine, brought down the U-2. Unfortunately, the Soviets also shot down one of their MiG-19 jets that day, killing the pilot, a victim of one of the many SA-2's launched at the U-2. The MiG was in pursuit of the U-2 and was near the spy plane. Mr. Powers ejected from his crippled, descending aircraft as it passed through 15,000 feet and was captured by the KGB, resulting in internment and interrogations. In February 1962, the United States obtained Powers' release, as part of a prisoner exchange, for Soviet Colonel Rudolf Abel, a Soviet spy we captured in New York City in June 1957. Also released back to U.S. custody was Frederic Pryor, an American student, held by East German authorities since August 1961.

"A second U-2 spy plane was shot down on October 27, 1962 by another SA-2, this time over Cuba during the Cuban missile crisis. The pilot, Air Force Major Rudolf Anderson, was the sole fatality of that tense, highly stressful, on-the-verge-of-nuclear-war confrontation between the then two superpowers: the United States and the Soviet Union."

The discussion about Iran's air defense system concluded with these observations: first, relative to its size (slightly smaller than Alaska but two and a half times the size of Afghanistan) the number of Iranian surface-to-air missile batteries is not particularly noteworthy. Whatever the configuration of their defenses, they are going to be spread relatively thin. Second, their primary SAM systems are quite old; maintenance costs continue to escalate with time. Third, interoperability is an essential element of multiple weapons systems. Combining data from intelligence, surveillance, and communications networks into an integrated air defense system—or any defense system—is critical. Iran imported—purchased—weapon systems from various countries. These systems were not designed or built to work together.

DNI Powers summarized the intelligence community's view of Iran's air defense setup. "Command and control, systems integration, battle management systems and their associated data links, timeliness of data transfer, resistance to jamming and electronic countermeasures— these vital issues pose significant challenges to any country's overall defensive architecture. If you import systems and hardware from different foreign suppliers, connectivity and interface integration problems rise exponentially. We assess there is a significant opportunity to exploit Iran's systems connectivity vulnerability and we think we have the right assets in place to do just that."

11

It was now nearly 1430 (2:30 pm) in Washington; 2330 (11:30 pm) in Dubai, UAE. It had been approximately 3½ hours since *Nimitz* had secured her #1 reactor as flight operations were concluding and, shortly after that, something occurred causing the EOOW to shut down the #2 reactor. After some time adrift, *Nimitz* dropped her anchor, and locating information confirmed she had remained stationary. The president glanced at the time and assumed a thoughtful stare, eyes focused on nothing, brain thinking at full speed. He placed a hand on each arm of his chair, preparing to stand when the DCI spoke.

Grayson Harvey had been director of the CIA for two years and was very well respected for his leadership. "Mr. President, may we talk to you privately?" The "we" meant the director of national intelligence and himself; they wished to privately discuss some sensitive, compartmented information. The president looked down at the lower left section of the large screen before him where the DCI and the DNI were visible and paused briefly before replying in the affirmative. He stood up, as did everyone else. With a nod of his head to Pete Sanders and Martha Wheatley to follow him, he started toward the door leading to the smaller conference rooms. On the way out, the president stopped and turned to address the remaining attendees: "I'd like all of you ..."

"Achmed." Unintentionally uttered out loud—little more than a whisper. Frank saw all eyes in the room suddenly turn toward him. It seemed everyone was surprised, not so much by what was said but that he had interrupted the president of the United States. The only people not looking straight at Frank Warren were the DCI and the DNI—these two men were looking at each other. Who was this guy? How did he know the name Achmed?

Frank Warren, had, for the second time in under two hours, allowed his thought process to produce a spoken word. He'd been listening carefully to the discussion about U.S./Iran relationships. But part of his mind had been drifting to several topics: the Strait of Hormuz, Iranian military assets—how many, types, delivery platforms; diplomacy—how do we engage in conversation with a country's regime with no diplomatic ties to us? Is the *Nimitz* battle group about to be attacked? Are tankers transiting the Strait of Hormuz in danger—is there now increased risk about safe passage? Could this Iranian activity be related to the price of oil? Frank remembered the per barrel price of oil being in the low $70's back in July (July 10, 2006: $73.61). Now it was in the low $50's? (January 12, 2007: $52.99). Could oil prices possibly be a part of Iran's decision to put all those boats to sea along with two Kilo submarines? The most important and pressing question persisted: what were the Iranians up to?

While reviewing these things in his head as he listened to the previous discussion, he recalled his visit to the CIA, set up by his buddy and former fellow C.O., William "Will Call" Stimson, and the tour of the Langley facility, escorted by Anthony Darnell. But there was that moment in a room with several files. One in particular he quickly scanned out of curiosity. It contained several bits of interesting data, including a name—the first name, he thought, not the surname—of an individual: Achmed.

Automatically rising with the others, Frank had been so entrenched in his thoughts he didn't realize he had quietly

said the name out loud. His first understated utterance—
"hook" —had resulted in a brief discussion about *Nimitz*'s
anchor and the act of anchoring, which was later
confirmed. So, all was well—then. Not this time.

The president, his tone and demeanor now more
serious and official, took a step toward Frank and
addressed him: "Mr. Warren, do you have something to
share?"

"Achmed, sir."

The DCI broke in—remotely: "Mr. President, I think we
should ..." He was cut off by a wave of the president's hand
and stopped talking in mid-sentence.

Frank Warren, addressing his commander in chief, said,
"Mr. President, I happened to come across the name
'Achmed' a while back. I didn't catch his last name; I
assume Achmed is not his surname. The name was
associated with Iran and Iraq—more specifically,
Baghdad—and that's about it. I sensed Achmed may have
been what we'd call a bad guy who was now enjoying our
hospitality as a guest of the United States."

That airy, almost flippant answer did not fit well with
the atmosphere in the Situation Room. Sharon looked
questioningly at Frank, and Admiral Donaldson fought to
control a grimace. The president seemed more curious and
skeptical than upset or angry. It was evident the name
"Achmed" held particular significance to both the
president and to his intelligence chiefs.

The president continued, "You 'came across' this
Achmed name, is that correct?"

Frank was a man on an island, and the tide was rolling
in. He was helpless, defenseless, and guilty as sin. In
aviation, you never want to be out of altitude, airspeed,
and ideas all at the same time. Frank was the perfect

analogy to that aviation adage: he had no explanations, no way out, and no ideas. No one could offer a hand or throw him a lifeline—nothing. His president had asked him a question, and who more than the president deserved an answer?

"Sir, Achmed's name is what I call 'guilty knowledge.' It was not something I sought or did anything devious or illegal to obtain. I know the name—the first name, I presume, and no other name, and that is all I know about him. Which is an assumption: that Achmed is a male name. I believe he is Iranian and in U.S. custody, somewhere. I assume I am not cleared for this information, but you, sir, Mr. President, are the only person I have ever discussed this issue with."

The president, pausing pensively, searched Frank's face and made his decision. "Very well, Mr. Warren. I am asking you and everyone here to refrain from ever discussing the name 'Achmed' with anyone, even those cleared to hear it. Please remain here and we'll reconvene shortly."

It was obvious the DCI and DNI had concerns about the clearance levels of the people in the Situation Room, specifically Frank Warren. The president, his secretary of state, and his chief of staff resumed their exit to another conference room to speak more openly to the heads of the U.S. intelligence apparatus. SecDef's and CentCom's screens went blank. Admiral Donaldson, General Townsend, Darren Ballinger, and Sharon Fleming all took their seats. Frank Warren, realizing he was the only one standing, also sat down. Everyone had their "eyes in the boat" —they looked straight ahead. Everyone except Darren Ballinger, who stared directly at Frank.

Frank stared blankly at nothing. He sensed Darren's intense gaze but oddly, he enjoyed an upwelling of confidence. He'd had some experiences that others in the room had not and felt he'd contributed to today's discussion. The "Achmed" comment, Frank assessed, was wholly inappropriate yet mildly satisfying. He felt like he'd gained some special status points amongst the upper echelon attending today's meeting. He was also naïvely oblivious of the significant security questions he'd just raised about himself which were probably, due to the president's "very well, Mr. Warren" comment, never going to be asked of him.

It's one thing to possess unique knowledge, even "guilty" knowledge, but what did he know? He was aware of a name: Achmed. There was a mountain of information he didn't know about the man; no one currently in the room had any knowledge about him. It was reasonable to assume, however, the CIA and the president knew all about Achmed, thus the admonition not to discuss the name with anyone. Obviously, too, the information associated with this man was highly classified and sensitive. It wouldn't be a stretch for everyone in the Sit Room to assume "Achmed" was now a central figure in the discussions going on in the smaller conference room. And everyone would be correct.

12

Achmed Farhad Ahmadi was a self-employed salesman, whose product line included various weapons, all of them classified as illegal. He sold to anyone who had money to buy. Not constrained by ideology or strict religious affiliations, Achmed was, first and foremost, a businessman. Before the U.S. invasion of Iraq in March 2003, his business had been good, sales were increasing, and Achmed did quite well. Following the invasion, he did even better.

Formerly from Bandar Abbas, Iran, Achmed limited his arms sales to Baghdad, Iraq and his home town. Bandar Abbas handled approximately 90% of Iran's commercial containerized shipping traffic, including the export of arms and related material, which, it was alleged, violated numerous United Nations Security Council resolutions. Achmed, however, wasn't concerned with United Nations inspectors, resolutions, or constraints, and continued to expand his enterprise, primarily through repeat business and word-of-mouth advertising. "I know a guy ..." was the most often repeated advertising slogan in his line of work, said either in Arabic, in Iraq, or in Persian, (Farsi), in Iran. Achmed spoke both languages—a decided advantage in his line of work.

A core principle and requirement of his business model was the proper vetting of potential customers and his contacts. "Trust" was not a word found in the lexicon of successful illegal arms dealers. The primary metric for how successful one was in Achmed's business was one's survival—staying alive by being excessively cautious (if that's possible) and trusting absolutely no one. How does one properly "vet" a potential customer in the illegal arms business? You had to develop familiarity with the client and establish a "meaningful" relationship. That is how Achmed Farhad Ahmadi came to meet Mr. Michael Wheeler and his wife, Shannon.

Michael and Shannon, both of mixed heritage and ethnicity, were Christian missionaries associated (quite) loosely with the Methodist Church, but affiliated with other non-partisan and non-political aid organizations. This was the cover, or "legend," of the two CIA operatives. With dark skin and black hair, and fluent in both Arabic and Farsi, they attempted a natural, unforced, friendly connection with Achmed (a "bump") when they happened to sit near him one day in a café in Baghdad. While sipping tea, the couple eased into some light conversation with Achmed on a day when the city was unusually quiet— there was hardly any sound of mortars, gunfire or explosives. One might consider this an average day, if such was possible in Baghdad during the U.S. presence there.

Michael and Shannon Wheeler, admittedly advocates of the Christian faith, but deeply respectful of the Muslim religion, professed no opinion of the on-going U.S. involvement in Middle East events or the affairs of senior Iraqi officials. The primary purpose of their lives was to help others, like the oppressed people of Iraq who had endured great suffering. If Achmed's business could somehow help those in need, then they saw the good in his efforts and praised his soul, and, by extension, his professional enterprise. Their first meeting ended cordially, and upon parting, Achmed said that he hoped they might meet again. Michael and Shannon both replied, almost in unison, *"Insha'Allah,"* Arabic for "If Allah wills."

They did meet again, but even the most devout believers should question God's involvement in their second "coincidental" encounter. Michael and Shannon were strolling along a street, heading toward a local hospital. Achmed was pleasantly surprised when he saw the missionary couple walking toward him, appropriately not touching each other yet still walking together. When Michael and Shannon's eyes met Achmed's, they expressed immense joy in their luck in once again seeing their new friend.

"As-Salaam – Alaikum," said Michael (peace be unto you), broadly smiling as he extended his right hand to greet his friend from the café. Achmed smiled and offered his right hand, repeating the same greeting as he eased toward Michael for a customary cheek kiss, right cheek first, then left. Michael had hoped for that degree of familiarity but had let Achmed take the lead. Achmed and Shannon then exchanged verbal greetings—but no handshake, of course—and, with Shannon standing to one side, the two men rejoiced at their good fortune of being able to renew their friendship.

Speaking in Arabic, Achmed had a suggestion. "Let us walk together and celebrate our reunion by having some tea. It is a beautiful day and a café is only a short walk away."

Michael agreed immediately. "An excellent idea, my friend. Show me the way. Praise Allah for bringing us together again."

Achmed took Michael's arm and led the way, Shannon walking behind them. The missionaries cultivated their friendship with Achmed Ahmadi, ensuring random "chance" encounters and having dinner with him in their apartment. The Wheelers noticed that Shannon's physical attractiveness and encouraging, slightly flirty personality appealed to Achmed and loosened his tongue. Through their conversations with him, they learned about his brother, Ali, who lived in Bandar Abbas, Iran, and worked "at the port"; this was all they could glean from Achmed. Some of their discussions with Achmed occasionally strayed into uncomfortable areas—talk about his brother being one.

Michael and Shannon Wheeler spent several months helping the injured and the inconvenienced people of Baghdad while developing a close friendship with Achmed. They learned a great deal about Achmed's enterprising business activities: where he purchased his weapons, who his suppliers were, who his customers were, how the money flowed, and how much money was involved. Achmed had few business partners—he was essentially a one-person operation—who contracted out certain functions and activities to others who specialized in their field of expertise. He had developed a network of providers, each seeking their slice of the illegal weapons pie. The AK-47 Kalashnikov was Achmed's number-one seller, and he used several suppliers to fill his orders. Like many people, Achmed talked about his work when he was in comfortable surroundings, and because Michael and Shannon were excellent listeners, these discussions became, over time, lengthier and more specific.

Early one pleasant evening, with light breezes and temperatures in the low 80's and the muffled sound of sporadic gunfire far off in the distance, Michael and Shannon Wheeler shared coffee with Achmed at an outdoor café. The Wheelers reluctantly advised him they were transferring soon to Bandar Abbas in Iran, a country that was 90-95% Shia Muslim and only 1-2% Christian.

The aid and assistance organization in Baghdad had made all their arrangements, they told Achmed, and they were scheduled to depart in a day or so. The Wheelers expressed their sadness about leaving Baghdad and their friends, particularly Achmed, but they were excited about their impending move to Bandar Abbas, over 800 miles away, and looking forward to their new challenges with hope and anticipation. Achmed replied, *"Masha 'Allah"* — expressing his joy about the Wheelers' good fortune in being sent to Bandar Abbas. When it was time to depart that evening, Achmed shook hands with Michael, kissing both cheeks of his good friend. He advised him and Shannon that he had told his brother Ali about them, and encouraged them to contact Ali once settled in their new location. The Wheelers said their heartfelt goodbyes, *"Ma'a as-salaama,"* assuring Achmed they'd be in touch with Ali, and thanking him again for his many kindnesses and friendship.

The Wheelers left Baghdad the next morning, leaving their apartment empty with no trace of its recent inhabitants. That evening, roughly 24 hours after Michael and Shannon had said goodbye, Achmed Farhad Ahmadi delivered 20 AK-47 semi-automatic rifles and 2,000 rounds of 7.62 mm ammunition to a buyer he had done business with two previous times. An old, unremarkable flatbed truck made the delivery to an abandoned building. In an empty ground-floor room, one light bulb, miraculously illuminated by Baghdad's uncertain power grid, hung uncertainly from a sagging ceiling which seemed ready to give way at any moment. A single, battered table, perched on several rocks to offset the different lengths of the legs, sat in the dim light of the bulb.

Two old metal chairs were placed on opposite sides of the table.

When the truck arrived, the driver and his assistant unloaded five wooden boxes of AK-47s and placed them inside the room following Achmed's directions. They also dragged in four metal containers, each packed with 500 rounds of ammunition, and set them near the wooden rifle boxes. The driver and his helper quickly disappeared into the haze and heat of a Baghdad dusk after receiving payment from Achmed.

The buyer, who had been patiently waiting and watching the offload, inspected the ammo and rifles, after which he counted out the money to Achmed, adding the equivalent of an extra $100.00 US in Iraqi dinars (about 120,220 IQD). Under Achmed's watchful eye, he placed the bills neatly on the table in equal stacks for ease of counting. The buyer suggested Achmed carefully count the money for himself, even though Achmed stated he was satisfied with the transaction. After more encouragement from his customer, Achmed relented, saying something to the effect of "if you insist." He pulled out his metal chair and sat down to verify the payment. Comforted by the fact he'd previously done business with this buyer, Achmed was accompanied by only one other person at this meeting who served as a guard and lookout outside of the building while Achmed tallied his payday. Nearly done, Achmed suddenly gasped, looked up with surprise and anguish on his face, and brought his right hand up to his neck. His eyes bulged, and his mouth gaped open as his head started to fall forward toward the table. The small, dart-like device, shot from a gadget that resembled a taser, embedded in his neck and contained enough chemical to cause 90 percent incapacitation for about 10-15 minutes.

Two male individuals, with dark skin and beards, dressed in local garb, silently appeared from a back room. One forced a black bag over Achmed's head, preventing him from hitting the table, while cinching the bag around his neck. The other man grabbed his arms, yanking them backward, and quickly put handcuffs on his wrists. Achmed offered no resistance as his mind and body fought to overcome the temporary paralysis caused by the drug racing through his blood vessels.

Achmed's associate, hearing a slight commotion inside the room, returned to find his boss's hands bound and his head covered with a bag. He was also greeted by three guns, close in, all pointed directly at his nose. Faced with no good options, he stood dead in his tracks and raised both hands to head level, palms facing the three gunmen, his AK-47 hanging loosely from a strap over his shoulder.

The buyer's accomplice, who'd handcuffed Achmed, stepped forward, keeping his arm extended and his weapon pointed directly at the young man's face. In Arabic, he commanded the stunned individual to hand over the Russian-made rifle and drop to his knees with his hands laced behind his head. The terrified guard, fearing for his life, meekly complied. Achmed's covered head tilted forward and uttered bursts of indecipherable noises; he made no attempt to stand or raise his head. The buyer placed his weapon on the table, took a dark plastic bag out of a rear pocket and quickly filled it with the Iraqi dinars stacked on the table. The entire seizure had taken only moments without a word spoken.

The buyer held the bagged money in one hand and with the other reached into his trouser pocket to retrieve a small transmitter, stating quietly, in English, "Ready." He heard a reply, also in English: "Copy. One minute." The buyer returned the transmitter to his pocket, picked up his weapon and pointed it at the kneeling guard's head, ordering him, in Arabic: "Get up." The young man struggled to his feet and followed the buyer's motion toward the empty chair at the table. The buyer commanded, in Arabic, "Sit." The guard—a mere boy—complied as ordered. One of the buyer's assistants pulled handcuffs from his pocket and stepped toward the young captive, but the buyer, obviously the leader of the three, shook his head and said, in English, "Plastic." The metal handcuffs were replaced by plastic restraints, like zip ties. With practiced efficiency, the assistant quickly bound the boy's ankles together and then, with a second restraint, gathered the boy's wrists behind the chair and around a leg of the table. The young man's body started shaking involuntarily, his eyes wide with fear and anticipation. The assailants exchanged glances, knowing what the boy didn't: his life was not in danger, nor would he suffer any pain or extreme discomfort at the hands of the three strangers surrounding him. The buyer touched the boy's ankle restraints and asked, in Arabic, "Too tight?" Startled by the question and apparently questioning its sincerity, the boy shook his head "no." The buyer's assistant reached into another pocket and withdrew three different sized rubber balls. He selected the largest one and opened his mouth, indicating the boy should do the same. The boy hesitantly opened his mouth like he was in a dentist's chair, his body shaking with trepidation. The assistant stuffed the largest ball between his teeth and onto his tongue. Instantly the boy started to gag and shook his head violently while trying to shout his objections to the restraints and the rubber ball. The assistant placed his arm around the boy's head to stop the shaking and removed the ball from his mouth. He chose the next smaller ball and again indicated to the boy to open wide. This ball fit better, but still uncomfortably. The assistant raised his eyebrows, asking, "OK?" The boy nodded, his breathing more controlled and the inclination to gag absent. The assistant produced a colorful scarf from another pocket. He rolled the scarf, placed it over the boy's mouth and tied it behind his neck. The goal was to restrict the young man's ability to yell for help, limit his mobility for a brief period while the gunmen made their escape, and not inflict unnecessary discomfort or injury on him. If he suffered from runaway fear, anticipation and uncertainty—fine, but there was no need for anything more.

The three men, their work complete, surveyed the room, nodded to each other in agreement, and waited for their ride to arrive. An old, dust-covered SUV with worn seats, two cracked windows, and missing hubcaps pulled up outside. The leader, money bag in hand, exited the building, circled the SUV, and placed the money on the floor in front of the passenger seat. He and the driver loaded the AK-47s and ammunition into the rear of the SUV. Achmed—who'd been quiet and subdued during his friend's ordeal—found himself out of his chair and dragged to the vehicle, his legs and feet trailing in the dust. One of the men climbed into the back seat and pulled Achmed in behind him with help from the other assistant. The driver resumed his position behind the wheel, the buyer took his place beside him, and the last assistant jumped into the vehicle and propped Achmed up in the middle of the back seat. They drove into the increasing darkness with no one seeming to notice.

Back in the dimly lit room, the helpless, bound and gagged young man could only listen to the last sounds of

Achmed's kidnapping and the noise of the SUV vanishing into the uncertainty of a Baghdad evening. The unexpected turn of events happened quickly, suddenly—and so quietly. He sat there, trying to process everything that happened, his mind spinning, thanking Allah—profusely—for sparing his life.

In less than 24 hours after his abduction, Achmed was in his new quarters at a CIA black site[24] somewhere in Europe.

13

Bandar Abbas, an Iranian southern coastal city, was the home port of the Iranian navy, including their three Kilo submarines and many of their "small boats." Michael and Shannon Wheeler were among its newest occupants. Their primary raison d'etre was Ali Karim Ahmadi.

From Achmed, now the guest of the CIA, the Agency gradually learned, through repeated "talks, conversations, and discussions," more about his brother, Ali, a Bandar Abbas local employed by what Westerners call the port authority. In his employment, Ali was privy to useful information about specific port activities: arrivals, departures, manifests, and the operational status of various vessels. He also had access to changes in military support operations, notably increases in truck deliveries to naval units of food, parts, and ammunition of any kind.

The objective of "Michael and Shannon Wheeler" was to "bump" Ali Karim Ahmadi as they did his brother, Achmed, a task made significantly easier since Achmed had informed his brother of their impending arrival. Their hope was to glean useful, timely data about Iranian naval assets—data that would be helpful to the CIA and the Defense Department. The Wheelers immersed themselves into the daily life of their new, much smaller surroundings—a population of about 367,500 at the time, compared to Baghdad's over 7 million people—a new city, a new country, a new person of interest, and a new language: Farsi.

Shannon Wheeler gave the appearance of enjoying Ali Ahmadi's rugged appeal and magnetic personality. He was a single man, slightly older than his brother Achmed. At their first meeting, he told the Wheelers it had been a week or two—maybe even three—since he'd heard from his brother, a situation he found increasingly worrisome. Would the Wheelers, of whom Achmed spoke so glowingly, know of anyone in his brother's circle of friends in Baghdad who might know about Achmed's welfare? The Wheelers graciously offered their assistance and assured him they still maintained numerous contacts back in Baghdad.

Early on, the Wheelers discovered several of Ali's strengths and weaknesses. He was a Shiite Muslim and frequented a certain Shia mosque, identified by its two minarets compared to a Sunni mosque, not far away, which had only one. Ali, they observed, was something of a ladies' man who found Shannon most pleasing to look at and be around. Also, they noted, Ali enjoyed the fruit of the vine. Alcohol consumption, as is widely known, is not tolerated within Islamic practices; "intoxicants" are to be avoided and are illegal in Iran. In the relationship and environment cultivated by the Wheelers, Ali grew increasingly comfortable in their company—particularly Shannon's. He looked forward to visiting them in their apartment, especially when the heady combination of an intoxicant and Michael's coincidental absences occurred simultaneously. Increasing comfort levels, however, can lead one to abandon caution. Like his brother Achmed, Ali Ahmadi was being played by experienced, well-trained operatives. Achmed never displayed any personal character weaknesses worthy of exploitation, but Ali couldn't hide his growing infatuation with Shannon Wheeler, nor his fondness for wine.

Left alone together one evening, Shannon edged slightly closer to him on the couch in their apartment. Ali dared ask how the Wheelers obtained such excellent "intoxicants" in a Muslim country. "Very carefully!" she whispered, adjusting her hair and tilting her head, smiling in a way that suggested she was sharing a special secret with an extraordinary friend. They laughed. When Michael returned moments later, they raised their glasses in a salute to the wine, to the lady who had the ingenuity to find the forbidden nectar of the gods, to their friendship, and to Ali and his special place and status in the Wheelers' world.

Whenever they were together, Ali's gaze was squarely on Shannon. She was so naturally and effortlessly charming, he thought. The right setting, the right companion, mix in some "intoxicants" —Ali was smitten. He knew it; he liked it. The Wheelers knew it, and they played Ali Karim Ahmadi like a fine instrument in the hands of a master.

14

Oil has been a dominant influence in the Middle East and throughout the world since its discovery in Persia (now Iran) in 1908, in Iraq (1927), and then in Bahrain, Saudi Arabia and Kuwait (the 1930s). The Strait of Hormuz became, and continues to be, a strategic factor in the transport of not only oil but natural gas, too. Roughly two-thirds of the world's oil reserves are located in the Persian Gulf region, while 29% of the world's natural gas is produced there, as well. Destined primarily for Europe and Japan, 30% of the world's oil supply originates in the Middle East. East Asia, a significant oil consuming region, accounts for 85% of Persian Gulf exports.[25]

Darren Ballinger, the NSC staffer and Middle East expert, provided a gusher of background data to the others in the Sit Room in response to Lieutenant General Townsend's inquiry about the possibility of Iran attempting to close or restrict access to the Strait of Hormuz. Darren noted that 17 million barrels of oil transit the Strait of Hormuz each day, some heading to the United States, which receives 12% of its oil from this region. Western Europe gets 25% of its oil from Persian Gulf countries; Japan, 66%. Of the world's seaborne traded oil, 35% passes through the Strait, as does 15% of the world's commerce.

As the number two oil exporter (behind Saudi Arabia) in the region, Iran's oil production constitutes a massive portion of her economic footprint. In 2006, Iran's exports of crude oil and petroleum products accounted for nearly three-fourths (74%) of the total value of its exports and were equal to 29% of its gross domestic product.[26] Fluctuating oil prices had a significant impact on Iran's oil revenues: in 2004, a one-dollar increase (or decrease) in oil price altered (up or down) their income by $1 billion. Creating some level of uncertainty—perceived or real— regarding the safe passage of oil tankers through the Strait could cause oil prices to skyrocket on world markets, resulting in billions of dollars of additional income for Iran, and other Middle East countries.

It was now 1500 (3:00 pm) in Washington, D.C., midnight in Dubai. President Sheppard, Secretary of State Wheatley, and Chief of Staff Sanders had not returned to the large conference room. Five people sat at the table, complying with the president's directive to remain until he returned, listening to Darren expound on oil, the Middle East, and their relationship to the world's economy. Practically every think tank and consultant who ever studied the issue agreed that Iran actively attempting to close the Strait would be a classic example of cutting off one's nose to spite one's face, as it would deprive Iran of revenue and could invite international intervention. Agreement on this point didn't help explain Iran's intentions, but there was complete consensus on what they weren't planning on doing. The critical question— Iran's overall goal—remained unanswered.

Preparing for the Sit Room meeting, the departments of state and defense had not been idle. The secretary of defense and his staff had been in constant communications with CentCom in Tampa, who in turn was in direct contact with ComFifthFlt in Manama, Bahrain. Plans had been formulated and reviewed, rules of engagement discussed, some forces alerted, others activated, still others placed on standby. CentCom had transmitted to Secretary Collier and the Joint Chiefs a proposed concept of operations to deal with Iran's actions and their possible intentions. The Department of State had been busy, too. One of their two deputy secretaries[27], along with the undersecretary for political affairs and the assistant secretary of state for near eastern affairs were all at the State Department, working the Iranian problem. Despite the worsening weather, these three were able to reach the Metro, and with the department located on the corner of 23rd and C Streets NW, it was a short walk from the Foggy Bottom Metro stop to their offices. Since direct diplomatic channels between the United States and Iran ceased long ago, the State Department "talked" to Iran through an "interests section" which Iran maintained at the Pakistani Embassy in Washington, D.C. The United States kept a similar section at the Swiss Embassy in Tehran. Through these pseudo-diplomatic avenues, State sought explanations from Iran for their unprecedented naval deployments currently under way in the Persian Gulf. So far, the Iranians had not responded.

The president re-entered the main conference room followed by Pete Sanders, his chief of staff. Secretary of State Wheatley did not reappear, deciding instead to join her staff at the State Department to help coordinate their efforts. All rose as the president walked in and remained standing until he had taken his seat.

It was 1511 (3:11 pm) as President Sheppard addressed the group. "While I was in the other conference room I spoke with our intelligence experts and with SecDef and CentCom. We discussed some delicate information, as it wasn't obvious to me what everyone's level of clearance is." He looked at Frank Warren, the only unknown in the room. The large, four-quadrant screen came back to life as the president was speaking. "Based on our discussions in this room and those I had in private, we've developed a plan to respond to the Iranian action in the Persian Gulf. I think it will deter any possible aggressive actions the Iranians may be contemplating, keep our ships in a defensive posture while still maintaining their offensive capability, and maintain the highest degree of regional stability in the area. That's the broad overview. I'd like CentCom to review the details of the plan we've agreed to, so everyone is on board, and we can fine-tune the plan before we execute it."

At that moment, a Sit Room watchstander opened the door. "Excuse me, Mr. President. *Nimitz* has one of her reactors back online. She intends to remain at anchor for the time being as she works to get the other reactor back to operational status."

The president looked at Admiral Donaldson questioningly.

The admiral, reading the facial expression, explained. "The ship recently got everything back to normal; every aspect of the ship is now fully powered and online. The captain probably wants to ensure all equipment is functioning normally. When they do get under way, if still on one reactor, they'll be restricted to a reduced rate of aircraft launches. This limitation is especially true if the natural wind is light and the ship has to go fast to make its own wind." The admiral further explained that the limiting issue was the amount of steam that one reactor could produce, and that steam powered the aircraft catapults and drove the turbine blades that ultimately turn the four shafts and their four 30-ton, five-bladed bronze screws. The ship's captain, the admiral assumed, thought it would be better to stay where they were until both reactors were functioning before they weighed anchor and headed toward the Strait of Hormuz. Perhaps, too, Admiral Donaldson speculated, the captain would prefer a transit eastbound through the Strait of Hormuz in the daylight due to the reduced pucker factor with a daytime transit compared to one at night.

Frank Warren noticed the president's questioning look and would have answered the unasked question the same way. Smart captain, he thought.

General Karl W. Alexander, U.S. Army, the 4-star Central Command commander, began his description of the plan to counter what he, and others, thought was a significant threat, to the region in general, and U.S. forces in particular. "To start with, the USS *Abraham Lincoln* (CVN-72) and her battlegroup, consisting of two *Ticonderoga*-class guided missile cruisers (like the *Bunker Hill*) and two guided missile destroyers (like *Milius*), have been ordered to proceed at best speed, from their position in the North Arabian Sea, toward the Strait of Hormuz and the Persian Gulf. The *Lincoln* battle group had planned a one-day turnover with the *Nimitz* battle group in the Gulf of Oman after *Nimitz* and her escorts had transited the Strait eastbound, an event now canceled. Overhead surveillance satellites have been altered to provide increased coverage of the Strait of Hormuz area. A Navy SEAL team is en route to the area for possible insertion if the developing situation requires their capabilities. We have air force fighter aircraft and tanker assets forward deployed at bases in Qatar and Saudi Arabia, placed on alert, with some units able to be airborne in 15 minutes or less. A U.S. mine countermeasures ship, currently pierside in Jebel Ali (where *Nimitz* had been) has been ordered to get under way ASAP and proceed toward the *Nimitz* battle group. Rivet Joint, JSTARS, and AWACS assets, all located in theater, are on 30-minute alert status.

"With one reactor online and the second one surely to follow, the *Nimitz* airwing has regained offensive capability (when the ship gets under way) and has been ordered to prepare for bombing runs on the Iranian small boats and to arm their jets accordingly.

"Two RQ-4 Global Hawk unmanned surveillance aircraft (UAV's) stand ready for launch from Al Dhafra Air Base, located 20 miles south of Abu Dhabi. The UAV's are operated by the air force's 12th Reconnaissance Squadron out of Beale Air Force Base, near Marysville, California. These assets are now under my command, controlled by our forward area command center at Camp As Sayliyah in Doha, Qatar.[28] I have designated ComFifthFlt (the navy's 3-star admiral in Manama, Bahrain) as the on-scene commander with orders to coordinate and liaison with our area command center in Qatar. Iran's unusual naval activities have certainly commanded our attention, but as of now, no violations of international or maritime law have occurred. Furthermore, no Iranian forces have overtly threatened any U.S. assets, and commercial oil tankers continue to move freely into and out of the Persian Gulf via the Strait of Hormuz."

The mood in the Sit Room was somber and introspective. Each mind pondered the General's brief and the actions of the Iranians—despite the strangeness of their activities, were they indeed a threat to our vital interests? Would Iran dare attempt some unprovoked, provocative act that would guarantee a vigorous, likely lethal, retaliatory response from the United States, the Zionist sympathizer?

In light of the uniqueness of the Iranian deployment of forces, the uncertainty of their objectives, and the sheer number of assets and the inherent offensive potential such numbers represented, the U.S. had to be ready for any potentiality.

General Alexander continued his comprehensive brief, and the heads around the Sit Room table nodded appropriately, with similar looks of approval displayed on the screens by the intel gurus and by SecDef and the chairman. This entire plan, devised/drawn up/conceived by these same people, was being presented in "Reader's Digest" form primarily as a courtesy to those sitting at the table—except the president, who'd gotten a fuller version in the smaller conference room. The purpose of this briefing was to get everyone onboard, to get their "buy-in." Frank's opinion was decidedly not in alignment with what appeared to be the prevailing one. He had questions, but as the new guy with no pedigree to compare with the seasoned veterans involved in the discussion, he hesitated to voice his concerns. He squirmed in his chair, wanting to add another view point. He'd felt this way before, while on active duty, listening to a senior officer brief more senior officers, wanting to insert his thoughts into the discussion but was reluctant to do so for fear of the ridicule he might suffer for challenging those who had more experience— and rank.

His peripheral vision caught minor physical indicators of unease and uncertainty among the Sit Room members: Darren also shifted in his chair and fidgeted with his pen; Admiral Donaldson's face suggested he was uncomfortable with what he'd just heard; and Sharon's mouth was pursed. Perhaps his apprehensions were not so unfounded. One participant, however, had no concerns or questions: Lt.Gen. Walter Townsend, the director of the Joint Staff. Over the preceding months, he'd worked closely with General Alexander and his staff at CentCom to develop the very plan that was currently being briefed. Townsend, therefore, knew all the particulars of the plan, many of which were his ideas. He had minor issues with the final version being presented today, but none were worth challenging, especially in front of this audience. Besides, Karl Alexander was a friend, and West Point classmate, class of 1974.[29] Following graduation, the two officers pursued their respective careers and reunited when, as army captains (equivalent to navy lieutenants), both served under Colonel Beckwith during the failed Iranian hostage rescue attempt in April 1980. No good would come from the 3-star Townsend questioning his 4-star friend in front of the president of the United States, the secretary of defense, and the chairman of the Joint Chiefs of Staff. Frank Warren, however, thinking he had nothing to lose and going all in, gestured with a hand and posed a question to, unbelievably, the president of the United States.

"Mr. President, in light of the challenges with diplomatic discourse with Iran, are you satisfied that all avenues of contact with the Iranians have been fully explored?"

There were uniform looks of surprise on everyone's face, including the president's. This was not a question anyone expected, if they thought one would be forthcoming. Who questions the president of the United States? Frank thought that by posing an easily answered inquiry he might create a little momentum—an ice breaker, in a way—for others to join in.

"Mr. Warren, Secretary Wheatley has assured me that every possible diplomatic option with Iran is being tirelessly pursued, and I trust her skills implicitly."

Frank took this response as a gentle slap in the face by the president for questioning his, or the Secretary's, efforts at diffusing the tensions in the Persian Gulf. But it was a mild slap, not intended to inflict harm or bruising, which left him encouraged rather than defeated. Others in the room apparently felt the same.

Sharon Fleming stepped in. "I'm wondering if anyone can provide any insight into the continuing Iran-UAE squabble over the Greater and Lesser Tunbs and Abu Musa, and specifically if this issue is related to Iran's actions in the Gulf?"

DNI Rand Powers, on the video screen, offered a vague, uncommitted observation. "We have investigated this long-standing issue and continue to assess its impact on the developing actions in the Gulf."

Not exactly an answer with any teeth in it, but an answer, nonetheless.

Darren Ballinger, unaccustomed to being out of the loop on any Middle East issue, addressed his question to the DCI and DNI. "What intelligence have you obtained from this Achmed fellow that pertains to the current crisis in the Gulf?"

CIA Director Grayson Harvey, nodding knowingly, took this question. "All pertinent information obtained from this captive has been passed to appropriate authorities and they have incorporated this information into their operational plans."

The DCI, like the DNI, had mastered the Washington, D.C. way of talking without saying anything. Darren had a look of protest on his face, but with a confirming gesture from the president, he knew, like everyone else, there would be no further insights from the Achmed file.

There was no sign or indication that the president objected to questions, thus Admiral Donaldson directed one at CentCom's General Alexander. "General, Rear Admiral Donaldson here. Sir, I didn't hear submarines mentioned in your brief, other than the two Iranian Kilos who we seem to have classified as non-factors. Could you address the presence and possible uses of U.S. submarines in the situation developing in the Gulf?"

General Alexander paused to collect his thoughts and carefully choose his words. Comments involving submarine locations and possible employment of assets were usually stated cautiously, even among those who had the highest possible security classifications. Clearly, as demonstrated earlier, not everyone listening had such a clearance. "We are monitoring the Iranian Kilo submarines closely; both remain on the surface and we don't expect them to submerge. As you said, we do not believe they will be a factor going forward. Regarding our own submarines, we do have assets in the area and will use them if the situation dictates. At present, we see no need to utilize those capabilities and thus expose, and confirm, their location to the Iranians, and everyone else. We do have information the Iranians are aware that U.S. submarines are in the vicinity."

All participants seemed to take a moment to digest those comments. Many wanted more information, such as locations, types of submarines, and weapons loadout. All knew, however, that the general's comments effectively concluded the discussion about U.S. subs. President Sheppard looked at Admiral Donaldson and, by inference, asked if he had more questions. The Admiral continued.

"Okay, General. I have another question. To what extent do you think Iranian mines will figure into this situation?"

"Well, as I stated earlier, as a precaution we've ordered the mine countermeasures ship at Jebel Ali to get under way and proceed to the eastern part of the Gulf. This is the only MCM surface asset in theater. In our estimation we don't see mine warfare as a plausible option in Iran's planning. Perhaps I'm stretching the definition of the word 'plausible' by linking it with Iranian thinking; sometimes their actions don't seem well thought out. But mines, as we know, are indiscriminate killers. We think Iran's 'pain-to-gain ratio' is severely distorted: they'd lose far more economically deploying mines and disrupting tanker traffic in the Gulf and the Strait of Hormuz than they'd gain militarily by such actions."

"Roger that, sir. Finally, General, could you please discuss what rules of engagement are in effect as a part of this plan?"

As Frank turned from Donaldson back to the screen, he glimpsed the president's face in his peripheral vision. His expression showed his satisfaction with the questions so far and with the answers.

General Alexander's demeanor on the screen showed calm and confidence as his proposal underwent detailed scrutiny. He looked directly into the camera to answer Admiral Donaldson's question. "The rules of engagement (ROE) have been forwarded to all units for implementation. My guidance to commanders has been, and continues to be, to employ their weapons system as they have been trained and use it as it was designed. If any feel threatened, they should act. The individual who is on scene and experiences enemy hostile intent should, indeed must, respond accordingly. There likely will be no time to check with higher authority for verification of hostile actions or to seek authorization for full use of their weapons. By my orders unit commanders have the authority to engage an enemy whose actions threaten U.S. assets and lives. We have no requirement to suffer an initial salvo before employing deadly force.

"To be clear, exercising ROE can be extremely challenging as commanders evaluate the threats they encounter. The 1988 case of the *Vincennes* and her commanding officer, Captain William Rogers III, serves as a poignant reminder for all of us of the challenging, time sensitive decisions commanders must make. I think we all appreciate the immense disparity between reading the ROE and making decisions following them."

The General's statement was met with quiet acceptance and served as a fitting conclusion to the question and answer part of the briefing.

15

"That's the plan and scope of operations," President Sheppard concluded. "I appreciate your questions and realize you were hearing about this for the first time and there is a lot to digest. I had the luxury of reviewing the plan as the general went over the details. I think it's sound, it protects our naval forces, we minimize disruption to the sea lanes, and we're positioned to respond to Iran's next possible moves, whatever they may be. With that said, are there any more comments on this plan before I give the execute order?"

The eyes and heads of everyone seated in the Situation Room went into a kind of sector scan, each looking around at the others, each person nodding their heads slightly, eyebrows raised, lips pressed into a horizontal line across each face. Their silence showed no opposition, and, in essence, gave their assent. In fact, the silence was just that—silence.

Except they were not in total agreement. Sharon Fleming, despite the president's earlier comments, wondered if the State Department's overtures to Iran had been given enough time to bear fruit; diplomacy is rarely a speedy process and is especially dicey when dealing with Iran through intermediaries at the Swiss and Pakistani embassies.

Rear Adm. Donaldson wondered what impact the use of all these resources would have on the current operation under way in Iraq.

CentCom displayed confidence that everything he needed and requested to handle the Iranian issue would be provided immediately and work flawlessly, though he knew it seldom happens.

Frank Warren wondered where the plan was most vulnerable; where was its critical node? Would American lives be at risk? What was the percent chance of failure, and thus, the percent chance of success assigned to this plan? It was as if the operation had been taken from a file, dusted off, modified slightly, and presented as the gospel solution. If it were a previously devised plan, CentCom's staff had already what-if'd this event, going through the tedious grunt work of evaluating all credible alternatives and maybe even war-gamed their plan to some extent. If so, then kudos to them.

The president surveyed the silent room. "So, no further comments? We're all in agreement?" He didn't really expect to hear a dissenting voice, now, from anyone, as several questions had been raised and these concerns addressed. No plan is perfect—everyone in the Sit Room knew that, so none were inclined to voice their individual reservations. Yet, the conundrum before them was seeking the perfect, risk-free solution to an ill-defined problem posed by an unpredictable adversary. They had asked several reasonable questions about an operational plan that General Alexander had revealed was devised after months of planning and had been reviewed at every level of the Defense Department.

The president continued to look at each person at the table, seeing concurring looks, but also one face of doubt.

Frank, staring straight ahead, trying to keep his face expressionless, was determined to remain silent unless called upon by the president.

"Mr. Warren, even though the questions asked here have been answered, your face suggests you are deeply troubled. What's on your mind?"

Frank Warren took a deep breath and turned toward the president of the United States. Now he felt he had no choice but to leap into the dark, vast abyss. "Mr. President, I am hardly one to find fault with a plan that has been thoroughly thought through and vetted at every level of the Defense Department. But drawing on my limited experience, I do have some thoughts—some issues—with the plan proposed here today."

The mood in the meeting instantly turned from resigned to resentful. Of all people, how could *he* have issues with CentCom's plan? However, since the president solicited his opinion, those who thought Warren unqualified, even unworthy, to critique the carefully crafted plan withheld their opinion.

The president knew that any action taken by the United States in the Persian Gulf would be parsed and criticized around the globe. Another view, now, could make some difference—or not. "Okay—let's hear them."

"Thank you, sir. In general, I think this plan is overly provocative, not proportional to whatever we perceive the threat to be, and is unnecessarily complex. I feel we are bringing too much force to bear and we are responding too robustly, if that's possible. We might be giving the appearance, to Iran and other nations, that we're planning another war front. We may well be creating increased instability in an area that needs exactly the opposite.

"I don't see *Nimitz* as a target of Iran, but more an unexpected opportunity to exploit. Most of us have learned to be wary of coincidences, but I feel *Nimitz*'s propulsion issues played into Iran's hands with uncanny timing. There is no way, in my view, that so many Iranian vessels plus two submarines could have sortied on such short notice; this had to have been planned far in advance of today. The *Nimitz* breakdown is probably, in Iranian minds, their version of divine intervention. With little more than a gut feeling, my guess is that Mazdaki is trying to improve his standing on the world stage, in the eyes of the Iranian people, and in the opinion of Ayatollah Ghorbani. To do this, he has orchestrated some vague, loosely coordinated exercise involving a defense of Abu Musa and the two Tunb islands. With only my instincts and my limited knowledge of Mazdaki as references, I sense he seeks a broader, more visible and influential image to project to members of the GCC and is striving to increase Iran's standing and prestige among world leaders. In short, he wants Iran considered as a force—a power to be recognized and respected. The UAE's unusually tart, aggressive rhetoric at the latest GCC meeting gave Mazdaki an opening, maybe an incentive, to respond to the comments with an unmistakable show of force and strength. When word of *Nimitz*'s issues filtered up whatever chain-of-command they have, Mazdaki seized the moment and capitalized on it. Who knows—he'll probably claim, if he hasn't already done so, that Iranian forces, at his direction, forced the mighty *Nimitz* to stop dead in her tracks in fear and trepidation in the face of Iran's impressive armada. Or some other such foolishness. When you control 100% of the news in your country, you can make up a pretty convincing story."

The president thoughtfully responded, "Okay, I hear you. So far, the intel that I've received is silent on your theory; nothing I've heard supports it nor contradicts it. But it's an interesting take on the events that have unfolded. What do you propose?"

Frank continued, "First, while *Nimitz* is bringing her other reactor back online, and while still at anchor, I'd suggest they launch 2 S-3 Vikings, both carrying 3 MK-82 bombs loaded on a TER (triple ejector rack) on one of their wing stations. They typically mount an in-flight refueling store on the other wing station—there'd be no reason to remove that. Have them fly around low and slow—have 'em fly around the *Bunker Hill* and *Milius* and mill about for several hours so they can be heard and seen by the Iranian sailors. Even though it's night over there, they'll get noticed by the small boats and patrol craft, and I think the impact will be significant enough to cause confusion and uncertainty in the minds of the Iranians."

Rear Adm. Donaldson had a knowing look on his face, while Darren Ballinger couldn't help but respond. "That's crazy. You can't launch planes from an aircraft carrier while it's parked, or, I mean, while it's at anchor—while it's anchored. It must be moving to create wind, right? What a crazy idea—the plane would dive into the water after it's—what—sent into the air. This plan is nuts."

The president, with a quizzical look on his face, asked, "What about that, Frank?"

"Darren is correct, Mr. President, about aircraft carrier launches. All fixed-wing aircraft need wind over the deck in addition to the speed generated by the cat shot to have enough lift to fly after a launch. That is, all except the S-3. Due primarily to its high-lift wing, the catapult itself can provide enough end speed for the airplane to fly after being launched. No wind is required. It's a pretty good cat shot, to be sure, but it's doable. It can be done safely—and has been."

Rear Admiral Donaldson's face now showed a slight grin of satisfaction, maybe even a degree of admiration.

Darren, of course, wouldn't let go. "So this has been done before? Or is this some conclusion you've drawn based on a graph out of a book or something—some calculation you've made? How do you know this will work?"

"It'll work because I've done it."

"You've launched off an aircraft carrier while it was, what, not moving?"

"Yes, sir. The ship was at anchor."

"Anchored—like *Nimitz* is now?"

"Yes, that's correct."

The interest level in the room—and on the monitors—increased. Was this guy telling the truth?

The president prompted, "Tell us about your experience."

Frank took another deep breath and dove in. "My squadron was embarked aboard USS *Ranger* (CV-61) doing workups before a cruise, and, to use a favorite phrase, 'it was decided' to try a launch while we were anchored near San Diego—specifically, off the coast of Coronado. We launched two S-3s. I was one of the pilots. We recovered back aboard a couple of hours later, with the ship still anchored." He chuckled a bit, finishing with, "It was a lot of fun, as I recall."

Darren had to object. He couldn't believe the president was seriously listening to this self-important flyboy. "*Nimitz* is still with only one operating reactor. Don't you think it'd be wise to wait until both reactors are functioning before they try your little stunt?"

Frank was in his element now. "The U.S. Navy has to be flexible to meet the needs of each situation. One might call it a stunt when we did it, but now every aviator who flies off a carrier knows it can be done.

"*Nimitz* can go 20 knots and conduct a full launch on one reactor, albeit with a slower launch rate." Frank's recall was spot on, and he knew it. "But here, no steam is required to drive the ship through the water; all of it can go to the catapults, and I'm suggesting they only launch two aircraft—as long as they're S-3s. The whole point is to create a little shock value—surprise them—get 'em talking and wondering—even intimidate them. An anchored aircraft carrier conducting flight ops will certainly stump them.

"And you're probably wondering about the bombs. Why carry MK-82s? Primarily for effect. Again, it'll be dark out there, and the bombs may be hard to see. I anticipate, though, the crews of all those small boats will be surprised to see aircraft that launched from a carrier at anchor. Add a few five hundred pounders to the picture and Mazdaki's gamble, if I'm correct in my assessment, takes on a much different tone."

Darren Ballinger was not about to concede authority on the Middle East. "That's your plan? Fly a few planes around in the dark, carrying bombs that may not be visible but which the crew has no intention of dropping? You are recommending we scrap a plan devised by CentCom, approved by the secretary of defense, and is ready for implementation by the president—and in its place launch two ASW (anti-submarine warfare) aircraft and have them fly around for a couple of hours hoping the Iranians see them? That's your plan?"

The president looked from Darren to Frank, indicating he had related questions—and wanted answers—as did those watching from the monitors and seated around the table. There was no shortage of skepticism and doubt; both were increasing—rapidly. Frank remained confident but still uneasy in this role as a presidential briefer. The president was still listening, at least for the moment.

Frank broke the silence. "The S-3s are the first part of my proposed plan, and we're fortunate they're available. The *Nimitz* deployment is the last one for the aircraft; it is being retired from the fleet.[30]

"The second part of my plan is this: have an air force B-52 fly a low pass—actually two low passes—at sunrise, over the area of the greatest concentration of Iranian small boats. In fact, I suggest the Stratofortress fly its passes over the area at a low altitude, and slowly; maybe even dirtied up. This will create lots of noise; lots of engine exhaust. Her wings will be drooping: that's a 185-foot wingspan coming right at you—it'd be quite a sight. For added effect, I suggest the BUFF be loaded out with about 20 of my favorite bombs, MK-82s—all carried internally—and have their bomb bay doors open when they do their flyovers.

"Both passes will serve two functions: first, shock those small boat crews with an impressive display of U.S. military strength and power. Consider the sight of such a huge beast with those eight Pratt and Whitneys screaming over their heads, weapons bays visible with bombs loaded; imagine the stories they'll tell when they get back to Bandar Abbas. They'll be telling their grandkids about the day they witnessed the power and reach of the mighty Great Satan.

"The second reason for this flyover is that the crew will be looking for a clear area near the largest number of Iranian naval assets. To fully capitalize on the moment and sear an image of American military capability and awesomeness into each and every mind, the BUFF should, after its second pass, drop, in immediate succession, at the lowest safe altitude, a line of 12 MK-82 bombs. These bombs will explode upon contact with the sea, one after the other, creating an incredible 'wall of water.' It would truly be a memorable sight to behold. The aircraft will be far enough from any surface traffic to avoid the possibility of a boat being near the frag pattern, but the Iranian sailors will still be able to absorb the full effect. First, the bombs explode, and the wall of water develops; then they'll hear the explosions when the sound gets to them; finally, they'll feel the power of the blasts as the water shifts beneath them. I felt it standing on the flight deck of an aircraft carrier as I watched two A-6 Intruders, flying together in a section, drop their bombs, six each, one after the other, roughly a mile or so away. It was very impressive."

16

Frank Warren commanded the floor in the White House Situation Room and the attention of everyone in the meeting. He continued, "Following the bomb drop and the wall of water, I'd suggest the BUFF go to MRT (maximum rated thrust), clean up, start a gentle climb, and ease into an angle of bank to cast a silhouette of itself in the morning sky against the rising sun—for more dramatic effect—and then RTB (return to base). I anticipate there will be widely shared condemnation of these actions by the Iranians, and others, protesting our confrontational, taunting act of menacing, conflict-inducing showmanship. The United States, naturally, will have to be exceedingly contrite and deeply disturbed by the actions of our wayward B-52 crew. We will have to insist there will be hell to pay, throughout the chain of command, once we get to the bottom of this unacceptable display of cowboy foolishness, which we all so deeply, and profoundly, regret—or some similar statement."

No one offered a comment or question; all, including the president, were processing what they'd heard. Everyone knew the president routinely encouraged and considered alternate plans, proposals, and policies; it was his way of doing business, and was a blessing or an aggravation, depending on your viewpoint.

Frank summarized his proposal. "After getting her second reactor back online, I suggest *Nimitz* remain at anchor until about 0630 to 0645, at which time she should retract her anchor, launch two F/A-18s as escorts for the

BUFF, and then recover the S-3s around 0700, Dubai time. When I was notified of this meeting, I checked the time of sunrise in Dubai tomorrow morning, Sunday, January 14, and it's at 0707. We should order the B-52 crew to conduct their mission between 0715 and 0730 Dubai time. After they have carried out their orders and are on their way home, recover the Hornets, and *Nimitz* can then continue toward the Strait of Hormuz, along with *Bunker Hill* and *Milius.*

"The mission is quick, easy, simple, effective, and safe. It is also forceful, powerful, and creates maximum impact. And it sends the unmistakable message to Iran and others that *we could have, but we didn't.*

"I predict that all of the small boats, plus the two submarines, will be tied up in Bandar Abbas by noon tomorrow, Dubai time."

Darren Ballinger had taken in every word and was uncomfortable having to ask for clarification. He moved in his chair, swiveling to be in more direct eye contact. "Okay. First, you said something about the B-52 being 'dirty' or getting 'dirtied up'; please explain that."

Frank enjoyed feeling he had all the answers. "When an airplane 'dirties up' or gets 'dirty' it means to extend the landing gear and flaps—to get into the landing configuration. To do so, you must fly slower than usual; most planes have maximum speed limitations at which you can do this. Obviously, you want to fly much slower when you land, and by dirtying up in its landing configuration, the B-52 could fly relatively slowly over the Iranian small boats. It would take a lot of power to operate in this configuration, which means more noise and exhaust for all our Iranian friends to hear and see. Which is precisely the point."

Darren's discomfort had now faded. "What is it with you and MK-82 bombs? 500 pounds each, I think you said. And the B-52 should carry 20 of them but drop only 12. Why would they carry more than you suggest they drop? Why not some other bomb, if we're going to consider this idea?"

"The MK-82 is a standard, often used, proven weapon. I assume the S-3s and the BUFF will put snakes on them, or snake-eyes. These are fins that extend upon release and cause the bomb to quickly separate from the aircraft—get distance from the launch vehicle—and to have a steeper dive angle into the target, which in this case is water. Carrying 20 bombs—the B-52 could haul a heck of a lot more—adds to the visual impact and gives the crew a few backups if there's a drop issue. And the wall of water is the result of dropping the bombs in rapid succession, creating an impressive sight."

Darren Ballinger did not like being shown up. "You keep saying BUFF – what is that? Some code word?"

"It's the nickname the B-52 picked up—way back when—the plane's been around since 1955. It's the reason the Soviets built their SA-2 air defense missile systems. But the word BUFF is an acronym, and it stands for ..."

Donaldson, Townsend, Fleming, and Sanders—all shifted in their chairs, in cautious anticipation of what was to follow as Frank finished his explanation. "... Big, Ugly, Fat," he paused, finding an acceptable word, "Fellow. BUFF—Big, Ugly, Fat, Fellow." The relief in the room was palpable when Frank said "fellow," which is a more polite word sometimes substituted for the more crass "F" word often used for the second "F."

Darren pushed on. "Okay—I get BUFF. Now, where does one get a BUFF? If this plan has any chance of implementation, how are we going to get a B-52 over there? Where are they based?"

Lt.Gen. Townsend, the Director of the Joint Staff, answered. "There's a detachment located at Diego Garcia. I'd suggest we task them with this mission, if approved."

The general started scribbling figures on his notepad, and looked at Frank with a question. "What time did you say sunrise occurs in the Gulf?"

"Just after 7:00 am—I think at 0707; that's for Dubai."

"And what time zone is Dubai in?"

"They're plus 4."

Lt.Gen. Townsend continued to write as President Sheppard zeroed in on the big question. "Frank, you've reeled off a complete scenario here, with no time to prepare or prior knowledge of what was occurring."

Sharon Fleming jumped in. "Mr. President, Frank, Admiral Donaldson and I attended NDU at Fort McNair together years ago and participated in a joint war game with students from both ICAF and the National War College. Frank and I were on the same side, and Joe was on the opposing team. That war game scenario had some elements similar to developments we see here. While much of what Frank is proposing is from his overall knowledge and experience, there are a few threads suggested here from the plan we put together back then."

"That was some time ago, wasn't it?" the president replied. "Well, let me ..."

Lt.Gen. Townsend broke in. "Mr. President, I know Diego Garcia is approximately 2,500 miles from Dubai. According to my rough figures, at a flying speed of .8 Mach, I estimate a flight time of around 5:15, five hours and fifteen minutes, depending on the winds. Dubai is +4 from GMT and I know Diego is +6, local time here is about 3:30

pm; that makes it currently about 2:30 am tomorrow morning in Diego Garcia. The crew will gain two hours flying to the northwest, so if the B-52 launches by 0400 in D-GAR, which is 5:00 pm here—in about an hour and a half—they'll be on station in the Gulf around 0715, Dubai time, just after official sunrise. The flyover, if ordered, would occur around 10:15 to 10:30 pm tonight, Washington time."

"So, as proposed by Mr. Warren, the B-52 option is doable, according to your math," the president stated.

"Yes, sir, Mr. President."

Frank had previously considered a flight from Diego Garcia to the Gulf and he silently agreed with Lt.Gen. Townsend's flight calculations.

Peter Sanders, with a nod toward the door to the small conference room, interrupted his boss, "Mr. President, a word?" Such was the position, power, and influence of the president's chief of staff, and the level of esteem and respect the president held for him, that a brief, cryptic request for a private moment was granted without hesitation. Everyone stood as President Sheppard and Sanders departed for a private conversation.

Once inside the small office, the president began, "Pete, what do you think of this Warren guy?"

"He seems okay; not sure why he's here. His alternative plan may have some merit, although using a high-altitude bomber in a low altitude scenario seems unusual, which might be the point."

"Yes, I was thinking about that. Sharon invited him, by the way. I didn't know about their history at NDU; didn't know Donaldson was there, too. Didn't Donaldson ... uh, didn't SECNAV and the CNO (Chief of Naval Operations) recommend a third star for him?"

"Yep, they did."

"Ah, that's good. He's very sharp. Good for him."

"Yes, an excellent choice.

"Getting back to the issue, Ed, the Iranians are giving us a gift on a platter. CentCom's plan is a good one. All the players are on board; it's practically already in effect. We get to show off on the world stage and make Mazdaki look like a fool. I don't see a downside. And with the time zone differences, this will have plenty of play on the Sunday talk shows tomorrow morning. Honestly, I'm surprised you're even thinking about Warren's plan. Can you imagine all the dead fish and sea life that would be floating in the Gulf after those bombs go off? It won't be a good optic, that's for sure. So why the hesitation?"

"I don't know, Pete. Something bugs me about General Alexander (CentCom) and his grandiose operation. Honestly, I'm not sure if it's him or his plan; it seems every time I hear him talk, he acts like he's the smartest guy in the room—he talks down to people. I always sense that he's trying not to tap his foot as he waits for others to catch up to him."

"Well, you would probably be surprised, but what I've heard is he's one of the best commanders to work for and with; he's highly thought of by peers and subordinates alike. SecDef likes him, and so does the Chairman. You know, I was down in Tampa not too long ago; I had an informative brief by his staff, and he jumped in often, too—not shutting down the briefing officer but adding some depth and context to the presentation. He's a good one, Ed. Maybe you're reading him wrong."

"Yeah, perhaps I am. What do you think his reaction would be if I choose Warren's plan over his? And by the way, what are his politics? Did you get a feel for that when you were down there?"

"On the second question, I have no idea. He seems apolitical but completely supportive of his president and the secretary of defense; he's a team player, unquestionably. Those are the only cards he shows, and the only ones he plays. On the first question, he'll support you like I mentioned. If you're leaning that way, maybe a heads up to SecDef would be wise."

"I should call him anyway. And I'll get the DCI and DNI on the line, too, and get their perspectives." The president picked up a phone, told the watch officer what he wanted, and within moments he was conversing on a secure line with his top advisors. After the call was complete, the president turned to Sanders, his longtime friend. "Pete, I'm going with the B-52, augmented by the electronic monitoring mentioned by CentCom. I'm inclined toward being more proactive rather than reactive. I like Warren's plan—maybe too much. That "wall of water" would be cool to see, don't you think?"

Pete Sanders now felt compelled to support the plan the president decided on. "Can you imagine what a B-52 would look like, coming at you, low and slow? I think there'll be some soiled underwear out there tomorrow morning! And I like how Warren substituted 'Fellow' in the BUFF explanation—that was decent of him. Ol' Darren bought it like it was on sale. Pretty good stuff! Of course, we'll have to send out the usual suspects tomorrow morning to the media to calm everyone down and defend your decision, but I think we can manage that."

The two men smiled briefly at each other. They genuinely respected each other and had years of history between them. They made many decisions when they were alone; this was one. They nodded at each other, acknowledging it was time to rejoin the others. Pete Sanders reached for the door, turned to his friend and boss and remarked, in a slightly mocking tone, "You know, Mr. President, I'll have to object in there when you announce your decision; the others, CentCom in particular, must see me disagree with you."

"Of course, Pete, I get it. Just don't go too hard on me, OK? Remember, I'm a sensitive guy." With a wink and a pat on his chief of staff's shoulder, they reentered the main conference room.

17

The president took his seat at the head of the table. Darren Ballinger sat to his left, then Rear Adm. Donaldson and Pete Sanders. On the president's right was Lt.Gen. Townsend, then Sharon Fleming, and Frank Warren. It was decision time. Local time was 1540 (3:40 pm) in Washington, D.C.; 0040 (12:40 am) Sunday morning in Dubai.

In Diego Garcia it was 0240 (2:40 am) Sunday morning. Often called D-GAR, this atoll in the Indian Ocean is among the 60-island Chagos Archipelago located in the British Indian Ocean Territory. Positioned 7 degrees south of the equator and over 1,100 miles south-southwest of the southern tip of India, D-GAR has been leased by the United States from Great Britain since the early 1970s and has been developed as a joint U.S.-U.K. air and naval refueling and support station.

With everyone settled and the video conferencing monitors back up, the president addressed his advisors. "I want to thank all of you for your efforts in providing me— on relatively short notice—with excellent insight and advice on the situation in the Persian Gulf. None of us can be sure of the purpose or intentions of Iran's unusual deployment of its naval assets. It's hard, therefore, to assess their objectives. I feel a response is necessary, and I know State is pursuing every diplomatic channel available to ascertain Iran's goals and objectives. From some highly classified and usually reliable sources we are informed that Mazdaki may be attempting to gain favor in the eyes of their Supreme Leader and with the Iranian people through the exploits of the Iranian navy based in Bandar Abbas. Whether *Nimitz* or any other U.S. naval ship or military asset is a target of any plan—we still don't know. I think we need to demonstrate force without being overly provocative; show that we're aware of and concerned about their actions while being cognizant of the fact they haven't violated any international laws. So, I am ordering CentCom to immediately implement what I'll call the B-52 option—the alternative plan briefed by Mr. Warren. I think ..."

"Mr. President!" Pete Sanders seemed to rise several inches above his chair as his face turned red with veins nearly popping out of his neck. "Sir, CentCom's plan, which has the support of both the secretary of defense and the chairman of the Joint Chiefs of Staff, is a forceful, balanced, and appropriate plan of action, parts of which are ready to be implemented immediately. While this alternate plan is not without merit, I must, sir, urge you to reconsider your decision and weigh carefully the compelling aspects of the previously briefed and fully vetted plan put forward by the Central Command. It is, I think most of us would agree, the superior choice."

The president, a man practiced in making big decisions and confident in his abilities, spoke evenly, unemotionally, and steadily. "I appreciate your thoughts and counsel, Pete. Your points are germane and may prove to be prescient. But I think a little less, in this case, will mean a bit more. We can show Iran, and others who will be watching, with two flyovers and a little demonstration at the end, that the United States is a force to consider and respect. The results will be dramatic—and significant. If the need arises, we will employ our considerable military assets. I view Iran as the bully of the Middle East—and I detest bullies. This action, which I am ordering, is restrained while being openly bold. We could have the S-3s do their mission and be done with it. That might be enough; everyone, especially the Iranians, should be bewildered and captivated by airplanes somehow launching from a carrier at anchor. So, I think that's a promising idea. The B-52, though—that's making a statement. We're telling the Iranians no, not here, not anywhere—we're not standing for this.

"I can handle the political and media repercussions— there will probably be, as Mr. Warren pointed out, likely fallout. But I think Iran will reconsider any future threats—real or perceived—toward the United States, our allies in the region, and to international waterways, particularly the Strait of Hormuz. If Mazdaki gets some mileage out of our actions, so be it. But I think he'll also get a clear understanding of our message. He'll never admit that, of course; he'd lose face if he did. So, while it's hard to communicate with Iran through diplomatic channels, the actions we are about to take will speak their language clearly; and what we don't do, in the face of what we potentially could do, may speak the loudest."

The president looked directly at his secretary of defense on the TV monitor: "Mr. Secretary, execute the plan as briefed."

The secretary answered, "Yes, sir, Mr. President. I'll execute it immediately."

The exchange was more formal than functional. The president, during the conference with his chief of staff, had discussed his decision while on the phone with SecDef, CentCom, and the DCI and DNI. General Alexander at Central Command voiced his concerns with the B-52 option, more as an experienced observer rather than trying to change the president's mind and opt for his operational plan. The more the general talked, the larger the error, the president realized, of his judgment of this officer. In the end, the president stuck with his decision and CentCom and his staff, in accordance with the president's and Secretary Collier's orders, instantly went to work to make it happen. Thus, when the president announced his decision in the Situation Room, there was no visible reaction by CentCom to hearing that his plan, the one meticulously and painstakingly put together over several months and the same one SecDef had previously approved, was being put away for future use. Its replacement was an unvetted, untested, back-of-the-envelope operation suggested by some two-bit low-level Pentagon staffer (and former U.S. navy pilot) whose sole claim to any expertise in warfare planning was participating in a war game exercise that occurred maybe 15 years ago. If that was a bitter pill for the 4-star general to swallow, he did so gracefully and professionally with no fanfare whatsoever. The president had decided and spoken, and it was time to move forward and execute. Frank, personally excited that his suggestion was adopted, but as surprised as anyone that it had been, thought his work complete and he'd soon be on his way home.

President Sheppard turned back to the room: "Once again, thank you for your inputs. We'll conclude this meeting now; please keep me informed of any changes or developments in the situation in the Gulf.

"By the way, any word on the second reactor onboard *Nimitz*?"

Secretary Collier replied, "Yes, sir. During your decision briefing I was notified that both reactors are now online, and all related systems are functioning properly. *Nimitz* will be remaining at anchor, as we discussed, and is preparing for the launch of the two Vikings. A full report is forthcoming."

"That's good news. Send me that report when it's available. Understanding how one troubleshoots a nuclear reactor should be interesting. I wish you all a safe holiday weekend, and again, thank you for your assistance today."

The president stood up, as did everyone else. He turned to shake hands with Darren Ballinger, thanking him for his contributions to the discussion. He then extended his hand to Lt.Gen. Townsend and thanked him for being a part of the decision process. Rear Adm. Donaldson, Sharon Fleming, and Frank Warren began moving toward the door. Pete Sanders indicated all could leave the conference room. It was nearly 1600 (4:00 pm).

Townsend and Ballinger were departing when President Sheppard motioned to Donaldson, Fleming and Warren to stay behind. Pete Sanders stayed as well. The TV monitors were all blank; only five people remained. The president gestured for all to sit.

As they were adjusting themselves in their seats, the door opened, and a watchstander took one step in. "Mr. President, I wanted to let you know the Ravens-Colts game starts at 1635 (4:35 pm) this afternoon. Someone mentioned you thought it started at noon, but we're about a half hour from kickoff. Just passing that along, sir."

The mention of the Ravens-Colts playoff game momentarily took Frank's mind out of the White House to M & T Bank stadium in Baltimore, Maryland, and to Tom Worthington, Policy's principal deputy, and his date, Denise Emerson. She, not he, was the source of a simmering unsettledness in his gut. It had been nagging him for some time, but he had not yet uncovered the cause.

"Ah, good—I thought I'd missed it." When Frank's attention returned to the Sit Room, the watchstander had retreated and closed the door. "I want to talk to the three of you about this B-52 flight," the president said, looking pensive and concerned, like someone suffering from buyer's remorse. "As I said earlier, I want to take some action in the Gulf rather than just respond to Iranian exploits. Now Frank, you think two passes—two flyovers—is enough? Is that your suggestion? Do I understand you correctly?"

18

"Yes, sir, Mr. President," Frank Warren focused on answering the president's question. "Depending on when they launch, my hope is that the flyovers occur closely after sunrise, so the B-52 crew will have good visibility while locating the Iranian boats, which I assume will still be gathered in groups. At that time of the morning, the crew should also be able to find a clear area for their bomb drop away from Iranian and commercial traffic."

Sharon added, "Doing this after sunrise allows the Iranian navy to have an unobstructed view of the BUFF as it flies over or near them, which is the whole point of the flyovers." Most everyone saw the logic in her statement.

The president continued with a question he'd already raised with the military leadership while in the small conference room; he wanted Frank to address it as well. "How do you see this failing—what bothers you about this plan you recommended, and I've ordered?"

"One worry is if a bomb goes astray and hits some vessel—be it an Iranian small boat or a commercial oil tanker. If that happens, Iran and the international community will collectively, and appropriately, condemn the United States. Another scenario I worry about is some sailor pointing his .50 caliber machine gun straight up and firing as the BUFF flies overhead. That has the potential to bring down the B-52. They'll claim it was self-defense. Finally, I'm concerned about a suicide small boat attack achieving success against the *Nimitz* or one of the other ships in her battle group. These are my main concerns."

Donaldson and Fleming agreed.

Frank continued. "I think the flyovers will accomplish all that we desire—the message to Iran will be loud and clear and impossible to misinterpret. And yet it demonstrates restraint by showing the potential and unquestioned power of other actions not taken. The bombs and the wall of water add a huge degree of emphasis—like a giant headline above the fold." He indicated size with his hands. "I think you can achieve your objective without the bombs, but with them, all doubt is removed. The message is sent and received, no question."

"Thank you, that's a good explanation." Continuing, and looking directly at Frank, "If I recall correctly, the B-52 should launch soon, possibly within the hour. SecDef confirmed he'd task a B-52 detachment at Diego Garcia with this mission. I want to call the aircraft commander before he launches to ensure he's aware of the sensitivity and delicacy of this mission. We simply can't accept any screw-ups in the Gulf."

"There's no question about the international pushback if things go south; it'd be intense and unanimous. So, they should be rolling in about an hour, at around 5:00 pm our time. The flyover should occur around 10:15 to 10:30 pm, Washington time."

The commander in chief looked at one of the time panels. "So, there's about an hour before they launch, if your math is correct."

Taking his cue from the president, Pete Sanders jumped up and asked a member of the watch team to come into the conference room.

"Could you get the aircraft commander of the B-52 in Diego Garcia on the line for me, please?" Technically, the president asked a question; in reality, he gave an order.

The White House is known for being able to find anyone, anywhere and connecting them with the president.

"Yes, sir, Mr. President."

To the group, the president said, "I want to impress upon him how important this mission is and how critical it is that he complete this assignment as ordered—no mistakes." The president glanced at the other four people in the room, looking for indications of concurrence. One face troubled him.

"Mr. Warren, you play much poker?"

"No, sir, Mr. President, I don't."

"Good thing—your face is a blatant tell. You don't agree with this phone call I'm about to make?"

"Mr. President, I don't have a problem with the call. I just don't believe you should be the one making it."

Four sets of eyebrows went up with that statement, and the president followed with the obvious question: "Who do you think should?"

"Sir, if you talk directly to the aircraft commander, I think you will inadvertently place this entire flight and mission at risk. What soldier, marine, pilot, grunt—pick one: what military member has ever had their president— their commander in chief—call them, talk to them before an operation or mission, to emphasize the importance of what they were about to do? Few, if any, would be my guess. Everyone knows who ordered this operation; heck, every order issued is technically from the president of the United States but delegated down the chain of command. When I was on active duty, and I told a sailor to get a haircut, by the strictest interpretation of every officer's oath, that order had the backing and full authority of the commander in chief. If the aircraft commander of this B-52 hears directly from you, from his president, and later one of his eight engines quits on him, what's he going to do? My guess is he'll press on, thinking he has seven other good engines—what's the problem? Then he gets a low oil pressure caution light on another engine, and the emergency procedure calls for an engine shutdown—now what? Well, 6 out of 8 engines operating normally is still pretty good. And it may be; I'd bet the BUFF can fly safely on six engines, maybe even fewer than that. It may not be smart, may not be exactly safe—but my president called me personally. I think a call from the commander in chief may unduly influence his perspective on safety and mission accomplishment."

Again there was silence in Situation Room. Another one of those rare moments in time; a sort of tipping point, a decision point. The president was making his. "I didn't look at it that way, Mr. Warren.

"When we're connected, you do the talking."

19

A Situation Room watchstander advised the president it would take no less than 30 minutes for the B-52 aircraft commander to get to a facility with secure telephone capability. Or he could be connected with a crewmember immediately on a non-secure line. The president decided on expediency.

After a moment the watchstander advised the president a B-52 crewmember was standing by and the Sit Room speaker phone came to life.

"Yallow! BUFF Dude 1, at your service—who can we bomb for you today?" "Dude 1" and other B-52 crewmembers were sitting in a small conference room in the BOQ (bachelor officers quarters) at Diego Garcia.

Frank, having been charged by the president to speak, proceeded. "Hello, this is Frank Warren calling from Washington, D.C.—are you a member of the B-52 crew that's standing alert there in Diego?"

"Yes, sir, indeed—we're alert, ready and able to bomb the target of your choice into the next century." Based on the twang and rustic, sing-song voice coming through the phone one couldn't help but conjure an image of a young man in jeans, t-shirt, cowboy hat and boots and an ice cold long-neck in his hand. Maybe the White House had misdialed? Is that possible?

Frank shared surprised looks with the others, as the voice on the line continued its casual rant.

"You say you're callin' all the way from D.C.? You a DoD dude from the Puzzle Palace? Them SOBs been callin', like, every ten minutes—how's a guy supposed to get any god damn sleep, anyway? Hey, you callin' about them I-rain-ees gettin' all excited up there in Bandar A-bass? Sounds like someone kicked a hornet's nest and now they're all pissed."

Frank spoke to the speaker phone as clearly as he could. "Yes, well, I am calling to see, to confirm, you've received a tasking order for an operation in the vicinity of the Strait of Hormuz. And I'm calling from the White House—the Situation Room—and you're on speaker phone with ..."

Much of Frank's last sentence was drowned out by: "Hey Georgie—yo Nav—hey, dude here's callin' from his house, which he says is white, and that he's got a situation ... yeah, I know ... our situation? No, he's calling about *his* situation ... he didn't tell me what his ... hey, Nav, we got any f...in' orders or tasking to do somethin', or what? Oh, hi Boss—what's happenin'?"

Despite it being the middle of the night in D-GAR, a well-groomed, freshly shaven, official looking U.S. Air Force pilot in his flight suit entered the room where his (good ol' boy) co-pilot had fielded a telephone call. "Another call?" he asked, dropping into a swivel chair.

"Yeah, same ol' shit. Except this guy says he's in his house, says it's white like I give a flyin' f... what color his house is, and he's got a 'situation' —like I'm supposed to know what that is; I mean, really, ya know?"

With a voice and tone fitting of the figure he cut in his flight suit, the "Boss" accepted the phone from BUFF Dude 1. "This is Major Barnes, may I help you, sir?" Barnes' voice was remarkably clear, though originating half a world away.

"Yes, Major, good morning. My name is Frank Warren, I'm calling from Washington, D.C. and I'm trying to confirm you received an operational order, or tasking order, for a B-52 crew. I think it's likely I have been connected to the wrong number, so if you have a better one for a B-52 crew member, I'd appreciate it."

"This is a good number, Mr. Warren. And about BUFF-One—he sometimes comes across as a bit rough around the edges, and his telephone protocol can at times sound in need of some tightening up, but Willie has a good soul and knows his way around the BUFF quite well. My apologies if he presented himself less professionally than you were expecting. He's sort of, well, an acquired taste, so to speak."

"Not a problem, Major. But I would think if anyone were to call themselves BUFF-One, it'd be you, not, uh, Willie."

"Yes, well, that's Willie for you. William Robert Washington, III, Captain, U.S. Air Force. He recently put it on—he's a brand new 0-3. Interesting fellow, to be sure. His father was a BUFF pilot and retired as a 2-star, and his grandfather was a navy admiral. So, there's quite a lineage of service that goes back many years, but I do sometimes wonder about some apples not landing properly when they fall from their trees. All that aside, sir, what can I do for you?"

"I need to confirm receipt of the tasking order and review those orders to provide you with some background and context to ensure you know exactly what is desired up there near the Strait."

In the background, Willie commented, "... time for swim-call in the Gulf. Don't forget your towels. Oh, that's right—they've already got them around their heads—good planning..."

Major Barnes gave Captain William Robert Washington, III, USAF, a cut motion across his neck to stifle the chatter. "I apologize for the noise here. You were saying something about our tasking order?"

Frank continued, "Yes, Major. What we're trying to do with your mission is tell the Iranians that their present course of action, their conduct on the seas near the Strait of Hormuz, is of grave concern to us; that it would be in their best interests if they were to terminate their current actions and remove themselves from the vicinity of the *Nimitz* and the shipping lanes in the eastern part of the Gulf. In short, they're not playing nicely, and we'd like them to stop it—for the betterment of all concerned. To reinforce our request, and as a demonstration of our strength and resolve, we thought a flyover by a B-52, a low flyover, that is, might send the right message to the Iranians—one they'd understand—without any doubt as to how dangerous we think the situation is."

Major Barnes nodded to himself. "Okay—I got it. Low and slow—what, maybe two runs? I think that's what's in the op order."

"Yes, two runs. And without trying to fly your airplane for you, I was thinking you could have your bomb bay doors open on both runs, flying as low and slow as you're comfortable with—to enhance the whole effect. I'm sure you'll be providing the thrill of a lifetime to many of those Iranian sailors. We think this could make a strong statement to our Iranian counterparts without antagonizing them."

"I follow you, sir."

"Let me address what our goal is after the second run." Frank's voice intensified. "You can think of your first pass as a sort of clearing run—see where the surface traffic is and where any open areas might be. You should expect to see numerous civilian tanker ships under various national flags in the area—they are *not* the focus here. While not prohibited, we accomplish nothing by overflying them. The Iranian small boats and two Kilo submarines are your primary contacts of interest during your flyovers. On the second pass, at an altitude as low as safety permits, in a clear area with no surface traffic present, but still as close to the Iranian small boats as is feasible, we'd like you to drop a line of 12 MK-82 bombs, one right after the other, creating, as they detonate, a wall of water that's visible to the maximum number of Iranians possible. Then accelerate, climb, and be on your way. All of this to say to Iran: 'This could have been you instead of a bunch of fish.'"

Barnes imagined a slightly different visual. "You know, we'll be loaded out with about 20 MK-82s. I mean, we can drop more than 12—and we can certainly make a bigger splash than what those 500 pounders will do; how about some 1,000 or 2,000 pounders—wouldn't they make a nice visual?"

Willie added his own ideas about creating an ACE parking lot out of Bandar Abbas to truly get someone's attention, suggesting that would be a good day at the office.

Amid some grimaces and smirks around the table, Frank's voice was steady, and his tone firm. "Let's stick with the 500-pound bombs. Please tell young Captain Willie Bob Washington thank you, from all of us, for his generous offer and energetic attitude, but that's exactly what we're *not* interested in. In fact, on your second run, the live bombing run, if you don't like what you see, don't release. A so-called error on the side of caution is no error at all. Simply close the doors and depart the area. No harm, no foul, no problem. The wall of water is intended as a point of emphasis but not a provocation. More of an exclamation point instead of a period.

"In any event, please understand this other important aspect of your mission, Major; upon completion, we expect there to be public uproar and widespread condemnation for the very actions you are being ordered to take. The president, the secretary of defense, the secretary of the air force, the air force chief of staff—they will be dismayed at what has happened and will all agree on a detailed inquiry into your unwarranted and undisciplined actions. Major, that's the nature of the PR game on the international stage, and you and your crew have nothing to worry about; the public furor will pass soon enough. But to be sure, if a small boat capsizes, or someone takes some shrapnel from the detonations, there will be—to put it politely— consequences. To start with, you'll have to trade your green flight suit for an orange jumpsuit and start living with several other similarly attired gentlemen in a room the size of a broom closet. At some point your head will be put on a stick and used for lawn art at the now former air force chief of staff's new residence, wherever that is, after he "resigns" his post. Willie's testicles will be bronzed, suitably engraved, and hung from the former chief's rearview mirror, as a constant reminder of our young captain's service to his air force and our country. So, Major, with those thoughts in mind, are we on the same page? Are we singing the same song from the same sheet of music?"

The reply was firm, polite, and to the point. "You're loud and clear, sir. I got it. We'll take care of business for you and get your point across to the Iranians."

"One more thing," Frank added. "Expect to have escort aircraft on either side of you during your two runs—two Navy F/A-18 Hornets, one on each wing. They're not solely for show but in case someone doesn't understand the friendly nature of a flyover by a mammoth, low flying aircraft with its bomb bay doors open and live armaments ready for deployment."

Major Barnes replied, "Two navy guys, huh? Couldn't we make this an all-air force event? What's the harm in that?"

Back in the Situation Room, both Donaldson and Frank grinned broadly. "Well, Major, we're nothing if not a joint force. You know the navy thinks you air force types are always trying to steal the limelight. So, play nice with your navy brethren, and they'll make sure you're well taken care of. Any more questions?"

"Yes, sir, just one. It's been gradually dawning on me about what Willie said when we first started this conversation: that you were calling from a white house about a situation—you wouldn't happen to be calling from a residence on Pennsylvania Avenue, would you?"

Everyone had a smile on their face. "Yes, Major, that's where I am. I don't live here, but the individual who resides here let me use his phone. He, along with a few other guests have been listening in; all have contributed to the plan we've been discussing, and we all hope for its successful execution."

"Ah, well, yes, thank you all for your support, and we'll try not to embarrass anyone."

In the background, Willie was practically screaming, "C'mon Boss, party time—let's saddle up!"

Finally, Major Barnes said, "Mr. Warren, before I hang up, one last question: Were you, or should I say, are you former navy?" Frank raised his head up a few inches when he heard the question as he continued to stare at the speakerphone in front of him. Every head turned, and every eye in the situation room focused directly on him.

Frank responded, "Yes, Major, I am former navy—retired a little over ten years ago. Something give me away?"

Chuckling softly, the major replied, "I don't know many navy guys, sir, but the ones I do know talk ... differently, like you ... they're not like air force people—you navy folks have interesting ways of saying things, and I find it kinda refreshing. You make your point and convey the essence of the issue in an off-beat, yet straightforward way. The phrases 'head on a stick' and BUFF One's testicles 'bronzed and engraved' —that's good stuff, sir; that's how a navy guy would say it. That's what I picked up on."

Smiling, Frank replied, "Very well, sir. I hope you understand I wasn't kidding about your head and BUFF's privates if this thing goes south—that'll be the opening act with more severe repercussions to follow!"

Laughing heartily, Major Barnes said, "Oh, that's good, that's very good."

"One last comment, Major. Navy folks, particularly pilots, well, they're sort of an acquired taste."

"Got it, sir. Very good."

"Uh, Major, standby just a moment." President Sheppard had motioned to Admiral Donaldson for pen and paper, using a signing motion, like asking for the bill at a restaurant. The president wrote:

1st pass – B/B doors closed

He pushed the paper in front of Frank and pointed at the speaker phone.

Frank nodded, understanding the message.

"Major, still there?"

"Yes, sir. Anything else?"

"Yes, we want to make a slight change to the plan. On your first pass, we suggest you have your bomb bay doors ..." Frank stopped in mid-sentence when he noticed the president shaking his head side-to-side.

He tried again. "Major, we recommend you ..." He stopped again, the president still not satisfied. President Sheppard reached for the paper and wrote one word: "ORDER."

Nodding, Frank continued. "Major Barnes, on your first pass, you are ordered to have your bomb bay doors closed. How copy?"

"Bomb bay doors closed on the first pass. Wilco.[31] Makes sense. No need to overly excite our Iranian friends, not that a low flying B-52 screaming over their heads won't cause their hearts to skip a beat. Got it—no bombs visible on the first pass."

Frank was about to conclude the call when the president intervened with a slight wave of his hand.

"Major, this is the president. We have every confidence in you and your crew. We're counting on you. Have a safe flight."

Major Barnes' posture suddenly straightened. "Thank you, Mr. President."

The line went dead, and a humbled air force major, eleven time zones away, quietly placed the phone in its cradle. In Washington, silence permeated the Situation Room. Small room, few people, big decision. Now it was time to execute the plan.

20

It was 4:10 pm (1610) in Washington; 0110 Sunday morning in Dubai, UAE; 0310 in Diego Garcia. Scheduled launch time for the B-52 was 2200Z, 5:00 pm in Washington and 0400 in D-GAR. The BUFF should be near Dubai and the Strait of Hormuz by 0315Z. Sunrise in the Dubai area would occur at 0307Z or 0707 local. The flyovers should take place from 0715 to 0730 local (10:15 to 10:30 pm in Washington), after which the B-52 would return to Diego Garcia. Nearly 11 hours in the air for the B-52 crew for roughly 15 minutes of low altitude, on-station activity. Sensible? Practical? Appropriate use of an asset? Safe? Smart?

The president rose from his chair with everyone else rising in unison. He looked at his chief of staff, then turned to Rear Admiral Donaldson and thanked him for his contributions to the discussion. He thanked Sharon Fleming for her participation. Those two started for the door, and Peter Sanders fell in line behind them. Frank headed toward the door, too, but stopped short of it when he observed a gesture from the president to stay behind. The chief of staff closed the door when he exited, and now Frank Warren was alone with the president of the United States.

"Frank, thank you for your views and comments today. I appreciate the delicacy of the situation when I asked about your alternate plan that was contrary to CentCom's proposal. I think you handled that well and obviously, I thought you had the superior plan."

"Thank you, Mr. President."

"You think all of this activity in the Gulf is a ruse, a show of force by Mazdaki? Iran flexing its muscles and demonstrating its willingness, its desire, to be a factor—a major player—in world events?"

Frank considered all he had read and written about over the years regarding Iran, particularly since he'd recently reported to the Pentagon. "The Iranians are difficult to figure out, sir. For starters, they have severe economic sanctions imposed on them. With this bold display of naval activity, my first thought was they were trying to influence commercial traffic in the Strait of Hormuz, which hurts them more than other nations and thus makes no sense. Then I thought they were responding to the UAE's comments at the recent GCC meeting in Abu Dhabi. That feud has been going on so long I sense everyone's tired of hearing about it, except the UAE, of course, although I feel Iran is on the wrong side of justice in that matter. When *Nimitz* went dead in the water, that changed my whole perception of the situation, and my biggest fear became a suicide small boat attack against *Nimitz*, like the USS *Cole* in Aden. That still concerns me, and that often-stated adage applies here: they only have to be successful once, while we must be perfect every time. On the other hand, they haven't violated any international laws, and they're still, as far as I know, cloistered in groups and milling about in the dark. I can't make much sense of it. I think the surprise appearance of the S-3s followed by the arrival of the B-52 will widen their eyes and get them praying to Allah. Hopefully, our actions will leave a lasting impression on the Iranians and influence their future decisions."

"Let's hope you're right." Then changing the subject, Sheppard asked, "You've known Sharon Fleming and Rear Admiral Donaldson since you were students at NDU?"

"I met Sharon there, that's correct, sir. Admiral Donaldson and I were in the same air wing many years ago. His career path has taken a slightly different course than mine did." Frank said this last statement with a polite smile and a slight head shake.

The president nodded. "They are both exceptional people. By the way, I have felt all afternoon that at some point in the past *our* paths may have crossed—that we've met somewhere along the way. Do you have any recollection like that? Just curious."

"Well, sir, if it happened, perhaps it was in London. I have some vague memory of being there with my boss, ComSixthFlt, at the same time a U.S. senator and his assistant were passing through—but I made many trips to London back then; I can't be sure."

"Well," the president stated, indicating a conclusion to the discussion, "I certainly can't recall, either. But thank you, again, for your thoughts and recommendations today. I guess now we'll wait and see how everything works out."

President Sheppard gestured toward the exit. Frank opened the door and walked out of the Situation Room, grabbing his backpack and retrieving his cell phone from the lead-lined cabinet. Sharon Fleming and Rear Adm. Donaldson had decided to wait for Frank and sat waiting in the hallway. When the president walked past, each offered to remain in the vicinity and return to the Situation Room when the flyovers were scheduled. Since the main event would not be happening for over five hours, the president dismissed all three, stating watch teams at the White House, the Pentagon, and the CIA were set to monitor the action. With the president's thanks, they stepped into the cold, overcast, late afternoon D.C. weather, and headed toward the Metro Center station. With collars raised and leaning into a biting wind, they crunched their way through the hardened snow, silent in their thoughts, each thankful the winter storm had passed. Lucky for them, an Orange Line train rumbled to a stop moments after their arrival, and they found seats close to each other. Sharon pushed the hood of her stylish coat off her head and with one brief touch smoothed her hair back to perfection. Joe removed his cover, and his hair looked freshly combed and styled. Frank put his backpack on the floor between his feet as other passengers boarded. Many seats remained empty which surprised no one.

It was approaching 5:00 pm, which made it nearly 4:00 am in Diego Garcia, Sunday morning. The BUFF should be airborne by now, or taxiing for take-off if it wasn't already en route toward the Strait of Hormuz. Then five hours or so later, it would be show time in the Gulf.

21

The Orange Line train left the Rosslyn station and headed westward toward its first stop, Court House, and the seven subsequent stops, concluding at Vienna. Sharon Fleming, Rear Admiral Donaldson, and Frank Warren had contacted their spouses and arranged for pickups at their respective metro stations. Snow plows had been busy all day, and most of the streets had at least one lane available for passage. The three DoD employees were rethinking the day's events and wondering if the B-52 option would be as effective as they hoped. Time would tell—the flyovers were scheduled to occur in about five hours.

Rear Admiral Donaldson, his gold two-star shoulder boards glistening on his overcoat, hunched forward and spoke to Sharon. "Tell me about your daughter and son-in-law. How are they doing these days with your grandson's condition?"

Frank tried unsuccessfully to suppress a look of surprise; he didn't know Sharon and her husband were grandparents; in fact, he couldn't remember anything about their kids—how many, or how old.

Sharon sighed as she responded thoughtfully, "They're holding up pretty well. At least they caught it early on. They were fortunate their pediatrician had already seen a case of infantile spasms. The disorder is so rare that some pediatricians never treat a case of it during their whole career. Those who do might see one or two cases, tops. So, they got a correct diagnosis at the start with an EEG (electroencephalogram) and followed that with an MRI. Reed, my grandson, tolerates the ACTH (adrenocorticotropic) hormone treatment well, although his cheeks are chunky now. We're all hopeful for Reedy's recovery, but it's hard to ignore the fact that, overall, there's about a 30% fatality rate with this disorder. The doctor thinks his chances of survival are good because of the early detection, but we'll have to face the high likelihood that he'll be developmentally disabled, to some degree. Our first grandchild, Reed's sister Olivia, is perfectly fine and doesn't seem to mind having to wear a facial mask at home, for the time being, because Reed is so susceptible to infections. It's a tough situation, but my daughter and her husband are handling it pretty well—better than me, sometimes!"

The admiral inquired again, "And Ronny—how's he getting along?"

"Well, as they say in sports, he's day-to-day, Joe. Frank," Sharon said as she turned toward him, "we're talking about my son, Ronald, Jr., the younger of our two children."

Frank, completely unaware of Sharon's family situation, nodded and uttered, meekly, "Oh, yeah. Of course."

Sharon continued, "We've been lucky to be able to hire some excellent assistance through the years, so Ronny has had first-rate help dealing with his autism. We think Brooke, our daughter, is such a good mother to Reed because of her experiences growing up with Ronny and his issues. They're both such beautiful kids. But with Ronny, some days we're laughing so hard with him we get tears in our eyes, and on other days, we just have the tears. We're blessed in so many ways and consider ourselves fortunate to have two extraordinary children."

"Well, Sharon," Joe replied, "I know it's been a tremendous challenge for you and Ron, and how you pulled off raising those kids with all of the demands of your professional lives—I don't see how you keep it all together. I've known you a long time, and I've always considered it a privilege to work with you and to call you my friend."

Frank was desperate to apologize for the less than flattering thoughts of Sharon he'd fostered in his mind over the years; he felt ashamed for not knowing of Sharon's family struggles. He offered, sympathetically, "You've traveled a challenging path, Sharon. I admire your ability to juggle the professional demands with those of your home life. I agree with the admiral—how you keep all the plates spinning is a real testimony to your character and your commitment to your family. Your kids and grandchild are lucky to have you in their lives."

"Thank you both for your kind, encouraging words," Sharon replied. "But we have lots of help, and we work with many people who contribute their skills to Ron, Jr.'s development and Reed's march toward recovery."

Returning to their present setting and reflecting on that day's events, Sharon continued, "You know, today was a good example of people working together, too, this time so we could develop a plan for the president."

Rear Adm. Donaldson nodded in agreement. "I want to compliment both of you for your efforts. Each of you displayed an impressive grasp of the complexities that define the Middle East. Even our disagreements were constructive and non-adversarial. Trying to complement rather than compete is a tough ballet to perform considering the seniority and positions of the folks in the Situation Room. We saw how a constructive and effective plan could be conceived, developed, and then put into action. I believe we did excellent work today."

Sharon concurred. "You're right, Joe. No one—at least none of us—tried to "top" each other or score some point of approval at the expense of someone else; we were all pulling in the same direction. And, importantly, we listened to each other. I thought the views you expressed, Joe, and yours, Frank, were right on point. And Frank, who would have dared to challenge a fully developed plan put forth by CentCom with the secretary of defense looking on? I give the president credit for fostering an atmosphere where a contrary opinion is not subject to criticism or pushback, and I give you kudos for not only speaking up when asked but for having a well-conceived plan already in your head. Apparently, you haven't limited your work to solely personnel issues since you've been back in the Pentagon, and I'm glad you were able to attend today's meeting."

During these comments, the Metro train stopped and started as it traveled toward the Vienna station. Frank was beginning to understand he'd experienced the most professionally challenging and rewarding day in his life. At the highest levels of our government—in the company of seasoned, experienced professionals, including the president of the United States—he'd been a participant in the development of a plan to thwart a threat posed to U.S. military assets on the other side of the world. To have others value his thoughts—his inputs—at this level was very satisfying. An "admiral" —the president, in this case—listened to a "lieutenant," a GS-14 with less than a year at the Pentagon. Sharon's gracious words were comforting, gratifying, and unanticipated. Frank realized he had greatly misjudged her.

Sharon and Joe looked on expectantly. "Yes," Frank finally replied. "Today was unlike any other that I've had—

ever—in my life. Thank you, Sharon, for your kind words. I was pleased to be asked for my views, and I want to thank you both for allowing me to participate in today's events. I'm sure one of you," he gave Sharon a knowing glance, "had to convince someone to allow me into the Situation Room—then to let me speak, and even brief the president—that was special."

Admiral Donaldson added: "Your comments and the briefing of your plan were right on the mark, Frank. Well done."

"Yes," Sharon noted, "you spoke quite well, and you had the president's and everyone else's attention. You know, Frank," she continued, "I got the impression that the president thought he recognized you from somewhere— sometime in the past. He kept getting a quizzical look on his face. Is that true? You two ever cross paths while you were on active duty?"

Frank replied with measured words. "I have a vague recollection of seeing him once in London at the CinCUSNavEur[32] headquarters at Grosvenor Square. The president was then an assistant to a senator from Virginia and was accompanying his boss on a trip to various military installations in Europe. I was there with my boss, the commander of the Sixth Fleet, on a visit to his immediate superior. So yes—I think that must be what the president had in mind; we were in an outer office together for maybe 10 to 15 minutes, as I recall, then he and the senator left for their next appointment. That's the sum of it; that's all I can remember." A statement which wasn't entirely accurate, but close enough. Regarding the president, when he saw the senator's assistant leave the navy's Grosvenor Square military headquarters that evening in the company of a young, single female ensign assigned to the Deputy CinC's staff—the two of them, no senator in sight—Frank was left to draw any conclusion he chose. The one he selected was that they were simply having dinner somewhere, since his boss was dining with the CinC. Throughout Sheppard's political career—3-term congressman, elected twice to the Senate, representing Virginia—and then his run for and election to the presidency—never had there ever been the slightest hint of any untoward personal behavior. To offer up now even the thought of some questionable past activity on the president's part would be inexcusable and inappropriate. Truth be told, what did he know for sure on this issue? Absolutely nothing.

Joe and Sharon both nodded to themselves and Sharon noted, "He has a pretty good memory to recall such an insignificant moment."

Frank nodded in agreement, "He sure does—it's a heck of a lot better than mine."

The train decelerated as it approached the next stop, West Falls Church. Even though Frank thought he saw Joe and Sharon board at different stops this morning, both started to bundle up for the chill awaiting them when the doors opened. They stood up as the train slowed, making some final adjustments to their outerwear. Frank rose, too, although he had two stops to go before departing. Admiral Donaldson looked directly at Frank, his cover (hat) placed perfectly atop his head, the two rows of "scrambled eggs" extending out over his eyes and nose.

He cuts an imposing figure, Frank thought. The admiral leaned forward slightly, offered his hand, and said, "Nice work today, Frank."

Frank grasped his hand in a firm clasp. "Insightful comments, constructive criticisms; it was a real pleasure working with you, and you, too, Sharon, of course. Today was a good example of working together and no one caring who gets the credit for the product."

Handshake complete, Sharon offered her hand to Frank as the admiral stepped toward the nearby door, which opened, letting in a gust of the wintry elements. "Yes, Frank," she said, as he shook her hand, "Joe is right. You know, someone may ask you about this Achmed fellow, but you'll get no questions from me!" She punctuated this declaration with a wink and a sneaky smile. "I hope we can work together again, under less stressful conditions. Excellent job."

Frank responded, "Sharon, Admiral, thank you both; I was honored to be included today, and I know it was a stretch to get me into the room. Sharon, I hope all good things come to Ron, Jr. and your grandson, Reed. I know they are special people."

Sharon looked at Frank and smiled warmly. "Thank you, Frank. That's kind of you."

22

They were about to step off the train and say their final good nights, when Frank again spoke up. "Admiral Donaldson, I want to offer you my congratulations on being nominated for your third star and the position of Sixth Fleet commander. It's a great assignment and a most deserved promotion, sir. A numbered fleet command is about as good as life can get, Admiral, and I think you are the perfect pick for the job."

"Wow—you do have some sources, Frank," Donaldson replied, wide-eyed and an inquiring grin on his face. "That information is supposed to be very close hold; how in the world did you hear of it?"

"Well, sir," Frank sheepishly replied, nodding toward Sharon, "this source I can reveal: she told me—today!" Sharon had stepped off the train but was a few feet away as the admiral momentarily straddled the door, one foot on the train and the other on the platform.

Sharon broke into a broad smile, stating, "It's hard to keep a secret in Washington, but Frank, please do keep this one. It's too early to let this tidbit start circulating. Joe, I join Frank in offering my sincerest congratulations on your third star and the ComSixthFlt job. Ron and I think you and Karen will love Gaeta." Gaeta, Italy, a small coastal town of about 25,000 people, on Italy's west coast between Naples and Rome, is the home port of the flagship of the commander, Sixth Fleet.

"Ah," Joe nodded at the mentioning of the congressman's name—Sharon's husband. "Now I see how the word must have slipped out." Sharon's grin only widened. "Well," Donaldson continued, "Karen and I are delighted with this opportunity; and Frank, you mentioned being in London years ago with your boss—were you SixthFlt's aide?"

"Yes, sir, I was. It was a great two years, and Gaeta is the perfect place to live. The locals are so nice—a few words spoken in Italian will create inroads wherever you may be. Watch out for the month of August—it seems that most of Europe and practically all of Italy go on "holiday" and all of them try to squeeze into Gaeta; that's how it feels."

The admiral had a thoughtful, pondering look on his face, with feet spread, one foot in the metro car, the other on the platform, blocking the movement of the door. For some reason, the doors weren't trying to close; the train sat there. The wind had all but disappeared. It was still cold—about what you'd expect in the middle of January, but almost pleasant. Admiral Donaldson, head slightly bowed, spoke quietly, looking at neither Sharon or Frank but addressing them both: "For Karen, this will be a return, of sorts, to the place where tragedy struck her years ago."

Frank, anticipating an important moment, grabbed his backpack and motioned toward the platform. "Admiral, let's step off the train and let the doors close. I'll catch the next one in a few minutes."

Admiral Donaldson nodded, and he and Frank joined Sharon on the platform, allowing the doors to close and the train to continue on its way. They stood quietly, their breath visible in the dim lights of the station. An inner warmth, generated by their close, professional relationship, enveloped them.

The admiral continued in measured tones. "My RIO (radar intercept officer) Bobby Hickman— "Stogie" to his many friends due to his preference for an occasional fine cigar—and I were on a routine, day, air defense hop off the *Dwight D. Eisenhower*, good old CVN-69. The ship had been anchored off the coast of Naples for over a week, and our schedule called for another port visit near Toulon, France, after only ten days at sea. Many of the squadron's wives had organized a trip to Italy and France to coincide with our port visits and were planning to visit other parts of Europe during the short at-sea period.

"This was day three since leaving Naples: clear skies and calm seas—perfect flying weather. Stogie and I got a good shot off the cat and were on station when suddenly the number one engine started running rough and then quickly failed. Among the caution and warning lights, it looked like we had a complete loss of oil pressure in the left engine. Once I got my stomach out of my throat, I realized I also had a flight control problem with my rudders and spoilers. I suspected the failed engine shed a few parts which probably cut some flight control hydraulic lines. With number one engine failed, I needed extra right rudder to counter the torque of the increased power required from the number two engine. But the hydraulic system commanded full left rudder and allowed me limited control movement; the stick would not move to the right— only forward and aft and to the left. I reduced power on the right engine, number two, to lessen the torque while I tried to relight number one, even though I presumed it was unlikely to work. Of course, we were descending now, the relight was failing, and an increase in power on number two only exacerbated the situation due to the full, uncommanded left rudder. I had no right turning capability and using trim to compensate helped slightly, but not enough. Stogie was with me through the whole event, calling out our altitude and airspeed and offering emergency procedures and other suggestions. I barely maintained control of the jet and passing through 10,000 feet we ran out of time, altitude and ideas. We made a MAYDAY call; I reduced #2 to idle and attempted to straighten my right leg, as I'd been trying to do throughout the ordeal, to get some rudder in to reduce the left torque. After a moment to get ourselves in an appropriate position in our seats, Stogie, with my concurrence, pulled the ejection handle. Out we went; each of us got a good chute, and we drifted down toward the Mediterranean Sea. As you can imagine, there are tremendous forces on your body as you're shot up the rails during an ejection and having the correct posture in the seat before it fires is critical. I have no reason to think the ejection system malfunctioned in any way, but I could see Stogie in his chute as we descended, and his head was down like he was looking at his flight boots. I removed my oxygen mask and yelled at him—I think I was close enough for him to hear me—but he didn't respond. After water entry, I got in my raft and used my hands to paddle toward Stogie. As I approached him, I could see he was turned away from me with his face in the water. I grabbed his flight helmet and pulled his head back, out of the water, and saw that his oxygen mask was missing from his helmet. How that happened is unknown and bothers me to this day. I don't know if his face was in the water the whole time. Stogie's life preserver inflated upon contact with the salt water and looked to have functioned properly.

"We weren't in the water long—I'd say no more than 30 to 40 minutes. I think someone either heard our emergency call or saw our chutes and notified the ship. The SAR (search and rescue) helicopter responded and headed to our area. The helo crew put a swimmer in the water, and he quickly determined that Stogie should be picked up first. After they hoisted me aboard, I could see a crestfallen, fatal look in the rescue swimmer's eyes—and when I saw Stogie, well, it didn't look good. When we got back to the ship, they took Stogie to sickbay where the ship's medical doctor examined him and pronounced him dead. Listed as the primary cause of death was a broken neck with drowning listed as a secondary cause. The water where we ejected was too deep to recover the jet, so the accident mishap board was unable to determine, with any confidence, what caused his injuries. Bobby Hickman's wife, Karen, was among the squadron wives visiting in Naples during the ship's in-port period, and the group was in Rome when she was located and told of Stogie's death. I wasn't the casualty assistance calls officer (CACO) assigned to Stogie, but my skipper allowed me to assist the CACO and accompany Stogie, and Karen, back to the United States."

Admiral Donaldson paused briefly. Time seemed suspended. Respectfully, Sharon and Frank kept silent.

Donaldson continued. "There was a large funeral; many family members attended—his personal one and his navy family. Practically all the squadron wives were there, including those of the enlisted men who knew Stogie. Most of the wives who were in the tour group decided to return home and skip our Toulon port visit. The family opted to bury him in a family plot outside Norfolk instead of requesting he be buried at Arlington. I rejoined the squadron, after about a week stateside, and finished up the cruise. I realized when I got back to the ship that we all grieve in separate ways and at different rates; the process may be similar but is unique to each of us. When we completed the cruise, the entire squadron had to work through the adjustments to being home again after a six-and-a-half-month deployment coupled with the added burden of Lt. Hickman's death. Not long after we returned, I visited Karen and her parents. I stayed in touch to see how she was coping with all the lingering details that persist when a spouse passes away. Over time, our visits became friendlier, and we realized we had developed feelings for each other. We were married about two years later.

"So, that's a little background on our upcoming move to Gaeta. Sorry to dampen the mood after the day we've had—but I wanted both of you to know. I don't tell that story to just anyone."

A moment passed, and then Sharon spoke, lightly touching the admiral's arm, "Thank you, Joe, for sharing that portion of your life with us. I know the two of you will enjoy your time in Italy—it'll work out fine."

Frank added, "I had no idea, sir. I appreciate you telling us."

Admiral Donaldson straightened, his body language indicating the conclusion of the personal moments. Briskly, he said, "Okay—off we go. There might be some exciting eleven o'clock news tonight; if not, tomorrow morning's news shows should be quite lively. I hope the operation goes well. Frank, have a safe drive home when you get to your stop." Then, with a smile, he added, "Hey, I could give you a lift home from here—wanna ride? I have plenty of gas!"

Frank smiled broadly, which told the admiral he remembered, too, saying, "Thank you, sir, but Mary is waiting for me." With that, Frank Warren, retired navy captain, came to attention and saluted, stating, "Good night, Admiral. All the best to you and Karen."

The admiral, surprised by this unexpected gesture of kindness and respect, returned the salute, remarking, "Thank you, Frank. Thank you very much."

Admiral Donaldson and Sharon Fleming exchanged a brief glance and departed toward the waiting cars, engines idling and their exhaust circling upward into the darkness. The occupants of two cars, parked near each other, had witnessed the final exchange between Frank and Joe Donaldson, the prospective Sixth Fleet commander. They stepped out of their vehicles to greet their long-awaited partners. Introducing themselves to each other, they realized they had connections to each other through their spouses. Of course, Congressman Ronald Fleming was (much) more familiar with the lady's husband, having met him years before at a White House function when he was a lieutenant. He also knew the admiral would soon be needing some new shoulder boards (with *three* stars).

When Joe and Sharon arrived, the four exchanged brief pleasantries in the frosty night air and reviewed the day's events. Several collar adjustments later, they said their goodbyes and departed.

Frank watched the introductions from the station platform and boarded the next westbound train. His thoughts concentrated in the same area as Sharon's and Rear Adm. Donaldson's. The giant B-52 was still well over four and a half hours away from displaying its prowess as Frank reflected on his president's style and interpersonal traits—his ability, his desire, perhaps even his insistence, for different and opposing views. No one felt diminished, or humbled, or looked down upon if their perspective wasn't in favor with others. The commander in chief listened—actively—but each had to be concise, factual, and on point when offering their views. Rank, title, position, seniority, experience—all were respected and acknowledged, but none were an automatic pass to acceptance of proposed policies or recommendations. Everyone was important—that's how Frank felt—and as a GS-14 in a room of (much) more senior folks, he'd had a good sense-of-self today, and felt part of the team. The DoD's organizational wiring diagram would never suggest that he'd be involved or even consulted about events like those that occurred today. He'd misjudged both Sharon and Joe; calling him Joe 2-star wasn't going to work anymore. Sharon was in her element today, as was the admiral. His esteem for each of them continued to grow throughout the afternoon. In contrast, he realized his own assessment of others needed work.

The admiral's touching story of the loss of his RIO, Lt. Robert "Stogie" Hickman, was moving and poignant. He hadn't a clue about how the admiral had met his wife and the beginnings of their relationship. Such a remarkable story. And Sharon Fleming—he'd never known anything about her personal life—but now recognized her as a kind, caring woman.

The image of another woman sought entrance into Frank's mind as he fumbled with his iPod and considered checking the score of the playoff game in Baltimore. He couldn't rid himself of an uneasy sensation in his gut. He attempted to make sense of the image of an older, senior Pentagon official with a pulse on all defense policy initiatives together with a young, attractive female defense employee who lived beyond her means. Something was off there.

The Metro car doors opened at the Vienna station, the end of the Orange Line, where he had begun his morning commute. The cold, biting air greeted the Saturday travelers as they hunched their shoulders against the invisible wind and rushed to the parking garage or cars waiting with their engines running. Frank secured his backpack over one shoulder and hurried toward the warmth of his car and his wife, his breath visible in the night air and his mind racing in a review of the day's many events.

When he recognized the family car, he reminded himself of the pact with his wife to leave his work, the department of defense, the U.S. government, his e-mails, his correspondence—all of it—leave it at work. The ride home was his decompression time to review the day's events, make notes about tomorrow, mentally deal with all the issues currently vying for his time and attention—but leave work behind. When you're home, you're home—all of you, not just the physical body. Work will always be there, so leave it there. Frank resolved to tell Mary only the high points of the day; and, he admitted, there were quite a few!

He opened the rear door of their SUV to stow his backpack, then climbed into the front passenger seat beside Mary. He welcomed the warmth inside the car, and the kiss he shared with his wife, his closest and best friend.

"Well," she began, "from what little you put in your text message I'm guessing you had quite a day. Did you ever get a chance to meet up with your friend who called from the Comfort Inn?" He understood she really meant, did you meet with your CIA buddy? Even in the car or at home, they kept certain discussions coded in their personal and secret dialogue. They felt better talking this way so they wouldn't get complacent and say something inappropriate at the wrong time, and in the wrong place.

"No," Frank replied as Mary slowly headed home over the hard, packed snow. The plowed street still had an inch or two of compressed snow over most of it. At least it was no longer snowing. "We talked on the phone but didn't see a time when we could meet. Real nice guy, though, and we had a friendly conversation. Maybe next time he's in town, we'll get together."

Then Mary glanced over, questioning eyes searching his. "So, did Ed call sometime today? I thought you mentioned something about him today, maybe in a text; I can't remember."

Edward S. Scott was the Under Secretary for Personnel and Readiness, one of the five "Unders." Of course, there was another 'Edward' in government service: Edward Michael Sheppard, president of the United States. When referring to his boss, a few steps up the chain of command, he was known simply as "Ed." When the subject was the president, and not wishing to identify him verbally, they used the phrase "my good friend" or "my good buddy." Thus, Frank replied, "I had an occasion to meet with our good friend Ed. He sends his regards, Mary; it was nice to chat with him. It had been a while since I last visited with him."

Mary's eyes widened in amazement when she comprehended the magnitude of Frank's reply. She mouthed the word "wow," and Frank nodded. She asked, "Did Sharon and 2-star work late today, too?" Frank had mentioned earlier in the day that other people were going to stay at work for a while, not only him.

"Yes, they were there, too. In fact, they both got off the Metro at West Falls Church. 2-star offered me a ride; said he had plenty of gas!" Mary knew the story and smiled knowingly. "By the way, our call sign for Shooter Donaldson will soon be obsolete." Frank held up three fingers and tapped his shoulder, which Mary acknowledged in wide-eyed amazement. "He's going to be nominated to be ComSixthFlt. The word's not out officially, but Sharon told me. If you'd seen him today, you'd be in total agreement with that decision. Mary, I've had some lingering doubts and misgivings about him for a long time, and I now realize I was way off the mark. I formed opinions about him which were misguided and ill-informed. I've rarely shared those thoughts with anyone else—you may be the only one—I sure hope so."

Mary continued the drive home, Frank telling her the traumatic story of how Joe Donaldson met his future wife. Then he discussed Sharon Fleming, their history at NDU, the thoughts he'd kept to himself about her working relationships with subordinates, and finally the burdens she shouldered in her personal life. Silence crept into the car as they neared their residence.

Finally, Mary said, "Thank you for telling me about Karen Donaldson and Sharon Fleming; that was touching."

She took a deep breath, and, getting their thoughts back to the present, stated, "We're going to my folk's house tomorrow morning. I told them we weren't coming today, so they're expecting us bright and early tomorrow."

"That sounds great. I'm glad we're staying home tonight, Mary. This has been one Saturday I'll never forget."

It was 6:30 pm (2330Z; 0330 Sunday morning in Dubai) when the Warrens pulled into their driveway.

23

Like a small town, an aircraft carrier has its own rhythm and pulse; it has unique sounds, smells, and routines, such as the shrill of the bos'n's pipe marking certain events throughout the day. Catapults firing and thirty to forty-thousand-pound aircraft landing on your head become commonplace. Sailors adjust to the gentle rolls and pitches that the sea induces on its 100,000-ton visitor. The hiss of the air conditioning system is always present as the ship drives on with purpose and anticipation. At anchor, the ship sings a different song, slightly off-key. *Nimitz*, tethered in place for hours but with all systems now fully functional, felt poised to spring back into action, like a restless animal seeking to escape an unnatural confinement. On the bridge, the ring of the navigator's phone punctured the silent darkness.

"Navigator, sir." Commander Josh Stoner spoke in a clear, confident voice which belied the weariness he felt throughout his body. He'd returned to the bridge at 0300 to ensure all was ready for the 0330 launch of two S-3 Hoovers. Naturally, swinging on the anchor, there would be no maneuvering of the ship seeking wind for the S-3s, scheduled to use the waist catapults that morning. No wind was required—any would be a bonus. Commander Stoner anticipated a call from his captain, requesting (ordering) he oversee the forthcoming launch while he, the *Nimitz* commanding officer, remained in his at-sea cabin, resting.

"Good morning, Gator." The Captain's voice was firm and direct, despite the time. "Any updates from the plant?"

Captain Charles S. Hathaway, U.S. Navy, commanded the mighty *Nimitz* and referred to his navigator as "Gator," as did everyone, from seamen to the embarked admiral.

"A few minutes ago, the EOOW reported that both reactors continue to operate normally. They are ready for the S-3 launch and are standing by for underway operations whenever ordered."

"Very well. Cover the Viking launch, Gator, and I'll be on the bridge for the 0630 events. You can get some rest after this launch."

"Aye, aye, sir. Good night, captain." *Very considerate*, the Gator reflected. Cdr. Stoner possessed a letter from his commanding officer authorizing him to fulfill all functions of the Captain when he was absent from the bridge. Overseeing flight operations was one such event. That same letter also authorized the navigator to relieve the officer of the deck of his duties and assume that role if the need ever presented itself. So far, it hadn't.

The navigation bridge of any navy vessel is a bastion of quiet professionalism. Commands are given and repeated using precise verbiage to avoid confusion and uncertainty, especially in challenging times (man overboard, for example). For the several hours following anchoring, there had been a distinct lack of challenges, except for one: boredom. There had been no surface contacts to contend with, no course changes for the helmsman to steer, no speed changes for the lee helm to request from the propulsion plant, and no flight ops. Stoner had allowed personal conversations among his watchstanders, and a more relaxed atmosphere prevailed on the bridge. He'd recommended to the captain that a full watch team remain in place should the need arise to weigh anchor and quickly get under way. The captain agreed, having reached that conclusion long before his navigator suggested it.

Stoner eased to the left side of the bridge and climbed into the captain's chair, where he could view the entire flight deck. An array of phones and indicators provided the captain the ability to reach practically anyone on the ship (or off it, such as the Pentagon) and to swiftly assess *Nimitz*'s tactical situation. A tone rang from one of the phones, demanding Stoner's attention. "Captain's chair, navigator, sir," he said, knowing that only one person on the ship—the captain—used a single beep when he called. The time was now 0325.

"Has the Air Boss requested a green deck?" inquired Captain Hathaway.

"Not yet, Captain. Should be any moment."

"Okay. By the way, Gator, this isn't the first time an S-3 will be launched from a carrier at anchor, right? Someone said this had been done before. You're an S-3 guy; can you confirm that?"

"I can confirm that, Captain. It happened back in the '80s, off the *Ranger*, I believe. They called it FLANKEROPS [flight at anchor operations], as I recall. It happened about the time I was commissioned, so I've only heard about it. I don't recall there being any issues, either with the cat shot or the trap when they recovered."

"All right. Thanks."

After a moment Stoner placed the phone in its cradle and watched the S-3s maneuver toward the waist cats. An orchestra of personnel arrayed on the flight deck monitored the movements of the aircraft. Another distinctive tone sounded, this one from the Air Officer (Boss) one deck above the bridge, requesting a green deck to launch aircraft. Stoner pushed a button, granting the request, and announced to his bridge team, "Green deck," informing them of imminent flight operations.

Neither Cdr. Stoner nor the bridge watchstanders gave the Captain's absence from the bridge a passing thought. The Captain's at-sea cabin, located about ten feet aft of the bridge, contained an assortment of TVs, radar repeaters, and navigation aids which assisted him in maintaining situational awareness. While not physically present on the bridge (and supposedly resting), he was actively engaged.

24

The Iranian small boat contingent, estimated at approximately 50 vessels, had organized itself on roughly three different radials with 15-17 boats on each: a cluster of boats at around 10 o'clock, 12 o'clock, and 2 o'clock all relative to the *Nimitz* and roughly 10 miles from her. *Bunker Hill* and *Milius* were three to four miles from *Nimitz*, at approximately 11 o'clock and 1 o'clock respectively, performing a modern version of guard duty—deadly guard duty, if need be. It was a clear, warm (66 degrees F; 19 degrees C) Persian Gulf night, with a sea state of 1 (smooth, glassy seas). All eyes and ears, human and electronic, were peeled in a northerly direction, searching and listening for any activity that looked or sounded odd, suspicious, or out of place. *Nimitz*, with both reactors online and functioning normally, was now a full-up round, and still, by choice, tethered to her hook.

Two S-3B Viking crews convened at 0130 local (Dubai) time in their ready room aboard *Nimitz* to brief for their 0330 launch. A warm, odd silence greeted them on the flight deck when they emerged from the catacombs of the massive warship and proceeded to their aircraft. Light, pleasant breezes swept across acres of aircraft parked on flat, steel decking, the quiet an enjoyable reprieve from the blustery environment common to carrier flight decks. No aircraft engines were turning, and no planes were being towed to startup positions because it was a two-plane launch, both S-3s.

After engine starts and systems checkouts, the two Vikings crept slowly in the darkness toward the catapult, their high by-pass engines moaning in the manner befitting their Hoover (vacuum) nickname. Vigilant yellow-shirted taxi directors provided directions to the pilots with flashlights fitted with yellow cone extensions, their wands directing precise movements of the airplanes. On the catapult, the director signaled the pilot to spread the aircraft's folded wings and extend the launch bar, a device connected to the front of the I-beam-like nose wheel that the catapult shuttle engages prior to activation. The director then circled one flashlight over his head, the night version of the daytime 2-finger power signal, and motioned the other flashlight toward the bow of the ship. The pilot advanced the throttle to full power, disengaged nosewheel steering, cycled the control stick and rudders through the limits of their travel (wiped out the cockpit, in navy phrasing), and ensured the parking brake was off. Both pilot and CoTac confirmed their feet were off the brakes and the heels of their flight boots were on the cockpit floor. The only thing keeping the plane in place while at full power was the holdback fitting, a small, dumbbell-like device attached to the rear of the nose wheel strut and extending to a fixture in the catapult, designed to break when the catapult fired. A small portion of the fitting remained lodged in the nose strut receptacle throughout the flight and was discarded over the side of the ship on the plane's next flight, when the launch sequence was repeated.

The Viking crew checked their instruments, and when they were ready, the pilot turned on the aircraft's exterior lights, signaling their readiness for launch. The catapult officer stood to the side of the aircraft, in view of the plane's crew, moving a vertically held green-lit flashlight side-to-side in front of him, the night signal for full power.

When the aircraft's navigation lights illuminated, he moved the flashlight in an exaggerated arc over his head toward the bow of the ship, touching the deck with the flashlight, and then lifting and holding it horizontal to the flight deck. That lifting motion directed the deck edge operator, standing in the catwalk on the side of the ship, to complete one final safety look forward and aft, and then depress the fire button. Moments later, the catapult fired, breaking the holdback fitting, thrusting the crew members into their seats and, less than two seconds later, they were climbing toward the millions of stars in the Persian Gulf sky.[33]

It was exactly 0330 when the first Viking launched, followed moments later by the second aircraft, the catapults acting like powerful slingshots as the two Hoovers began their see-and-be-seen mission. They flew at pre-briefed altitudes that were never less than 1,000 feet apart to avoid any chance of collision. It didn't take long for the S-3s to confirm the location and estimate the number of boats assembled on the three different axes centered on the *Nimitz*. Commercial tankers transited the international waters, too, and the S-3s also reported their positions. Soon the combat plots on the three U.S. ships had a complete and accurate picture of all surface activity in the eastern part of the Gulf. And so it went, the Iranians remaining in their clusters, the S-3s flying about in the beautiful night sky. The Vikings adopted a large oval pattern by flying eastward, then completing a gentle 180-degree turn, now flying westward for a while, then another 180-degree turn, and so forth. In addition to altitude separation, they also maneuvered to be directly out of phase with each other—one aircraft flying east, the other west, using turns to the left to help the pilot, seated on the left, to better see his counterpart.

It didn't take long for this to get routine. The S-3s changed altitudes and airspeed and asked *Nimitz* for any additional taskings or missions that needed their assistance. Otherwise, they continued to fly their basic oval pattern, similar to a large civilian aviation holding pattern. Around and around they went, continually flying over the nests of Iranian boats and sailors, the aircraft's presence (and hopefully their armaments) impossible to miss. Soon the beginning of sunrise started to appear in the east, first visible to the pilots because of their altitude.

Nimitz scheduled their recovery time at 0630, approximately forty minutes before official sunrise, meaning they'd trap, in the morning twilight, with the ship still anchored. The vessel intended to commence raising its anchor when the second Viking was "on the ball," or on the final portion of the approach for landing. *Nimitz*'s four mighty screws would then begin churning the Persian Gulf waters, thrusting the massive warship through the calm morning seas, once both S-3s trapped aboard.

When she had achieved the required wind over the deck, *Nimitz* was scheduled to launch 2 F/A-18 Hornets which were to join the U.S. Air Force B-52 and escort her through her low altitude maneuvers. Once the mini airshow concluded with a point of emphasis at the end, the Hornets would recover aboard the ship, and the BUFF would return to D-GAR following a few sips of liquid gold—fuel—provided en route by a KC-135 U.S. Air Force tanker.

Everything had been planned, coordinated, and briefed. Phase one, the Vikings' patrol, was under way.

25

Preacher Johnson frowned as he reviewed the air plan from his chair in Ready Room 3, where squadron pilots gathered for meetings and flight briefings. A note regarding the 0630 launch of two F/A-18 Hornets stated it would follow the recovery of two S-3B Vikings. Normally launches preceded recoveries; the reverse was scheduled this morning.

Lieutenant Pete Johnson had been "ordained" by his fellow pilots with the call sign "Preacher" when word spread that his father was a Baptist minister and his wife's father was a Lutheran pastor. His interest in Islam, more a curiosity than a religious pursuit, conveniently aligned with his moniker. Through word and deed Preacher demonstrated he hadn't wholly embraced the principles of his father's or his father-in-law's calling.

Lieutenant Commander Alton "Husker" Cobb, the designated flight lead, and Lieutenant Jared "Swamp" Marsh joined Preacher in the ready room. Preacher was the designated spare for the other two go birds; he'd launch if either Husker's or Swamp's aircraft developed a mechanical problem.

That day's squadron duty officer, Lieutenant Michael "Hoss" Cartwright, addressed the three pilots. "Good morning and welcome to the 0430 brief. The aircraft assignments are on the board. Husker is the flight lead, Swamp is his wingman and Preacher is the turning spare. The plan is to recover two S-3s at 0630 while we're still anchored, raise the hook, and then launch you guys. I'm told the ship will start raising the anchor when the second

Viking is on the ball and get under way while you're taxiing to the cats. Expect to use the waist cats after the Hoovers land as the bow is full of aircraft."

Hoss's forced interest and sardonic tone were not surprising considering the time of day. "The mission this morning is to hold hands with the air force and make sure they don't screw anything up and delay our start home. More specifically, you'll be accompanying a B-52 as it makes two passes over some Iranian small boats and then drops some Mk-82s as a show of force, or just as a show. More details are in the briefing packets you received last night; I've received no changes or updates. The weather remains perfect, also known as Preacher's personal minimums (smirks all around). The skipper sends his regrets for not being here personally to encourage you to be on your best behavior this morning while making sure the air force can find their target, which I take to mean anywhere in the Persian Gulf. The ship is expecting to recover you around 0800 and requests you contact them ASAP if that time looks in doubt. Once you're back aboard, the *Nimitz* battle group will head to the Strait of Hormuz, provided the nukes don't let us down again, and we'll depart the lovely confines of the Arabian Sea. Or is it the Persian Gulf? Which is it, Preacher?"

"I pray you choose wisely the term describing the sacred waters of the Middle East, my friend." Preacher's mock sincerity brought grins and head shakes from the others.

"Okay," Hoss stated, "here's the emergency question of the day from the flight schedule: what are the memory items associated with a Left Oil Pressure caution light? Anyone?"

Swamp took the question. "Throttle – affected engine – idle. Then refer to the PCL (pocket check list)."

"You were all over that one, Swamp. Nice job," Husker taunted his wingman. "Anything else, Hoss?"

"Nope—that concludes my portion of the brief." A long time Star Trek enthusiast, Hoss fashioned Mr. Spock's familiar hand sign and declared, "Fly well and prosper."

Lcdr. Cobb addressed the other two pilots. "Let's brief this thing and then see if wardroom 1 has anything to eat." Husker referred to the squadron standard briefing guide and made quick work of the items. At this point in the deployment, the pilots needed little amplification on the topics listed in the guide.

Preacher Johnson shook his head in growing disgust as Husker finished briefing. "Who the hell thought up this stinking plan? Got to be an air force puke. A B-52 dropping 12 MK-82s is like skipping stones on a lake. Why would you send a BUFF all the way from D-GAR to the Persian Gulf, loaded with pebbles, when we could do the same thing and drop boulders? They'll probably spend over 10 hours in the air for about 15 minutes of on-station time. And hope they *don't* hit anything when they drop their load. All this about a bunch of Iranian ragheads trolling around the Gulf in the equivalent of motorized rowboats. How did this plan ever get approved?"

Husker Cobb offered some perspective. "Sometimes, Preacher, the visual trumps the practical in certain situations. Occasionally you can accomplish more by doing less. We exercise a little restraint, and the other side gets the point. We avoid dead bodies, lost equipment, and possible world condemnation and still get the message across."

"Jesus, Husker, is there any Kool-Aid left in Newport or did you drink it all while you were at the Naval War College?" Swamp Marsh chided. "We ought to load these Hornets up, pay a visit to Bandar Abbas, and demonstrate what can happen when the Iranians piss us off one too many times. I'm so tired of 'measured' or 'proportional' responses. We sit here, discussing an escort mission where the mere presence of a B-52 and a waterworks display is supposed to be an influencer and force multiplier. It's timid, weak, and pathetic. We have an entire air wing at the ready, and the deep thinkers dream up this goat rope. And Husker, your thought is 'we can accomplish more with less?' What seminar did that come out of?"

"Swamp, I get what you're saying, and I don't disagree, to a point. But simply by having power and capability, and the threat of using it, one can often convince your adversary to modify their behavior in the way you desired all along. You save bullets, and both sides, especially ours, avoid funerals. Not always a path that's available, but certainly, one worth considering."

Preacher tried to lighten the mood. "So, Husker, when you make 0-4 (lieutenant commander), is the lobotomy optional or just par for the course?! And we're still waiting for an answer on the Kool-Aid."

"Someday you will both realize that the navy's Kool-Aid tastes different the longer you stay on active duty. I'd recommend the war college to anyone. It's a great time to think about things and learn different viewpoints about our profession. But for now, let's get something to eat."

The three pilots set off for the forward part of the ship, stepping over numerous knee knockers, the bottom part of the oval-shaped openings which were about a foot higher than the deck. These were spaced approximately every 10-

12 feet in passageways throughout the ship. They neared the door to the wardroom in a red-lighted alcove when Husker turned to Lt. Johnson. "Well, Preacher," sarcasm dripping from each word, "what's the good news for our last Sunday in the Arabian Sea? Enlighten me, because I'm really going to miss this place."

Preacher paused momentarily before answering as the other two studied their fellow pilot in the darkened shadows.

"I will cast terror into the hearts of those who disbelieve. Therefore strike off their heads and strike off every fingertip of them."

"Well, that's hardly uplifting," Husker replied quietly.

"That passage comes straight out of the Quran, chapter 8, verse 12. There are over one hundred verses in the Quran that speak of war with non-believers and over 160 verses that talk about *jihad*."[34]

Husker stated, "So, if I'm a, say, Methodist, and thus a non-believer of Islam, a Muslim is instructed to remove my head and fingertips? Kind of a dark thought, don't you think?"

"I don't buy that Muslims as a whole are bad people; it's the ideology that's bad. I read this stuff to get a better understanding of the world we live in, not that I embrace what I read."

Heavy thoughts, considered Husker Cobb, as the three pilots walked into the wardroom and were served eggs to order, if you like your eggs scrambled.

26

At around 0530, with the BUFF less than two hours from its planned arrival time, one of the S-3s radioed the three ships. It appeared at least one Iranian small boat had detached from its group, located at the 10 o'clock position, relative to *Nimitz*, and was headed toward the vicinity of *Bunker Hill* and directly at the aircraft carrier. *Bunker Hill* had been monitoring the coordination frequency and copied the S-3s transmission. The Viking modified its pattern and flew in a circle around the suspicious vessel, which kept its navigation lights on and appeared to be a patrol boat. A few other small boats started inbound from the same location in a ragtag manner, not seeming to care about the increasing distance between their vessels and the lead patrol boat.

It would have been impossible for the Iranian boat not to be aware of the aircraft orbiting above it, and it must have assumed all U.S. units were mindful of its actions. The craft kept its course and speed, apparently not in a hurry to get anywhere quickly. *Bunker Hill* and *Milius*, both informed of all activities since *Nimitz* went DIW, assessed this latest unexplained action by the Iranian small boat to be enough of a potential threat that each commanding officer ordered their ship to go to General Quarters (GQ), a ship's highest level of readiness and its warfighting condition.

Bunker Hill maneuvered herself to be directly in the path of the Iranian boat if it didn't alter its course toward the *Nimitz*. All eyes on *Bunker Hill* were focused on this one boat, and those two or three loosely following. So far, no other Iranian craft had mirrored the actions of these few. *Milius*, along with the other S-3, kept its attention on the two groups of boats at 12 and 2 o'clock.

The lead Iranian vessel continued toward *Bunker Hill* when suddenly, it slowed, almost to a stop. The S-3 overhead could not discern why it had cut its engines. In the limited light of dawn, the pilot thought he saw crew members moving about in an unusual, almost frantic way. The Viking reversed course, banking hard to the right to give the right seater a chance to look at the patrol boat. A white object that looked like a T-shirt had been raised on the ship's mast. Though only dimly visible, there was smoke that was not engine exhaust. The Viking, at 1,000 feet, reversed course again, going back to a left-handed orbit and descended to 500 feet. From that altitude, the pilot confirmed his crewmember's report: he could make out a white object—a flag or T-shirt—on the mast, and could barely see some smoke rising from what looked like the engine compartment. The crew radioed their sightings to the *Nimitz*, climbed back to 1,000 feet, and increased the size of their orbit around the faltering boat to avoid appearing to be hostile or threatening, and continued to monitor the vessel.

The Battle Group commander embarked in *Nimitz*, with FifthFlt's and CentCom's concurrence, tasked *Bunker Hill* to determine the Iranians' intentions. It is well known the United States and Iran, like feuding neighbors, don't talk to each other, at least not formally, and hadn't since early 1980. That was the official, diplomatic position of the United States. However, it is a common custom and courtesy among fellow mariners on the high seas for seamen to aid a vessel in distress. With that concept in mind, along with appropriate levels of caution and skepticism, *Bunker Hill* launched its motor whaleboat on a repair/rescue mission to assist the ailing Iranian patrol boat.

Even though still at GQ, the ship assembled a contingent of sailors whose mechanical skills helped keep the *Bunker Hill*'s four gas turbine engines in top operating shape. The officer in charge (OIC) of the motor whaleboat taking these sailors to the Iranian patrol craft was Lieutenant Susan B. Anderson. Her call sign or nickname was Tony, or Lt. Tony, derived from Susan B. Anthony, the principal force behind the women's suffrage movement of the early 20th century.

Tony grew up in the suburbs of Philadelphia, the daughter of an auto mechanic father, and a mother who tended bar at a local bowling alley. She felt comfortable at her dad's workplace, an auto dealership where she learned how to build and repair motors and engines. In high school she earned better-than-average grades—B's with the occasional A and the rare C—but her SAT scores were over 700 for both math and verbal portions, suggesting untapped academic capability. Following graduation from high school, Tony enrolled in a local junior college—the Community College of Philadelphia—to reduce costs and remain close to home. After two years of academic life, Susan B. Anderson informed her parents that she wanted to answer a call she had felt for years to expand her horizons and try something different. Great, her parents replied; what do you plan to do? Her reply: I'm going to join the navy! Oh, they replied with forced enthusiasm, how wonderful.

Lt. Tony began her naval career with boot camp, then she attended "A" school and soon was serving on a *Ticonderoga*-class cruiser, where she quickly advanced to

2nd Class Petty Officer as a gas turbine system technician. Her professional knowledge, overall background in motors and machines, plus her excellent supervisory skills made her a perfect candidate for what the navy calls their Seaman-to-Admiral commissioning program, or STA -21, for the 21st century. The navy accepted her application and sent her back to college for two more years where she earned not only her bachelor of science degree but also a commission as an ensign in the U.S. Navy. Currently, in her second sea tour as an officer, Lieutenant Anderson served in the engineering department on board *Bunker Hill* and was a qualified Surface Warfare Officer. She was also the OIC of the ship's motor whaleboat, which was now en route to a disabled Iranian patrol boat, with a white "flag" of some kind displayed on its mast, and white smoke emitting from its engine compartment. Visibility was improving by the minute as the first rays of sunrise began to reach over the horizon. The sound of the overhead S-3 was nothing more than background noise. Lt. Tony and the senior enlisted member of her crew, a chief petty officer (E-7), each wore a .45 pistol on their hips, visible for all to see, and both were well trained in its use.

Before they launched on their mission, Lt. Tony addressed her all-male crew. "Gentlemen, our mission this morning is to assist an Iranian vessel which has indicated they are in distress. The exact nature of their problem is unknown. On the high seas, mariners help mariners, setting aside political or cultural differences."

One of her sailors, Seaman Johnson, interrupted her brief. "But Lieutenant, aren't all those Iranian boats the reason we're at General Quarters, ready for an attack? Why are we helping the enemy? And how do we know they're really disabled? Couldn't this be a trap?"

"Good points, Johnson," she replied, glancing at the young sailor. "They *are* the reason we've gone to GQ, and you're right, we know nothing of their situation. So we'll proceed with caution. The Chief and I are both armed, and we'll use our weapons if we need to. On the other hand, they know we could have already blown them and the other boats out of the water, so it's likely they really have a problem.

"I think our biggest challenge today will be communications, as none of us speak Iranian, or Farsi, as it's called, and there's a good chance none of them speaks English. Another issue might be their engines, if that's their problem. They'll be Russian-built and may look different from anything any of us have seen. One last thing: keep looking around and asking yourself if things look and feel normal. Different is okay and is to be expected. But if something is bothering you, let the chief or me know and we'll address it.

"Any other questions?" After a brief pause and a scan of her men, Lt. Anderson ordered them to load up.

The other Iranian boats that had followed the disabled vessel remained far away—at least initially. Once close to the Iranians, Lt. Tony's crew threw some lines over and tied up alongside, placing some fenders between the two boats to guard against damage as they bobbed in the gentle swells of the Persian Gulf. The Iranians had placed some lights around the engine compartment which illuminated that area and cast light on the T-shirt they used as a distress signal. These helped the S-3 pilots identify both the white object and the smoke rising from the engine area.

Lt. Anderson stood on a step in her boat and addressed the Iranians: "Good morning, gentlemen. We're here to help you. Does anyone speak English?"

The Iranians may not have known English, but their faces spoke volumes—an inability to comprehend, in their Muslim minds, the conflicting scene before them: an (attractive) woman, in a military uniform, wearing a (ship's) baseball cap, carrying a weapon, and acting like she was in charge. Their looks contained a salad of astonishment, amazement, and bewilderment sprinkled with a light covering of contempt and a pinch of admiration. Lt. Tony left out three minor briefing items that may have prepared her crew for the surprised reactions of the Iranian sailors to her presence: she was an officer, she was in charge, and she was a (pleasant looking) woman. The small boat sailors had difficulty processing her presence, and their stares and hushed mumblings confirmed the striking impression made by the navy lieutenant. Most U.S. Navy women (and men) agree the navy's khaki uniform doesn't contribute to or enhance the figure of its female wearers. There are exceptions, of course, and Lt. Tony was one of them. Add a .45 pistol to the visual and the result was, in the eyes of most male sailors, a compelling and pleasing effect. She knew it; she saw it; she dismissed it. Again, she asked, "Any English, gentlemen?"

All Iranian eyes turned to one young man with a scruffy beard and stained work shirt who took a step toward the edge of his boat. He said, softly but clearly, "A little."

"Okay. Trouble?"

He pointed at the engine compartment: "There."

The lieutenant replied, "All right—may we assist?" Her body language more than her words asked for permission to go aboard. She received a slight head nod and replied, "Thank you." She turned to her crew and directed, "Chief, you remain on board with me. Petty Officer Nelson, you lead the way, and the rest of you follow Nelson. Start with the easy, obvious stuff—check the oil and fluid levels for proper servicing."

PO1 Nelson (First Class Petty Officer, an E-6) ventured onto the Iranian vessel, stepping carefully from his boat to the other, the two boats moving like two people learning to dance, not quite in sync. Four more sailors joined him carrying toolkits and pouches; all were about to experience Russian ingenuity and craftsmanship.

The two boats continued to ride the minor waves and swells while Lt. Tony's men worked on the patrol craft's engine. She and her chief monitored the repair progress, advising and recommending but also carefully watching the movements of the Iranian crew. She surveyed the scene before her—her men and the Iranian crew—and sensed something was out of place; something didn't jibe—didn't feel right; an intuitive doubt crept through her body. It wasn't fear; she did not feel threatened nor did she sense the safety and security of her men to be compromised. She couldn't nail it down, but something was amiss. Two more Iranian patrol vessels eased toward the disabled craft but made no effort to help. Nor did they make any attempt to conceal their interest and fascination in the officer in charge of the American repair effort. They're kids, thought Lt. Tony, just kids. Wouldn't the gawkers be surprised to know the most seasoned and qualified individual to assess and repair the questionable engine was the very person who was the source of their fascination and fixation?

27

The F/A-18 pilots strapped into their jets in the darkness and quiet of the vast flight deck. When the first of the two S-3s commenced its approach to land, the Air Boss called for the Hornets to start engines. Preacher Johnson was less than enthusiastic about being the spare for the other two pilots, but his jet's systems performed flawlessly, and now he waited to see if he'd be needed. The second S-3 trapped and taxied toward the bow as flight deck personnel readied the waist cats for the Hornet launch. The three pilots, their canopies still open in the early light of the approaching dawn, felt a brisk breeze as the *Nimitz*, its anchor retrieved, plowed through the seas, creating wind for their launch. Preacher noticed several maintenance troubleshooters around Swamp Marsh's aircraft, leaning into the wind and shaking their heads, signaling a thumb's down. Swamp looked at Preacher, tapped his helmet near his ear, then showed four fingers held horizontally, a signal indicating the number nine. Preacher checked his communication card and dialed in the ninth frequency listed, squadron common.

Swamp broadcast, "Guess what, Preacher? I've got a low oil pressure indication on my number two engine. Looks like you're a go this morning."

"The work of Allah, my friend. Gotta be," Preacher replied.

Husker Cobb, monitoring the frequency, keyed his mic. "Preacher, we'll rendezvous and proceed as briefed."

"I'll be there, Husker, *Insha'Allah*."

Husker grinned and shook his head, acknowledging Preacher with two mic clicks.

*****

Official sunrise was still a half hour away as the work continued on the ailing Iranian boat. The S-3 Viking that had been circling overhead eased away for its recovery aboard the still-anchored *Nimitz*. The seas remained calm as the breaking sunrise brought more natural light to the area. Iranian faces came into sharper focus, and their mannerisms were easier to observe. The can't-quite-get-a-fix-on-it feeling persisted in Lt. Tony. She was reminded of a radio playing in her dad's garage, the music grating on her nerves because of the static from the station not being precisely dialed-in. Standing in her motor whaleboat, in the Persian Gulf as the sun started to rise, the "static" feeling would not abate. On the side of the Iranian patrol boat she was observing, new hull numbers had been sloppily painted over the old ones. The sailors' eyes troubled her, too; they didn't stare at her, they just stared—lost, unfocused—minds seemingly adrift, far from anywhere. She compared other nearby Iranian patrol craft to the one they were tied up to: how they rode the seas, how they "sat" in the water. The ailing boat under repair didn't ride or sit in the water the same way, notwithstanding the fact that the two vessels were joined. Something was indeed amiss.

"Boat 1, this is the XO, over." The radio attached to Lt. Anderson's belt cackled sharply, the volume turned up enough for all to hear.

She grasped the radio, brought it near her mouth and pushed the transmit button: "Boat 1 here, go ahead, sir."

The voice of the USS *Bunker Hill*'s Executive Officer (XO) came in loud and clear. "How're things going, Lieutenant?"

"Repairs are under way, XO. The engine apparently needed some oil, which we provided. Petty Officer Nelson thinks he'll have things buttoned up and be ready to give her a test run in another 30 minutes or so. Seas are calm with little wind, and overall vis is improving as we approach sunrise. I don't see a major mechanical breakdown here; we shouldn't need any parts from your end. Over."

"Roger that, Tony. I'd like to have you and your crew hoisted back on board by 0730; it's 0645 now—think that's doable?"

"Might be tight, sir; 0745 would be more realistic. We in a rush this morning?"

The XO didn't immediately reply. After a pause: "Zero seven thirty, Lieutenant. That's the target. Do the best you can. Be advised—you may see some unusual activity in about 30 minutes; nothing to be alarmed about—everyone will be safe—press on and get here as close to 0730 as you can. Copy?"

Her chief heard the transmissions, too—they exchanged questioning glances—wondering what was up. The lieutenant answered, "Copy that, XO. Boat 1 out."

Judging by the looks on the Iranian crewmember's faces, you'd think they'd heard and understood every word, particularly the "everyone will be safe" comment. Soon enough the blank stares returned, and the repair work continued.

At 0710, Petty Officer Nelson announced he was satisfied with their work and indicated to Lt. Anderson he wanted the Iranians to start up the engine. Tony caught the eye of the Iranian English "speaker" and gave him a 2-finger turn-up signal. The Iranian seemed to understand and nodded toward a shipmate who stepped to the patrol boat's control area, turned a key two clicks to the right, and pushed a red button. Immediately the engine came to life and purred like a kitty with no smoke billowing into the air. The Iranians smiled at each other, and then gave Lt. Anderson a thumbs-up while nodding slightly. Lt. Tony smiled at the English speaker and saluted the young man. This act was too much for the sailor, who kept nodding his head and mouthing the Farsi equivalent of *Thank You, Thank You.*

*****

Petty Officer Nelson and his team started back to the motor whaleboat, accepting a couple of handshake offers from the Iranians. Then, in perfect unison, every individual on the two boats stopped moving and slowly raised their heads, trying to force their ears to be more sensitive to a sound none of them had ever heard. Everyone, Iranian and American alike, adjusted their heads, attempting to determine what the noise was and from which direction it was coming. The sound, whatever it was, seemed to be growing louder. Suddenly, a young Iranian yelled out something in Farsi and pointed to the horizon, his eyes nearly popping out of his head. His chin dropped to his chest while his lips failed at forming words.

Lt. Anderson, seeing the man react, followed his outstretched arm with her eyes, and beheld a sight one's imagination could never have conceived: a flying monster—making a whining, screeching noise increasing in intensity with each passing moment—as it approached the still-tied-together vessels.

"Holy Mother of Jesus, what in God's name is that?" cried Lt. Tony, although no one could possibly hear her words.

The wings drooped at an anhedral angle with a wingspan that seemed to touch opposite sides of the horizon. With the flaps extended, landing gear down, and bomb bay doors closed, the aircraft appeared so low it seemed you could reach up and touch the flying beast of destruction. It had eight screaming engines, four under each wing, paired in twos, exhaust smoke trailing from each engine. A single F/A-18 Hornet was flying outboard of the wings on each side. It was an overwhelming sight. Crewmembers from both countries repeatedly squinted, trying to refocus their eyes because their minds were not accepting the image transmitted to it. Every sailor's ears were covered with the palms of their hands pushing hard against their heads, trying to protect their hearing from the piercing, penetrating, painful racket emitting from those gas-guzzling, ear-splitting engines.

When the BUFF was nearly overhead, the sailors—all of them—instinctively ducked even though they knew it was a senseless act, but their bodies involuntarily reacted to the moment. For both the American and Iranian sailors this was the definition of the then favorite phrase, "shock and awe." The immense aircraft—the largest airplane the Iranian sailors (and some American sailors, too) had ever seen—seemed capable, despite no evidence of weaponry, of eliminating entire cities if not whole civilizations. The XO's comment, "Everyone will be safe" rang in Lt. Tony's mind. Is this what he was talking about? What is going on here?

Every head turned to follow the path of the BUFF as the sound of its engines started to diminish following its flyover. They all stood motionless, staring. It was hard to figure out what to do after an experience like that. Comprehension was a fleeting concept among all the sailors; trying to make sense of the senseless made no sense at all. Every sailor heard the swirling sound of the wind created by the wingtip vortices; they smelled the exhaust from the engines as it descended in trails— approximating the familiar odor of car service bays, ship's engineering plants, and, for some of the American sailors, the flight decks of aircraft carriers. Here, in the (now) calm of a Persian Gulf sunrise, Lt. Tony assessed this surreal moment in her life: a massive, incredible, almost unbelievable flying apparatus had screamed over her head, and she vacillated between being scared beyond all hope or so damn proud it felt like her chest would explode. A smile spread onto her face as she recalled the movie "Apocalypse Now" and Robert Duvall, crouching on a beach with munitions exploding around him. Lieutenant Anderson stood tall, grinned, and softly proclaimed, *"I love the sight of a B-52 in the morning!"* The whole event was almost too much to comprehend.

*****

The air force crew of five[35] experienced an uneventful flight from Diego Garcia, taking off a few minutes after 4:00 am into the vast darkness of the Indian Ocean. For nourishment, they consumed a tasty box lunch before their descent off the coast of Oman where the navy Hornets joined up, outside the Strait.

The B-52's first pass was from east to west; after a left 90-degree turn followed by a right 270-degree turn, it headed back in an easterly direction, into the sunrise, for the second pass, flying over much of the same water they'd just traversed. The Iranian small boats were still gathered in three distinct groups on three separate radials, or spokes, with the *Nimitz* near the center, having moved slightly while launching the Hornets. *Bunker Hill* and *Milius* were stationed about where Major Barnes and Captain Washington expected. The only thing that differed from their briefing was a wayward patrol boat which was adjoined with a U.S. motor whaleboat. Commercial shipping was surprisingly light that morning, with several ships inbound in the northern traffic separation scheme and only two outbound vessels using the southern one, neither of any consequence for their upcoming bombing run.

Following the first pass, Major Barnes climbed a few hundred feet to a more comfortable—and safe—altitude for their second pass and bombing run. His co-pilot, the intrepid Buff 1, would fly the second pass and be at the controls during their bomb drops.

Inside the B-52, the two pilots discussed the bombing plan as they were setting up for the second pass and configuring the cockpit for their live run.

"You know, Boss, when I was doing the external preflight before takeoff, our loading crew offered to throw on some 1000 pounders and a couple 2000 pounders. They had 'em standing by, ready to go. Wouldn't have delayed us at all."

"I know, Buff, I saw them before climbing up to the cockpit. Master Sergeant Armstrong (the loading crew chief, an E-7) approached me and suggested we take some more fire power—just for effect. He thought twenty 500 pounders didn't do a BUFF justice; like loose change jingling in someone's pocket. I agreed with that assessment, thanked him for the offer, but turned him down. Loved his spirit, though."

"Yeah, and you know Senior Airman Tower? The dude from Lubbock, Texas?"

Barnes nodded.

"He's got a brother in some army outfit that's deployed to Iraq. Told me his brother recently got wounded and was sent home after a stop at an American hospital in Germany. Had to have several pieces of shrapnel removed from his leg and chest that they couldn't get out in Iraq. Souvenirs from his trip to the sandbox. Tower said his brother will make it and shouldn't lose his leg. In honor of his brother, he chalked a few "love notes" on a couple bombs right before they were loaded, even though Iran isn't our primary focus with the crap we're dealing with in Iraq. Gave him a sense of satisfaction—like he finally had a voice in this Middle East shit."

"Good for him. Tower's a good guy, and a solid loader."

"Yeah, you're right. So, to make sure we get the message across to the I-rain-ees, I figure we might as well drop all 20 of these puppies. I know the op-order called for 12, but what's a few extra bombs among friends? 12 was surely a compromise, right? I think we should drop 'em all, if just to honor Tower and his brother. What do you think, Boss?"

Major Barnes was steady in his reply as he banked the flying beast toward the live bombing run-in heading. The voice of his commander in chief, the president, resonated in his head, tempering his thoughts, and actions. "The order was for 12, Buff." he stated in measured tones. "Perhaps there's a reason for exactly 12, although I can't imagine what it'd be."

"Yeah, well, maybe. I figure, if 12 is good, then 20 is better. Who can argue that thinking, and who's out here countin', anyway? They want a wall of water, let's give the I-rain-ees something to write home about. It'll be like the water fountains outside the Bellagio in Vegas, minus the music, only to the N-th degree. What do ya think? Are ya with me, Boss?"

Barnes paused briefly, then sat up straighter in his seat when he made his decision. *If they want a wall of water*, he thought, *then by god, that's what we'll give them.* "You know, accounting was never my forte at the academy, and who can argue with your perfectly logical mind? We'll configure to drop 'em all. I am not inclined, nor do we have the time, to ask for permission. But we may end up begging for forgiveness. Hell, what's the worst that can happen? Be sent to Diego Garcia?"

Both pilots grinned and chuckled at Barnes' perfect use of the well-known adage.

Barnes continued. "And when we're done, let's accelerate and do a slight climbing left turn, the long way around, to the south, to about a one eight zero-degree heading. Might be a good picture for our favorite mariners with the BUFF turning and the morning sun in the background—kind of a ghostly flying silhouette."

"You got it, Boss. After I get done with my ecological cleansing of the Persian Gulf, if you'd close things up and then raise the flaps on schedule as my speed increases, that'd help me a lot. Then I'll give the aircraft back to you; we'll ditch these navy babysitters and then get us some gas from Texaco (the call sign for the KC-135, the in-flight refueling tanker). Sound okay to you?"

"Sounds good, Buff; excellent plan."

*****

After a few moments, the sailors on both boats started to resume what they had been doing before the BUFF interrupted the idyllic early morning setting. Lt. Tony's men reboarded their boat and stowed their tools. When everyone was ready, Lt. Anderson and her chief exchanged "thumbs up" motions and directed Petty Officer Nelson and one other crewmember to "cast off lines." But once again their surroundings were disrupted, and all activity ceased; the vessels remained secured to each other. Like creatures of habit they performed the same ear-protecting maneuver, but this time with a trained eye to the sky: they'd heard the sound before, and at least they knew the direction where the awful noise and incredible sight had flown out of view. Collectively, they all looked in the same direction, to the west, and their hunch proved correct. The inexplicable beauty of an instrument of death and destruction, but also of strength and peace, approached for a second pass. No less daunting and imposing than the first flyover, the BUFF seemed slightly higher than the first pass with its landing gear now retracted but with flaps again extended and bomb bay doors now open. The instinctive reaction to duck moved everyone as the wailing beast flew overhead. Palms were again squeezed against ears to mitigate the piercing, high-frequency squeal produced by the powerful, 17,000 pounds-of-thrust engines. The recovery time from the impact of the flyover was shorter this time, even though the effect was equally as forceful. The Iranians talked in whispers among themselves as they and the U.S. crewmembers finished untying the two boats. When the last line came free the entire world suddenly stopped in its tracks. Life seemed suspended. All who experienced the next few moments felt transformed into an altered state of existence.

No one saw the first few bombs fall from the mighty, massive metal bird; the rising waters obscured the remaining drops. One of the Iranian sailors, glancing toward the east after the flyover, saw the Gulf begin to explode, and stood motionless, one arm raised, pointing. Other sailors gradually followed suit, and soon all were watching in awed silence. The water leaped from the sea, grasping for the heavens, a veritable wall of water, erupting from the Gulf and stretching, from their vantage point, all the way to the sky and the horizon. Then came the unmistakable sounds of fury as the MK-82s, falling from the belly of the beast, exploded on contact with the Persian Gulf. One boom after another, the whole scene strangely disjointed because sight and sound didn't match as the visual led the aural, eyes seeing the seas rocketing upward and then one's ears recording a belated retort. When the sailors from both countries finally began to understand that disconnected sensation, a third sensory impact intruded itself into the event: a shaking and earthquake-like feeling—a sense that kettle drums were pounding under your soul, a never-before-experienced beating from under your feet.

The American and Iranian sailors had never witnessed an event like the two flyovers and the wall of water. They all found the experience challenging to process and comprehend. For the Iranians—that was precisely the objective, and the point.[36]

28

The B-52 crew configured for their bombing run, with their radar operator confirming the absence of surface traffic in the intended drop area. The bombs left the massive beast one after the other, spaced at approximately one-second intervals, each exploding on contact with the Persian Gulf. Water erupted toward the early morning sky, forming a continuous waterfall-like wall, except the water rose from the sea instead of falling from a higher source.

About 10-12 seconds into the roughly twenty-second run, the radar operator advised, "Boss, I might have a single target at about two o'clock, four thousand yards. Just got a blip."

Major Barnes replied, "Okay. We're looking. Keep me updated."

The drops continued; number sixteen, seventeen, eighteen. Number nineteen, however, didn't drop. Barnes quickly intervened and manually punched off bombs nineteen and twenty. His actions caused Captain Washington, at the controls of the BUFF, to glance his way, which resulted in a slight wing wobble of the B-52. The final two 500 pounders exploded on contact with the Gulf, but the "wall" had a small opening in it, caused by the slight delay in drops. The movement of the aircraft resulted in a deviation in the line of exploding bombs. These aberrations were hardly noticeable to anyone floating on the water. The view from the air, however, was another thing.

Once their bombing run was complete and they were heading south toward D-GAR, the B-52 crew informed their "escort service," the two navy Hornets, they were free to detach.

Hornet 1 (Lcdr. Husker Cobb) keyed his mic. "Okay, BUFF, nice flying with you today. From what I could see that was one dramatic waterfall you created back there. It looked to me that each bomb was perfectly on target— which means you found the Persian Gulf! Now that's some precision bombing!!"

Major Barnes stated, "Sometimes close is good enough! At least they all left the airplane, and I don't have any hung ordnance. So, we're going to get some gas and head to D-GAR. Have a slider for me when you get back to the mothership; enjoyed having you with us today."

Hornet 2 (Lt. Preacher Johnson) broke in. "And BUFF, this is Dash 2. In case we get asked once we get back aboard, how many MK-82s did I see you drop this morning—to make sure I'm consistent with the official report?"

Major Barnes replied, "Well, we were ordered to drop 12, we selected 12, and they all dropped, according to my indications in here. That marry up with your count?"

"Yep, that's what I saw. 12 for 12—pretty good average, even for the air force."

"And from Hornet 1, that matches my count, too. But I thought I noticed a little hitch in your giddy-up near the end of the run. Was that my imagination, or was there a glitch in the delivery system?"

Barnes and Washington glanced at each other. Barnes answered, "Yeah, you're right. I had to punch the last two off manually. We had a minor hiccup in the auto (automatic bomb release) drop system so I released them manually. Was it that obvious?"

"Not really. Looked like there was room for a small door in the wall. Down on the water, I'm sure no one noticed. At any rate, good flying this morning, BUFF; nice workin' with you. We'll peel off to the right, descend and RTB. Have a safe trip to D-GAR."

Major Barnes answered, "Always a pleasure, gentlemen. Safe flight to you also. BUFF out." The two navy F/A-18s, now joined as a section on the B-52's right wing with Husker in the lead, rolled smoothly to their right and started a descent to ensure separation from the massive bomber. *Nimitz* was already steaming into the wind when they arrived overhead. 15 minutes after detaching from the B-52 they trapped aboard. It was nearly 0800 on a bright, warm Sunday morning in the Persian Gulf.

In the cockpit of the Stratofortress, Buff 1 observed, "Nice to know we had some navy guys with us this morning who can count to 12."

Major Barnes said, smiling, "Nice to know they can't count to 20."

*****

There are consequences, some not immediate nor intended, resulting from a country's foreign policy decisions, including the use of military force. Varying degrees of uncertainty—known as the "fog of war"[37] — always exist during the execution of plans, diplomatically and militarily, despite the efforts of commanders at every level to minimize its impact. Unexpected things happen; expected things don't. Two bombs from the B-52 didn't drop when scheduled. On the surface, one Iranian small boat experienced a mechanical irregularity and signaled a request for assistance.

On another boat, in the third "swarm" at the two o'clock position relative to *Nimitz*, two Iranian sailors, Farzin Hassan, its "officer in charge" or Iranian equivalent, and Arman Kazem, Hassan's assistant, had for months discussed their growing agitation at Western foreign policies. They harbored a hatred of Israel, and a desire to achieve religious purity. The seamen met when both were assigned to the same small boat crew months before.

They discovered they shared similar family histories—and influences. Farzin Hassan's elderly grandparents were on a bus that was detained the evening of April 24, 1980 at the hostage rescue rendezvous area known as Desert One. Through the years they often retold their night of terror in the Hassan household. Arman Kazem, on the other hand, had an uncle who left his family and joined an Iranian-backed "support group," later identified as Hezbollah, the Iran-supported and financed terrorist organization. Kazem learned his uncle played a key role in the two Beirut, Lebanon suicide terrorist attacks against American personnel in 1983: the April 18 truck bombing of the American embassy that killed 63 people, including 17 Americans and several CIA officials, one on her first day at work[38]; and the October 23 attack against a Marine barracks, killing 241 military personnel, when a Shiite terrorist with ties to Iran exploded a truck near the building containing explosives equal to 18,000 pounds of dynamite. In a separate suicide attack two miles away, 58 French soldiers, part of the multinational force (like the marines) charged with overseeing the Palestinian withdrawal from Lebanon, were also killed.[39]

The two Iranian shipmates learned of their current at-sea exercise days prior and were excited and determined to fulfill their ultimate destiny if the situation allowed.

Once under way, both noticed the different handling characteristics of their heavily-ladened boat and concluded their vessel, among a select few, had its bow specially loaded with unusual, unmarked material.

Farzin Hassan, hands on Kazem's shoulders, solemnly confided in his friend Arman prior to departing Bandar Abbas. "It is our glorious mission and our fate to further the work of our brothers-in-arms and join those who have gone before us in the wonderment of ever-lasting paradise."

"Allah will guide us and rejoice with us when we achieve our magnificent objective," replied Kazem.

In the Islamic tradition, suicide is a sin. However, killing oneself as a part of jihad to harm non-Muslims is, in the radicalized view, an act of deep piety and makes one a martyr, guaranteeing the highest rank in paradise.[40] Since the U.S. invasion of Iraq in March 2003, the simmering hatred of the western goliath residing in Hassan and Kazem had begun to boil, and their assignment to the same boat was an unmistakable endorsement of Allah's many blessings and desires.

The final confirmation came when a gargantuan, flying monster emerged out of the early morning sunrise and screamed over their heads, seemingly just out of reach. All crewmembers, fearing for their lives, crouched in horror and disbelief, engine exhaust and the stench of burning oil lingering in the dawn air following the flyover. The aggressive, offensive display of arrogance and superiority by the Great Satan enraged both Iranian sailors, who felt the United States had effectively extended its middle finger at their country, their religion, and themselves. Hassan and Kazem nodded to each other in prayerful unity, each realizing, and accepting, that their ultimate fulfillment was about to be realized.

Hassan, in charge and at the helm, had achieved some separation from the other boats in his group, and with the concurring approval of Kazem, advanced the throttles to full speed ahead and assumed a course toward the American warship scarcely visible on the horizon. It was not the American aircraft carrier *Nimitz* they had heard about whose distinctive shape they could easily discern, but any U.S. vessel manned with non-believers would prove suitable. The other crewmen, younger and less experienced, looked at each other and accepted the decision of Hassan to leave their cluster and proceed at full power toward the American warship (the *Milius*), unaware of his ultimate objective.

Every crewmember's attention suddenly jerked to the west upon hearing the first bombs explode when the flying monster started its second pass. Their disbelieving eyes witnessed the seas erupting to the heavens followed by the sound and rumbling under their feet from the exploding 500 pounders as the flying death creature lunged toward them. Hassan and Kazem and their crewmembers again involuntarily squatted and plugged their ears with their hands as they watched the relatively small instruments of destruction fall from the massive bays, the snake-eye fins extending immediately, causing the bombs to twirl downward to the salt water, exploding upon contact, one after the other.

It appeared the beast would fly directly over them, but then Arman Kazem noticed a slight delay, or gap, in the sequence of drops; perhaps they were finished? The gigantic machine momentarily wobbled its wings and appeared to raise its nose slightly as its wings fluctuated in the air. Suddenly two more bombs fell from its bottom as the immense bird started to climb and the doors of its underbelly closed. Hassan and Kazem and their crew watched as the B-52 began a turn to the north and ultimately circled the entire fleet of small boats and headed south as it climbed. Their attention, however, was quickly riveted back to the area directly in front of them when the two errant bombs exploded. They were headed straight toward the rising mini-wall of water as they heard and then felt the report of the explosions. Farzin Hassan quickly retarded his throttles. His boat slowed as he stood quietly in the morning calmness of a now-gently rolling sea, evaluating the torrent of emotions and images in his mind: ascending to paradise after killing countless non-believers and the mysterious rising of the seas in front of him. Could this water eruption be a sign from Allah, standing with his arm out straight, the palm of his hand signaling "stop"? Hassan and Kazem exchanged inquiring looks, each searching for an answer from the other. Kazem slowly began turning his head from side to side. Hassan gradually submitted and reversed course toward the other boats which had commenced the short transit back to Bandar Abbas. Allah had spoken: not now, not today.

Prussian General Carl von Clausewitz called it the "fog of war." In modern parlance it would be: stuff happens.

29

The troubled Iranian patrol boat, now running smoothly with no apparent mechanical problems, returned to her original group of small boats which had already begun to depart for Bandar Abbas, as did the other two collections of vessels. Lt. Anderson and her crew returned to their ship which hoisted them aboard around 0745. *Bunker Hill* then picked up her speed to rejoin the *Nimitz* battle group, which had maneuvered to recover the Hornets. The XO greeted each returning sailor, welcoming them back on board and informing them the mess decks were still open as the ship had secured from GQ. The motor whaleboat crewmembers could not stop talking about the massive air force B-52 they'd seen "up close and personal" and the explosive display of water they'd witnessed from sea level.

Lt. Tony's crew departed for the mess decks, and she and her chief debriefed the repair effort for the executive officer, who wore the gold oak leaves of a lieutenant commander, an 0-4.

Lt. Tony concluded her summary and looked at her XO with a troubled face. "Sir, something is bothering me about this morning's mission, and it has nothing to do with that incredible air force power demonstration—that was unbelievable! Chief, I want you to hear this and then tell me and the XO what you think."

The XO shifted his weight and prepared to listen. "All right, Lieutenant, what's up?"

"The whole time we were tied up to the Iranian patrol boat, I thought something was off. The looks on their crews' faces—it was much more than seeing a woman in charge; it was the way the boat sat in the water, plus the sloppy paint job where they painted over their equivalent of a hull number. I am convinced that if I'd asked them for a tour of their boat, they would have adamantly refused. When the other two Iranian patrol boats got close to us, they didn't offer to assist their sister boat—nothing at all. It was as if that one boat was off limits. When we departed, I got a quick look at her bow; it looked like it had been re-built. I could tell it was different from the rest of the hull. Finally, this mechanical problem they had. It wasn't the engine. My guys added some oil and tightened things up, that's all. They made a show of things, to a degree, and did more cleaning than fixing. The basic upkeep of the motor in that boat needed lots of attention—I could see that from where I was standing.

"I'm not sure what all this means, if anything. But I think it's possible they were hiding something or scared of something; they were visibly uncomfortable and were failing at trying not to show it. I can accept some level of discomfort, or uneasiness, even embarrassment, with the fact that foreigners—Americans at that—were on their vessel attempting to fix their boat. But I sense something else was not right. I know this is vague, but I wanted to mention all of this to you. Chief, did you get any vibes similar to what I've mentioned?"

Her chief petty officer echoed many of her thoughts, and he, too, questioned the construction of the patrol craft's bow. He added his observation that the patrol craft was over grossed; the way it moved through the water suggested it was burdened with too much weight. There was nothing visible to the chief that could explain or cause this condition.

The XO listened intently to these two seasoned sailors. This was years of experience talking to him; both had lingering suspicions of something being amiss, and he trusted their judgments without reservation. "First, thank you both," he replied, "for your work on that vessel and bringing all of this to my attention. I have a friend on the CarGru staff who is an intel officer. I'll send a summary of your observations and concerns to him and let him take it from there. I need both of you to write down your thoughts. Do it separately; don't compare notes and don't consult with each other—your individual views and opinions are what's important here. Do it this morning, while everything is still fresh in your mind. Get something to eat first then start writing—don't type it up—no need for formality here. After I've read your comments, maybe we'll get together and review a few things and see if that triggers something else that you saw or inadvertently left out. Thank you both—again—for your professionalism this morning; it was impressive. I'm hearing this whole episode is garnering a lot of attention—your repair efforts and that B-52 show. You had ringside seats—for both events! So, press on, get some chow, and then get your pens working."

In unison, they replied: "Aye, aye, sir."

Bunker Hill's XO went straight to the ship's bridge and briefed his commanding officer about what he'd learned. The captain agreed with the XO's plan to send a report ASAP to the staff on *Nimitz*; if needed, they'd send an amplifying message after reviewing the comments from Lt. Tony and her chief. He ordered the XO to write it and send it—there was no need to chop it through him before releasing it.

The message left the *Bunker Hill's* comm center at 0845 local (0445Z/GMT/UTC) which is 11:45 pm in

Washington, D.C., still Saturday night. The admiral embarked in *Nimitz* (the CarGru or Carrier Group Commander), and his staff forwarded the XO's report, in its entirety, with amplifying comments, to ComFifthFlt in Manama, Bahrain. FifthFlt's intelligence department watch stander briefed his admiral and immediately forwarded the complete package to CentCom headquarters in Tampa, Florida, with a copy transmitted to CentCom's forward headquarters located at Camp As Sayliyah in Doha, Qatar. CentCom forwarded the report to various entities within the Pentagon and to the "U.S. intelligence community," which included, not surprisingly, the Central Intelligence Agency, and others.

One of the recipients of the report that night was Anthony Darnell, the longtime friend of Bill Stimson (Will Call) and relatively new friend (and CIA tour guide) of Frank Warren. The CIA operations duty section read the message, and then, with Anthony's assistance, composed their version of the *Bunker Hill* XO's report, with all accompanying comments, and transmitted it, with relevant additional observations ... to others with a "need to know."

The message went to two such others in Bandar Abbas, Iran, who, fortunately, were in their apartment when a very high priority message arrived via some extraordinarily highly classified communication equipment. Michael and Shannon Wheeler—undercover operatives living as missionaries currently doing the Lord's work among the one or two percent of Iran's population that was not Muslim—sat on a couch in their apartment and carefully studied the report. The time: 1:00 am (0600Z) in Washington, D.C.; 10:00 am in Dubai, UAE. In Bandar Abbas, since Iran is 3:30 ahead of GMT, the local time was 9:30 am Sunday. It took one hour and fifteen minutes for the entire chain-of-command to read, analyze, comment on, and forward the XO's message. The report and endorsements went halfway around the world—and back—ending up in the hands of the exact people who needed it the most.

30

After reading the report, Michael and his "wife" Shannon left their apartment on foot to attend church services, as was their habit on Sunday mornings (even though Sunday was the first day of the workweek in Muslim-dominated Iran). They were quiet people, reserved and unassuming, whose circle of friends continued to expand as their acceptance into Iranian society, despite not being Muslims, became more widespread. Iran tolerated faiths other than Muslim, but many felt they weren't entirely accepted.

Michael and Shannon had chosen a location near the massive port of Bandar Abbas to attend services, held in a nondescript, two-story building. The second story was the reason for their choice, as it had an unobstructed view of the port. Shannon and her "husband" mingled with some acquaintances when they arrived. Neither missionary noticed any difference in their friends' words or actions that would suggest they'd heard about that morning's events on the Persian Gulf. Michael, seeing a friend across the room, excused himself, briefly greeted his fellow church-goer, then climbed the steps to the second floor. He stood back from the window to avoid being noticed and scanned the port using a telephoto lens on his CIA-provided camera. It was 10:30 am in Bandar Abbas; approximately 3 ½ hours had elapsed since the B-52 flyovers.

The port was alive with inbound traffic as all the small boats returned to their berths. The two Kilo submarines, Michael observed, had returned to port earlier (never having submerged) and were already tied up. It appeared the flyovers had achieved the desired result as the small boat crewmembers swapped stories and impressions with their fellow sailors, using their hands to imitate the impressive B-52. Later, U.S. intelligence experts reported that Iranian military and civilian officials lit up the phone lines (which the U.S. was monitoring) between Bandar Abbas and Tehran. Michael Wheeler, however, was looking for one specific patrol craft among many either already moored or returning to do so. Using his special camera like a set of binoculars, he scanned the port in search of something different, something unusual. It wasn't long before he found a target of interest—and interesting it was.

A select group of workers offloaded some boxes of material from one small boat and stacked them on the pier. No other vessel had anything resembling these boxes positioned near where they tied up. The boat's crew stood by and watched; they neither offered their help nor was it requested. Michael took numerous photographs, documenting and likely confirming the data in that morning's top secret dispatch. Lt. Anderson's name wasn't mentioned, but the report noted that the *Bunker Hill* motor whaleboat crew had observed how the Iranian small boat "sat" in the water; they described the looks on the faces of the Iranian crew members, the appearance of the apparently rebuilt or modified bow, and the oddly haphazard painting of her hull numbers—all suggesting this vessel was a suicide boat laden with explosives in its bow. Judging by its original heading, its goal was to ram the USS *Nimitz*, detonating on impact. One of her escorts, USS *Bunker Hill* or USS *Milius*, would have been an alternative target.

Michael Wheeler took a few more pictures before rejoining Shannon. Long before they arrived—first in Baghdad, Iraq, and then Bandar Abbas, Iran—they had developed and practiced various hand signals and gestures to communicate with one another—a personal sign language. As Michael approached, he pulled up his left sock to alert Shannon he had a message for her. By adjusting his trousers and then moving his backpack to the opposite shoulder, he indicated they needed to get back to their apartment forthwith. Shannon understood his signals as if he'd spoken the words, but they were in a challenging situation: the service was about to begin, and it would look unusual if they suddenly claimed they had to leave. They agreed to remain for the service, and once seated, happily participated and thoroughly enjoyed the celebration of the Lord's word—or so it appeared to the other members of their small congregation.

They were saying their goodbyes in the lobby of the building after the service when an Iranian couple whom the Wheeler's had befriended invited them to their apartment for a light lunch and continued fellowship. Through forced smiles and half-hearted attempts to deflect the kind invitation of their friends, the Wheelers finally succumbed and joined their acquaintances in the short walk to their residence. Some of the route was up a slight incline, and before arriving at the apartment, everyone stopped momentarily to enjoy the splendid view of the harbor and port of Bandar Abbas. As they took in the expanse of boats and commercial vessels, Michael noticed two more patrol boats being unloaded by the special crew he had seen before. He didn't use his camera; no need to draw unnecessary attention to his unique equipment and he didn't need its telephoto lens to confirm the scene before him. It appeared there were now three specialty boats. Were there more?

Michael Wheeler had valuable information which needed to get to Langley, but it was not so important that he should risk compromising his standing and position among his Iranian friends. Training and professionalism prevailed, and the American missionary couple strived to be gracious and engaging guests of their Iranian hosts. When the social event concluded, they ambled on their way home to give the appearance of not having a care in the world, in case anyone was watching—which, more than likely, they were.

By the time Michael finally transmitted his report and pictures, it was 5:00 pm (8:30 am Sunday morning in Washington). The CIA analysis branch went right to work, examining and reexamining every picture and every word contained in the transmission filed by their missionary agents in Bandar Abbas, Iran.

EPILOGUE

Beware of false knowledge; it is more dangerous than ignorance.

-George Bernard Shaw

31

Sunday
January 14, 2007

It was 12:00 pm in Catoctin Mountain Park, roughly 62 miles north-northwest of Washington, D.C., on a bright, cold, January Sunday. Earlier that morning, in a 30-minute helicopter ride from the White House, the president of the United States returned to Camp David and was about to eat lunch with his wife in their private quarters. He sat on a couch in the living room, a crackling fire adding warmth to the room. With the remote, he turned on the television. CNN came on the screen.

The secretary of defense, with the chairman of the Joint Chiefs of Staff, sat in a VIP lobby at Travis Air Force Base northeast of San Francisco waiting to board a flight to Andrews Air Force Base in Washington. The TV was on, and they were watching CNN.

Rear Admiral Joseph Donaldson and his wife Karen were, like the president, about to eat lunch and they, too, had CNN on.

Sharon Fleming and her husband, Congressman Ronald Fleming, were clearing dishes from their kitchen table following a late brunch. Their TV was on, and CNN was beginning a noon-hour newscast.

In Middleburg, Virginia, Frank and Mary Warren were setting the table for lunch at Mary's parents' house. A TV was on with the sound muted. On the screen, a newsperson stood outside the White House, holding a microphone with the "CNN" emblem facing the camera. He appeared ready to conduct an interview.

B-52 aircraft commander Major Wesley Barnes and his co-pilot, Captain William Robert Washington, III, were enjoying the warm Indian Ocean breezes and the refreshing taste of icy cold American beer while seated at the bar in the officer's club at Diego Garcia. It was a minute after 11:00 pm, local time. They were reflecting on their eventful day when the TV showed CNN starting another hour of news.

After their return to D-GAR, the B-52 crew submitted an after-action report (which stated, militarily, "... the assigned mission was safely and uneventfully completed with the deployed payload creating the desired effect ...") and then split up for the day with plans to meet around 2000 (8:00 pm) for dinner. While they were eating, the Sunday morning news shows in Washington came on the air, and they found themselves the center of attention and the topic of the day.

As predicted and expected, the military in general, the air force in particular, and one specific, deranged B-52 crew were harpooned from every corner of the earth. The naysayers admonished the pilots and the entire chain-of-command for having lost their minds, their senses, their professionalism, and their judgment for pulling such a dangerous and life-threatening stunt near innocent Iranian navy sailors and commercial vessels under way in the international waters of the Persian Gulf. The outrage was universal and oddly uniting. Elected officials from both parties, anxious to feed at the trough of an unexpected publicity opportunity, where they could display their self-enhancing outrage, jumped in front of any available camera to demand immediate, complete, detailed investigations into the despicable, unconscionable, and reprehensible conduct of the two B-52 pilots. Not everyone, however, shared this opinion.

For their part, the major and his happy-go-lucky copilot couldn't buy a drink that night in D-GAR as they had become the most talked about rock stars on the island. Somehow, amid all the buzz and adulation ricocheting around D-GAR, the loading crew who'd armed the B-52 with 20 MK-82s and were scheduled to download the unexpended ordnance upon its return, became afflicted with the same condition the Navy F/A-18 pilots had suffered: difficulty in counting beyond the number 12. How do 8 MK-82s slip through the cracks and become lost in the system? Well, from the navy's perspective, you'd have to ask the air force!

At about 1702Z, the CNN reporter was joined by another individual outside the White House for an interview about the intensely discussed story lighting up the news wires. The "expert" on the hot seat, in the glare of the camera, was none other than National Security Council staff member Darren Ballinger, stylishly attired with a cashmere scarf tucked perfectly under his woolen topcoat; his bow tie symmetrically situated and tied, and his beard meticulously trimmed.

The interviewer, in an accusatory, presumptive tone which suggested the impending demise of his guest, posed the anticipated question. "Mr. Ballinger, we understand you were part of the planning group that devised the unprecedented B-52 fiasco which took place early this morning in the Persian Gulf. Can you explain this departure from sanity demonstrated by the air force bomber crew?"

Ballinger's response was surprisingly thoughtful, cogent, and, most importantly, calming. "I believe the outcry in response to the recent actions of the United States in the Persian Gulf is unfounded, overblown, inappropriate, and ill-informed. Let me explain. By any country's assessment of the actions of the Iranian naval forces, Iran was demonstrating unannounced and dangerously provocative measures which anyone, including the United States, would interpret as needlessly reckless and potentially life-threatening. The only reasonable and cautionary assumption one could make about the intentions of the Iranians was that they planned to inflict significant and substantial damage on our Persian Gulf naval forces which were, we all agree, operating in international waters. The president solicited and considered numerous options of how to respond, including diplomatic overtures and military plans. All our efforts at a diplomatic resolution—together with requests for an explanation of their actions—were rudely ignored. The president feels, and I wholeheartedly agree, that Iran intentionally sought to instigate a response from the United States and they now take center stage in decrying the very reaction they hoped for. It's hypocrisy of a grand order."

Unmoved, the CNN reporter continued his questioning. "The Iranians appear not to have violated any international laws and enjoyed every right to be at sea like the United States. Do you honestly think using a B-52 bomber dropping 500-pound bombs in proximity to the Iranian boats was the correct proportional response to the situation over there? That seems inappropriately aggressive to many people, including some members of Congress."

Ballinger continued in his diplomatic demeanor. "The B-52, or BUFF, as it's called, is an incredible instrument of power, but also of peace and deterrence. We discussed at some length the inclusion of the B-52 and how it might dissuade or eliminate the reckless, undisciplined behavior ..."

The reporter, interrupting him, saw an opening and went hard for it. "Talk about reckless and undisciplined behavior; was the B-52 crew given carte blanche out there to drop as many bombs as they wanted to? Against small patrol boats? It sounds like the United States is the bully, not the Iranians, as the president often calls them."

Darren, remaining calm and composed, replied, "We had a nuclear-powered aircraft carrier in a vulnerable position yesterday and Iran reacted with a display of their so-called "swarming tactics," sending two submarines and nearly 50 surface craft in mere hours, taking up potentially threatening positions on three different axes, all centered on the USS *Nimitz*. The United States will not sit idly by and be menaced by such outlandish and overt, undisciplined actions. It is my belief that President Sheppard chose a measured, reasonable, forceful yet restrained course of action to demonstrate our resolve, our concern, our dismay, and, I should emphasize, our disappointment at the actions of the Iranian leadership. I think that, upon further reflection, the world community will soon see the wisdom in our actions and applaud our president's decisions in the Persian Gulf and thank him for standing up to the true bully of the Middle East.

"And let me remind everyone of the courageous and unselfish assistance the sailors from the USS *Bunker Hill* provided to the Iranian patrol boat which suffered a mechanical breakdown as the sun was beginning to rise this morning in the Persian Gulf. I don't think lending a hand to fellow mariners in distress on the high seas is characteristic of a bully, as you liken the United States to be." This last statement came as he turned his face from the camera in front of him and looked directly at his interviewer.

Darren Ballinger did not hesitate to continue. "And the MK-82 bombs? They should be viewed more as a symbolic reminder that no nation, including the United States, should be subjected to the offensive and harassing actions of another. The Islamic Republic of Iran should acknowledge our restraint, thank us for our assistance, and refrain from further acts of malevolence and aggression. I think the president effectively got his point across, delivered," —a smile crept across his face as he prepared to deliver his concluding punch line— "not with a period, but with an exclamation point!" Darren didn't think Frank Warren would mind his use of this analogy.

In numerous parts of the world, viewers and world leaders began to rethink their initial dismay and disappointment at the actions of the United States. At Camp David, the first lady inquired, "Is Darren the new spokesman for the administration?"

The president was surprised, pleasantly so. "I think that's the first time he's been interviewed, on TV or anywhere, for that matter. That was well done—very well done."

At Travis AFB, in the Donaldson and Fleming homes, and at the Warrens' in-laws' house, there was unanimous approval of Darren's even, forthright delivery and his undeniable support of the plan and the president.

In Diego Garcia, everyone in the bar, led by Major Barnes and his recently minted Captain co-pilot, filled their glasses preparing for a toast to a most unlikely recipient. CNN had scrolled the NSC staffer's name along the bottom of the screen. Wes Barnes stood and addressed the bar: "To Darren Ballinger, honorary BUFF pilot!" The response, yelled in unison as all glasses were raised: "To Darren!" And all downed their drinks in one motion.

The CNN interviewer appeared to be slightly taken aback by Darren's response but had one more question: "Mr. Ballinger, thank you for speaking with me today and for your candid responses to my questions. One last question, though; you called the B-52 the BUFF, spelled B, U, F, F, I believe. Could you tell our viewers what 'BUFF' stands for?"

Darren began, and every viewer who had a clue (including those watching at Camp David, Travis AFB, Diego Garcia and northern Virginia), leaned forward in their chairs to see how Darren Ballinger answered this bombshell of a question. "The term 'BUFF' has long been associated with the magnificent Stratofortress we know as the B-52. An endearing term always said with a degree of admiration and respect, 'BUFF' means B–for Big; U–for Ugly; F– for Fat; and the second F stands for (all inhaled and held their breath) Fellow. Big, Ugly, Fat, Fellow. A truly remarkable example of American engineering and ingenuity. I personally disagree with the Ugly and Fat descriptors; I think it's a beautiful machine and is perhaps a bit stocky, at best."

One could hear the collective sighs of relief as the president, the secretary of defense, the entire United States Air Force and many DoD employees around the world all exhaled and silently praised the man of the hour for his timely discretion. In D-GAR, however, the joyous and praiseworthy atmosphere previously displayed around the bar among the mostly air force crewmembers disintegrated into derision and ridicule as they mocked the government staffer for his distinct lack of gusto and fortitude. How quickly, as they say, the mighty can fall.

32

A phone rang in the president's quarters while he and the first lady were finishing lunch. The time was 12:50 pm. The president and his wife exchanged glances; they knew why the phone was ringing, just not specifically. President Sheppard took a seat in an easy chair and lifted the receiver: "This is the president."

"Good afternoon, Mr. President." By agreement, the caller didn't need to identify himself. The distinctive baritone voice and the slightly southern inflection in his delivery identified the caller as Randal Powers, the Director of National Intelligence. He got right to the point.

"We have information from reliable sources that indicate the Iranian small boat deployment may have, in fact, been a disguise of a suicide mission involving perhaps three patrol boats loaded with explosives with *Nimitz* as the primary target. The officer from the *Bunker Hill* who oversaw the repairs of the disabled Iranian patrol craft reported her concerns about how the vessel was riding in the water—how it appeared to be weighted down and carrying far more cargo that it was designed for. We later received photographs of what we believe to be explosives being off-loaded in Bandar Abbas from that specific patrol boat. Two other boats were observed off-loading similar looking material. Overhead imagery of the port was partially obstructed by coastal low clouds, but we did get some views; however, they are not conclusive due to the clouds."

President Sheppard said, "Maybe CentCom's plan was the way to go instead of the B-52."

"With what we knew at the time, I think you made the right choice."

"This action had to come from the top, from Ghorbani, don't you think? No way would Mazdaki try to pull this off on his own."

"We're trying to verify exactly who directed this and why, sir. They must know the scope and scale of our response if they even come close to executing this. Just our ante in this poker game would be the elimination of Bandar Abbas. Then we'd look at our cards and go from there."

"Good point," the president replied. "But reviewing yesterday, it appears that the mechanical breakdown happened to precisely the right patrol boat, and we had exactly the right officer report her suspicions about what she saw, and the report got all the way to you and then to our contact in Bandar Abbas. That's about as perfect as we could hope the system to work." He sighed and shook his head. "I think we were very fortunate yesterday."

The director concurred, "We may have dodged a bullet, sir."

"Well, I think Iran is the one who dodged a bullet. If their patrol boat had achieved any level of success, then the B-52's bombs would have served as an hors d'oeuvre for an 8-course meal served hot in Tehran. Trust me on that!"

"I hear you, Mr. President. I still need some closure on the nature of the small boat's breakdown; the report I saw stated that the lieutenant in charge thought the required repairs were so minor that she questioned the need for outside assistance. Also, we're working on determining what type of explosives were on board, and most importantly—that they actually were explosives."

"You're not 100% sure on that?"

"No sir, we're not. One of Grayson Harvey's analysts at CIA, Anthony Darnell, former special forces Army 0-6, top-notch guy, and a friend of that Warren fellow, is working on a theory. He thinks that one of the three patrol boats, which we've identified as being excessively overloaded, *had* explosives while the other two only appeared that way—but each crew thought their boat was the designated suicide vessel."

The president, briefly distracted by the association between Anthony Darnell and Frank Warren, which might explain some things, responded, "Like a firing squad where there is one rifle without a live round, and no one knows who has that rifle."

"Exactly."

"About the repairs being minor—if not a mechanical problem, then why the white flag?"

"One theory, sir: they were considering asking for asylum—that they thought they had the explosives but didn't want to die, and they'd face, well, a rude reception if they returned to Bandar Abbas with their ordnance unexploded."

"Interesting. Maybe the B-52 overflight gave 'em a free pass when they returned to port. I guess there's still work to do there. Anything else?"

"Yes, sir. One more observation to discuss. You recall that *Nimitz*'s underway time was delayed because some delivery trucks went first to a Dubai loading area thinking the ship was anchored off the coast instead of being pierside in Jebel Ali. When they finally got to the ship, the dock workers and crane operators had departed the area to work another ship's offload. We're investigating the possibility that those events were part of a greater coordinated scheme intended to delay *Nimitz*'s transit through the Strait of Hormuz until nightfall, when their small boat tactics, including a suicide ramming of one (or more) of our ships, might have a better chance of succeeding. Not mentioned yesterday in the Sit Room was the fact that the ship's flight operations were initially planned to commence *after* transiting the Strait of Hormuz. With the delay in getting under way, the ship decided to get its flying in before the Strait transit. Then with the reactor issue, everything changed again; it may prove to have been fortuitous from our point of view. The decision to anchor the ship and then remain anchored probably added to Iran's confusion and uncertainty about the whole situation. The radio traffic and other communications we've been monitoring continue to give us some useful information, but so far, we can't confirm our suspicions. What is clear is the volume of traffic increased dramatically between Tehran and Bandar Abbas after the B-52 flyover. We'll be working on all of this and hopefully have more definitive data for your PDB tomorrow morning."

"Okay, Director, thank you for the update. By the way, did you happen to catch Darren Ballinger a few minutes ago on CNN?"

"Yes, sir, I saw that. He may have earned himself a new job as the face of the administration; he spoke quite well, I thought."

"Yeah, I thought so, too. He did well in front of the camera. Do you think he knows what BUFF usually stands for?"

"My guess is, what he heard in the Sit Room yesterday from Warren is all he knows. Someone will clue him in soon enough."

"I suppose so. He's a good man who has done a lot of decent work for me. I'll tell him—better he hears it from me. By the way, I think I got some good advice yesterday in the Sit Room—do you agree?"

"Yes, sir, I do. They speak up because they know you'll listen to them, and it's okay if you don't agree with them. You've created a productive atmosphere, Mr. President, and we all thank you for that."

The president replied, "Thank you. I value everyone's opinion, even those I disagree with. Well, we'll talk again. Good day."

Director Powers signed off, "Thank you, Mr. President."

The president of the United States returned the phone to its cradle and sat in his chair, reflecting on the events of the previous 24 hours.

33

While the President and Director Powers were watching Darren Ballinger on CNN, other high-ranking, formidable individuals were doing the same all around the globe. Statecraft, intelligence gathering, diplomatic and military maneuvering and readiness never stop, though their pace may change; the world never takes a day off. The CIA and the Departments of State and Defense do not close their doors to celebrate a holiday such as Dr. Martin Luther King, Jr.'s birthday or the 4th of July. Vigilance is a constant, never-ending need and requirement.

Thus, the fact that Iranian Supreme Leader Ayatollah Hamid Javad Ghorbani was meeting with his Supreme National Security Council, which included Marzban Mazdaki, Iran's president, while Darren Ballinger spoke of the previous day's events should not surprise anyone (Tehran tapes such events for their review and analysis). The topic of discussion, however, might.

Some countries and analysts viewed the Persian Gulf event as an isolated incident; others, including intelligence expert Anthony Darnell, saw Iran's actions through a different lens. Iran's supreme leader is the commander in chief of their armed forces; he controls all intelligence and security operations, he can appoint and dismiss leaders of the judiciary, and he controls the state radio and television networks. It was unlikely that the Iranian naval activities that occurred the previous day and were completed around noon were conducted without his knowledge and approval. Anthony Darnell and other analysts at Langley knew this. The CIA and the entire intelligence community, however, were unaware that the whole event had been planned for months—even before the *Nimitz* battle group had entered the Gulf. Ghorbani had grown weary of the U.S.'s continual ridicule and self-righteous, virtuous, hubristic blather, and was tiring of Mazdaki's personal aggrandizement and self-promotion.

In secret discussions with Ali Ahmadi and a life-long friend who Ghorbani personally appointed to the Supreme National Security Council, the three devised a plan designed to give the Great Satan a horrendous black eye and wrestle the world spotlight away from the infidels from the West (and also from Mazdaki) and place it squarely on the Islamic Republic of Iran.

Once *Nimitz* and her battle group became part of the Fifth Fleet it was hardly an intelligence gathering challenge to figure out their operating schedule. Deployed U.S. aircraft carriers generally make port visits to only Dubai, UAE while in the Persian Gulf. This includes Jebel Ali (where a carrier has the luxury of tying up pierside instead of anchoring off the coast), a straight-line distance of about 21 miles to the southwest of Dubai and around 27 driving miles away. The best source of data regarding port visit dates and other ship information were taxi drivers and port services people. Food suppliers, truck drivers, restaurant owners, hotel owners, and nightclub owners could supply additional information.

Even though battle group schedules and port visit dates are classified, "everyone" knows when U.S. ships are arriving and departing, particularly aircraft carriers (with thousands of men and women sailors aboard) and Iran planned their "exercise" accordingly. In fact, it was a trial run, a dress rehearsal, the results of which greatly pleased the Supreme Leader.

The timing of events could be regarded as fortuitous or calamitous, depending on one's viewpoint. First came the UAE's surprisingly strident comments at the Gulf Cooperation Council meeting regarding the disputed Persian Gulf islands, an unexpected, diversionary blessing that played perfectly into Iran's forthcoming operations. The delay of *Nimitz*'s underway time was accomplished flawlessly even though the truck drivers appeared to be the only people in the Middle East who didn't know where *Nimitz* was berthed. They knew, of course, but a bribe in the amount of a year's salary—in cash—can affect anyone's sense of direction. The coordination and join-up of the many Iranian small boats went reasonably well as did the loading of explosives onto *five* of them, three primary vessels and two backups. The crews were told the explosives were not real but rather were similar in size and weight to the actual material. In fact, they *were* real explosives. Arming wires, however, had been removed to prevent any accidental detonations. Only three people knew that fact: first, The Supreme Leader, who gave the order; second, the close associate he appointed to the Supreme National Security Council; and third, Ali Karim Ahmadi. (Note that President Marzban Mazdaki was not aware of that important detail.)

Ali Ahmadi was not quite the amorous fool that Michael and Shannon Wheeler made him out to be. In a note to his brother informing him of the missionaries' move to Bandar Abbas, Achmed had cautioned him of Shannon's alluring personality and inviting, flirtatious demeanor. From the get-go, Ali suspected the two Americans were CIA operatives, not religious missionaries, as they claimed. But he played the attentive, eager pursuer to Shannon's enticing mannerisms and kept his handler on Iran's

Supreme National Security Council informed of all that transpired, who in turn informed the Supreme Leader. The Wheelers, and the CIA, knew nothing of this arrangement. Nor did they ascertain from any of the photographs or overhead imagery they possessed that the team leader of the special loading and unloading unit, working the unique cargo carried on five of the small boats in Bandar Abbas, was none other than Ali Ahmadi.

While the U.S. was convinced the B-52 flyover and impressive waterworks display deterred the Iranians from further action and caused their return to port, in fact, the anchoring by *Nimitz* was the deciding factor. Once word was received the mighty vessel had dropped her hook, the Iranians, exercising a pre-briefed abort option, canceled the remainder of their plan and waited for daylight the next morning before commencing the short trek back to home port. And what of the crew of the wayward Iranian small boat who received assistance from Lt. Anderson and her crew? They told their superiors back in Bandar Abbas they wanted to get a closer look at one of the American warships and that they really did suffer some mechanical problems. The crew's (life?) saving moment: "luring" the Americans out to their broken-down vessel. That was enough to overcome the suspicions of their supervisors and spared the crew severe disciplinary measures for a suspected defection.

The other errant boat, led by two radicalized believers, was intent on ramming a U.S. warship, the *Milius*, in an act of martyrdom or suicide, depending on one's interpretation. Had they successfully penetrated the barrage of bullets from the CIWS and actually struck the *Milius*, Farzin Hassan and Armen Kasem probably would have survived (and failed, in their minds), since the explosive material in their boat was not armed. In yet another intelligence shortfall, Iran's chain of authority had no knowledge of either boat's intentions. The B-52's two wayward bombs played a significant role in how the wall of water event concluded, but no one, with the possible exception of two Iranian sailors, would ever know. For the CIA and other nations observing these activities, a vast difference existed between their interpretation of the events and what was fact. However, the CIA director's hunch about the Iranian small boat crew's pursuit for asylum was spot on, though he had no data to confirm his thoughts, only his intuition. One can picture Major General Clausewitz in the background, observing the entire two-day event, head nodding, as his 175-year old "fog of war" adage proved itself again.

Similarly, Frank Warren's troublesome stomach discomfort caused by visceral thoughts about Denise Emerson's improbable lifestyle was equally on target, despite a lack of concrete confirming information. Denisha Emerson was born Naghmeh Mitra Zargari. On her seventh birthday, July 3, 1988, Naghmeh, at home under the care of neighbors, became an orphan when her parents, returning home to Dubai from Bandar Abbas after visiting relatives of her father, lost their lives. Two surface-to-air missiles, launched from a United States warship commanded by some crazed, trigger-happy killer (her words) blew their Iranian airliner out of the sky. A case of mistaken identity, she was told. Since that day, Naghmeh Zargari, later renamed Denisha Emerson by her mother's sister who raised her in the United States, harbored unbridled enmity and contempt toward the country that killed her parents. Motivated by animosity and spitefulness, she graduated from Howard University in Washington, D.C. with a diploma, a plan, and a goal: working for the government (and specifically the defense department) of the country she despised and detested: the United States. As payback for the misdeeds of the nation where she currently held citizenship, Denise Emerson served as an unrecruited spy for the Islamic Republic of Iran. Her work area contained a sea of classified information, and she mingled, professionally and socially, with unsuspecting sources (male and female) who were fountains of data, much of it useful, if not explicitly classified. She gave all information—copies of documents, summaries of conversations—to her aunt who sent it on a convoluted path for further dissemination, some of it ultimately arriving in Tehran. Denise received compensation for her efforts from Iranian intelligence officials which afforded her a lifestyle not supported by her GS-9 salary. She sought payback, retribution, and revenge—for a lifelong, unnecessary, unrepayable debt, and one for which an apology had never been issued.

In Tehran, during the dynamic debate among Iran's Security Council members, three questions remained unanswered:

1. Why did *Nimitz* anchor?
2. How did it launch aircraft while anchored?
3. Who was the female officer on the U.S. motor whaleboat?

The last question dumbfounded the Shiite elites and brought smiles of curiosity and introspection to their faces—and possibly (though they would never let on) a degree of intrigue and admiration. They carefully examined photographs of the young woman, taken by

Iranian sailors, pausing to "inspect" the details of each picture. Outwardly, however, they maintained the appropriate façade, agreeing she would have died like the rest of the infidels had their plan been executed.

Quite a Saturday—and Sunday—for the bullies of the Middle East. Next time, they agreed, there'd be arming wires ...

Acknowledgements

My editor, Lynn Tosello, provided expert guidance and an experienced hand in reviewing my manuscript. I owe her a deep debt of gratitude for her many suggestions and recommendations. Expert illustrator Steve Ferchaud crafted a working drawing which ultimately led to the final cover design. Both were supportive and encouraging during the preparation of this book and are members of the North State Writers branch of the California Writers Club.

Endnotes

Prologue

[1] The Supreme Council for National Security (SCNS) is Iran's highest national security body. Five of the nine members, including the top official, the Secretary, are appointed by Iran's Supreme Leader. Ayatollah Ali Khamenei, Iran's current Supreme Leader, also has a representative from his office as one of the nine members. Other members typically include the President of Iran, the Speaker of Parliament (*Majles*), the Chief of the Judiciary, the Chief of the Armed Forces General Staff (similar to our chairman of the Joint Chiefs of Staff), and ministers of Foreign Affairs, Interior, and Intelligence. Katzman, Kenneth. "Iran: Politics, Human Rights, and U.S. Policy." crs.com. http://www.crs.gov (assessed December 4, 2017).

[2] Assembly of Experts. An 88-seat elected institution similar to a standing electoral college. Chooses the Supreme Leader and has the power to remove him. Oversees the work of the Supreme Leader and can amend the constitution. Usually meets twice a year. Elections to the Assembly are held every 8-10 years. The selection of a new Supreme Leader customarily happens upon the death of the incumbent. Removal of the incumbent would normally be associated with a health crisis. There have been only two Supreme Leaders since the Revolution in November 1979: Ayatollahs Khomeini (1979-1989) and Khamenei (1989-present). Katzman, Kenneth. "Iran:

Politics, Human Rights, and U.S. Policy." crs.com. http://www.crs.gov (assessed December 4, 2017).

[3] Hostage rescue attempt, code named "Eagle Claw." The complicated two-day operation, April 24-25, 1980, to rescue the hostages being held at the American Embassy in Tehran left little room for errors or unforeseen circumstances. Led by Army Colonel Charles Beckwith, the plan called for a nighttime rendezvous of helicopters and airplanes at a landing area in the desert south of Tehran, named Desert One. There, the helos were scheduled to refuel before carrying the raiding party to hiding places just outside Tehran, arriving before dawn. The force would then spend the ensuing day in hiding, awaiting nightfall before assaulting the embassy compound on the second night, gathering the hostages and taking them to a nearby soccer stadium from which the helicopters would airlift them to a seized airstrip outside the city, where C-130 transport planes would fly them to safety and freedom. Eight RH-53D Sea Stallion helicopters launched from the USS *Nimitz* (CVN-68), cruising in the Arabian Sea, and six C-130 Hercules transport planes, with the approximately 130-man assault team embarked, departed from Masirah, an island off the coast of Oman. Enroute to Desert One a RH-53 suffered a rotor failure, landed, and was abandoned in the desert. Another helicopter incurred an electrical failure and returned to *Nimitz*. Several C-130s and helos encountered fine desert sand, called a *haboob*, while enroute to Desert One. The dust caused engines and compartments to overheat. The six remaining helos (the minimum required to execute the mission) and all six C-130s arrived at Desert One. To guard against mechanical

failures, the helicopters and C-130s kept their engines running, causing intense dust and sand storms, limited visibility, and impairing interpersonal communications. Despite the remoteness of the rendezvous location, two Iranian vehicles approached the area. The first one was a fuel truck with a pickup truck attached to it. A rescue team member fired a 66mm rocket into it, causing a huge explosion which illuminated the area. Then during helo refueling operations from gas stored in bladders onboard the C-130s, a bus carrying Iranian civilians approached on a road that ran through the rendezvous area. Rescue team members disabled the bus and detained the Iranians. Shortly thereafter, a helicopter crew reported their helo suffered a hydraulic failure and their aircraft was now unusable. All helicopter spare parts had been loaded on the helo that returned to *Nimitz*. Now with only five flyable helicopters, Colonel Beckwith aborted the mission. In preparation for departure from Desert One, the rotor blades of a repositioning RH-53, airborne at about 15 feet of altitude, clipped the top of a parked C-130. Both aircraft exploded, and the resulting inferno killed eight men and seriously wounded five others. The remaining assault force and wounded men departed on the five flyable C-130s. Left behind were eight deceased American servicemembers, a cache of secret documents, five intact helicopters, and much of America's military reputation. Many agreed that also consumed in the burning rubble was any chance of a second term for President Jimmy Carter. Glass, Andrew. "Iran rescue mission ends in debacle, April 24, 1980." Politico.com. http://www.politico.com/story/2017/04/23/iranian-rescue-mission-ends-in-debacle-april-24-1980-237422 (assessed March 8, 2018). History. "Hostage rescue mission ends in disaster." history.com. http://www.history.com/this-day-in-history/hostage-rescue-mission-ends-in-disaster (assessed March 8, 2018). Bowden, Mark. "The Desert One Debacle." theatlantic.com. http://www.theatlantic.com/magazine/archive/2006/05/the-desert-one-debacle/304803 (assessed March 8, 2018). Koehl, Stuart L. and Stephen P. Glick. "Why the Rescue Failed." spectator.org. http://spectator.org/34807_why-rescue-failed/ (assessed March 8, 2018).

[4] President George W. Bush signed the Fair Treatment for Experienced Pilots Act (Public Law 110-135) on December 13, 2007, raising the mandatory retirement age to 65 for pilots operating under part 121 (Delta, United, Southwest, FedEx, etc.) of the Federal Aviation Regulations.

Chapter 1

[5] Prior to 2005, the PDB was the responsibility of the CIA. Coll, Steve. *Directorate S: The C.I.A. and America's Secret Wars in Afghanistan and Pakistan.* New York: Penguin Press, 2018, p. 245. See also note 15.

Chapter 2

[6] A sixth line, Silver, opened in July 2014 and should be fully operational by 2020.

Chapter 4

[7] That number increased to 117 in 2016, to 125 in 2017, and to 129 in 2018.

Chapter 6

[8] NOBLE PROPHET, sometimes called Great Prophet; Iranian military exercises or demonstrations, started in 2006 and usually held annually, that often involve missile launches, naval swarm maneuvers, and tests of new weapons. The normally heavily publicized exercises are conducted by the Islamic Revolutionary Guard Corps (IRGC) ground and naval forces, separate from Iran's national armed forces, known as Artesh. The 2015 exercises included missile firings at an Iranian-built full-scale metal mockup of a *Nimitz* class nuclear aircraft carrier. Nadimi, Farzin. "Iran Keeps a Lid on Its 'Great Prophet' Exercise." washingtoninstitute.org. http://www.washingtoninstitute.org/policy-analysis/view/iran-keeps-a-lid-on-its-latest-great-prophet-exercise (assessed December 18, 2017).

[9] The Nuclear Regulatory Commission defines a "scram" as the sudden shutting down of a nuclear reactor usually by rapid insertion of neutron absorbing control rods into the reactor core, either automatically or manually. In 1942, Enrico Fermi supposedly coined the phrase Safety Control Rod Axe Man, describing the person who would cut the safety rope, allowing the control rods to drop into the core. The term has also been attributed to Volney "Bill" Wilson, who called the safety rods "scram rods." After they are

released, claimed Wilson, "you scram out of here." U.S. Nuclear Regulatory Commission. "Putting the Axe to the 'Scram' Myth." Nrc-gateway.gov. http://public-blog.nrc-gateway.gov/2011/05/17/putting-the-axe-to-the-scram-myth/ (assessed October 7, 2017).

Chapter 7

[10] Inmarsat was established in 1979 by the International Maritime Organization. It is a mobile satellite communications system originally designed to enable ships to stay in contact with shore establishments in case of an emergency. A fleet of 13 satellites allows worldwide communications for aircraft and ship users. Headquartered in London; there are six regional offices located in the United States, one on Connecticut Avenue, NW in Washington, D.C.

[11] In 2013, the school's name changed to The Dwight D. Eisenhower School for National Security and Resource Strategy.

[12] Navy selection boards meet annually to select officers for promotion to the next higher rank and for positions of command. The list of selectees is published navy-wide. All promotions to the next higher pay grade are for the following fiscal year. The captain selection board meets each January. The most senior 0-6 selectees will promote and start receiving captain pay as of October 1 of that year, the start of the new fiscal year. Each subsequent month, more 0-6 selectees promote and start receiving their new pay. This continues into the next year, even after the 0-6

selection board meets again in January. Thus, a new list of 0-6 picks (and other paygrades) comes out each year before selectees from the previous year's list are promoted to their new rank and receive their new pay.

Chapter 8

[13] GMT, also called Zulu or UTC, is never adjusted backward or forward. GMT is also known as the Prime Meridian, 0 degrees of longitude. It runs, like all lines of longitude, from the North Pole to the South Pole, at a right angle to the equator. This particular line passes through Greenwich, England. Washington, D.C. is in the U.S.'s eastern time zone and, in January, is five hours behind Zulu or GMT, or GMT-5 (during daylight savings time it's GMT-4). Dubai, United Arab Emirates, is four hours ahead of GMT, or GMT+4. 1300 (1:00 pm) in DC equals 2200 (10:00 pm) in Dubai; they are nine hours apart. The two local times reference Zulu time, 1800Z. Some countries adopt time practices which may seem unusual. China, despite its immense size, has only one time zone: GMT+8. Iran chooses GMT+3:30. 0700 local time in Dubai equates to 0630 in Bandar Abbas, Iran, roughly 150 miles north northeast from Dubai, similar to Cleveland's direction from Columbus, Ohio. India has one time zone, too: GMT+5:30. In addition to Iran and India, Sri Lanka, Afghanistan, Myanmar, Newfoundland, the Marquesas Islands (located in French Polynesia), Venezuela, and areas of Australia, all use 30-minute offsets. One town in Australia—Eucla—uses GMT+8:45. Nepal is 15 minutes different from India

(GMT+5:45). Finally, the Chatham Islands in New Zealand also use a :45 offset (GMT+12:45).

[14] A ninth unified combatant command, U.S. Africa Command (AfriCom), headquartered in Stuttgart, Germany, became operational on October 1, 2007. The tenth unified combatant command, U.S. Cyber Command (USCyberCom), headquartered at Fort Meade, Maryland, became operational May 4, 2018.

A unified combatant command is a United States Department of Defense command that is composed of forces from at least two military departments and has a broad and continuing mission. Currently there are ten unified combatant commands (CCMDs)—four functional and six geographic. Functional CCMDs operate world-wide across geographic boundaries and provide unique capabilities to geographic CCMDs and the armed services, while geographic CCMDs operate in clearly delineated areas of operation and have a regional military focus.

In 2002, Secretary of Defense Donald H. Rumsfeld banished the acronym "CINC" (commander in chief). Previously, the commander of the pacific fleet was called, "Commander in Chief, Pacific Fleet," or CincPacFlt. The commander of the Central Command was called "CincCent." Mr. Rumsfeld stated there was (and remains) only *one* commander in chief, the president of the United States. "Combatant commanders" replaced the term "CINC." The ten Unified Combatant Commands:

Geographic Commands (6):

Command	Acronym	Headquarters
U.S. Africa Command	USAfriCom	Kelley Barracks, Stuttgart, Germany
U.S. Central Command	USCentCom	MacDill Air Force Base, Tampa, Florida
U.S. European Command	USEuCom	Patch Barracks, Stuttgart, Germany
U.S. Northern Command	USNorthCom	Peterson AFB, Colorado Springs, Colorado
U.S. Indo-Pacific Command	USIndoPaCom	Camp H. M. Smith, Hawaii
U.S. Southern Command	USSouthCom	Doral (Miami), Florida

Functional Commands (4):

Command	Acronym	Headquarters
U.S. Special Operations Command	USSoCom	MacDill AFB, Tampa, FL
U.S. Strategic Command	USStratCom	Offutt AFB, Omaha, Nebraska
U.S. Transportation Command	USTransCom	Scott AFB, Illinois
U.S. Cyber Command	USCyberCom	Fort Meade, Maryland

[15] From 1946 to 2005, the Director of Central Intelligence was the head of the CIA and served as the principal intelligence advisor to the president of the United States and the National Security Council. Additionally, the DCI was the coordinator of intelligence activities among and

between the various U.S. intel agencies, collectively known as the intelligence community. In December 2004, Congress passed the Intelligence Reform and Terrorism Prevention Act; President Bush signed the act on December 17. The act reorganized the U.S. intelligence apparatus by abolishing the positions of Director of Central Intelligence (DCI) and Deputy Director of Central Intelligence (DDCI) and creating the position of Director of the Central Intelligence Agency (D/CIA). The act also established the position of Director of National Intelligence (DNI), who became the head of the intelligence community. In this narrative the term DCI refers to the director of the CIA.

Chapter 9

[16] 220 marines, 18 navy sailors, and 3 army soldiers.

[17] The coordinated 90-minute attacks targeted the American and French embassies, the Kuwait City airport, a Kuwaiti National Petroleum Company oil rig, the grounds of the Raytheon Corporation, and a Kuwaiti-owned power station. An attack outside a post office was stopped. At the American Embassy, a truck laden with 45 large cylinders of gas connected to plastic explosives broke through the front gates and rammed into the embassy's three-story administrative annex, demolishing half of the structure. Five people were killed: two Palestinians, two Kuwaitis, and one Syrian. Many lives were saved when the driver missed the more heavily populated chancellery building and only a quarter of the explosives ignited. An hour later, a car parked outside the French embassy exploded, leaving

a massive 30-foot hole in the embassy security wall. No one was killed, and five people were injured. At the Kuwaiti main oil refinery and water desalinization plant (Shuaiba Petrochemical Plant), 150 gas cylinders on a truck carrying 200 cylinders exploded 150 meters (492 feet) from the number 2 refinery and just feet from a pile of highly flammable sulfa-based chemicals. The perpetrators missed Kuwait's primary water desalinization plant, located within the premises, the destruction of which would have left Kuwaitis nearly devoid of fresh water. Other car bombs exploded at the base of the Kuwait International Airport (one Egyptian technician killed), the Electricity Control Center, and the living quarters for American employees of the Raytheon Corporation, which was installing a missile system in Kuwait. Americans suffered injuries, but no deaths, in the December 12, 1983 Kuwait bombings.

The Islamic Jihad Organization and the Islamic   Da'wa Party, consisting of senior Hezbollah operatives and their Iraqi compatriots, were responsible for the attacks. Following an investigation and a six-week trial, 21 defendants—17 that were captured and 4 tried in absentia—were convicted in March 1984, with 6 terrorists receiving the death penalty (3 in absentia); 7 were sentenced to life in prison; the remainder were sentenced to terms of 5 to 15 years in prison. The jailed convicted terrorists became known as the "Kuwait 17" (also known as the "Al Dawa 17"). The terrorists sentenced to death were to be hanged within 30 days, but the Emir of Kuwait never signed their death warrants.

When Iraq invaded Kuwait in 1990, the Iraqis released scores of inmates from Kuwaiti jails, unwittingly including the members of the Kuwait 17. (See note 32.)

In February 2007, the *New York Times* reported that Jamal Jafaar Mohammed Ali Ebrahimi, one of the three defendants convicted in absentia and sentenced to death, was later elected to Iraq's Parliament in 2005. The article, dated February 7, 2007, reported that Mr. Jamal had recently left Iraq and was reported to be in Iran. Lanz, James G. and Marc Santora. "Iraqi Lawmaker Was Convicted in 1983 Bombings in Kuwait That Killed 5." nytimes.com. http://www.nytimes.com/2007/02/07/world/middleeast/07/bomber.html (assessed August 13, 2018). Public Broadcasting Company. "Terrorist Attacks on Americans, 1979-1988." pbs.org. http://www.pbs.org/wgbh/pages/frontline/shows/target/etc/cron.html (assessed August 13, 2018). Levitt, Matthew. "29 Years Later, Echoes of 'Kuwait 17'." weeklystandard.com. http://www.weeklystandard.com/matthew-levitt/29-years-later-echos-of-kuwait-17 (assessed August 13, 2018).

[18] In 1996, expressing "deep regret" but no apology, the United States paid the Iranian government $131.8 million in compensation, of which $61.8 million went to the victims' families. Iran, in exchange, dropped its lawsuit against the United States in the International Court of Justice. It was an international out-of-court settlement, on a tragic scale. The agreed upon value of an Iranian life?

$300,000 per wage-earner, $150,000 per non-wage-earner. Reportedly, some years later the U.S. arranged to replace the Airbus A-300 with a used aircraft.

[19] Crowley, Michael. "Four Good Reasons Why Iran Doesn't Trust America." time.com. http://swampland.time.com/2013/10/15/four-good-reasons-why-iran-doesnt-trust-america/ (assessed October 23, 2016).

Chapter 10

[20] On October 12, 2000, the USS *Cole* (DDG-67), a guided missile destroyer refueling in the Port of Aden, Yemen, was attacked by two Al-Qaeda-operated small boats which were laden with explosives. One of the suicide terrorists, in a 15-foot-long skiff packed with several hundred pounds of explosive material, rammed the *Cole* mid-ships with the resulting explosion ripping a 35x36 foot hole in the ship's port side, killing 17 sailors and injuring 39 others.

[21] RC-135 V/W Rivet Joint reconnaissance aircraft—support theater and national level operations with near-real-time on-scene intelligence collection, analysis, and dissemination capabilities. Its mission is to detect, locate, record, identify, analyze, and geolocate signals throughout the electromagnetic spectrum and forward this data in a variety of formats to a wide range of consumers. The aircraft is an extensively modified Boeing C-135. The interior seats more than 30 people, including the cockpit crew, electronic warfare officers, intelligence operators

and in-flight maintenance technicians. Various versions of the RC-135 have been in service since 1961. (www.af.mil)

E-8C JSTARS – Joint Surveillance and Target Attack Radar System aircraft, a joint development project of the U.S. Air Force and Army. The system provides an airborne, stand-off range, surveillance, and target acquisition radar and command and control center. The airframe is a modified Boeing 707-300 series with a standard crew of 21 and up to 34 for long endurance missions. Based out of Robbins AFB in Georgia, JSTARS provides ground situation information equivalent to that of the air situation provided by AWACS. JSTARS can determine the direction, speed and pattern of ground vehicles and helicopters. (www.airforce-technology.com)

[22] AWACS – Airborne Warning and Control System. AWACS provides situational awareness of friendly, neutral and hostile activity, command and control of an area of responsibility, battle management of theater forces, all altitude and all-weather surveillance of the battle space, and early warning of enemy action during joint, allied and coalition operations. The Air Force utilizes the E-3 Sentry, a modified Boeing 707/320 commercial airframe. The Sentry is equipped with integrated command and control battle management (C2BM), surveillance, target detection, and tracking capabilities. The aircraft provides an accurate, real-time picture of the battlespace to the Joint Operations Center. The U.S. inventory totals 31 aircraft, 27 of which are based at Tinker AFB in Oklahoma City, OK. Four E-3s are located at Kadena Air Base, Japan and Elmendorf AFB, Alaska. The crew is composed of a flight

crew of four plus a mission crew of between 13-19 specialists. (www.af.mil)

The Northrop Grumman E-2C Hawkeye serves as the Navy's aircraft carrier-based AWACS. The all-weather aircraft is designed to give long-range warning of approaching aerial threats and provides threat identification, strike command and control, land and maritime surveillance, search and rescue assistance and can serve as a communications relay. Its 24-foot diameter circular antenna houses the Lockheed Martin AN/APS-145 radar which can track more than 2,000 targets and control the interception of 40 hostile targets. The crew of five consists of a pilot, co-pilot, combat information center officer, air control officer, and a radar operator. (www.defenseindustrydaily.com and www.naval-technology.com)

[23] The RQ-4 Global Hawk is an unmanned aerial vehicle (UAV). In operation with the U.S. Air Force since 2001, it is a high-altitude, long-endurance, remotely piloted aircraft with an integrated sensor suite that provides global all-weather, day or night, intelligence, surveillance, and reconnaissance (ISR) capability. Global Hawk is operated remotely by a three-person crew: a Launch and Recovery Element (LRE); a Mission Control Element (MCE); and a sensor operator. Global Hawk has a range of over 12,000 miles, endurance exceeding 30 hours, and an altitude ceiling greater than 60,000 feet. Its wingspan is nearly 131 feet. (www.northropgrumman.com and www.af.mil)

Chapter 12

[24] "Black sites" are secret CIA prisons located   overseas (Thailand, eastern Europe, Afghanistan, Romania, Poland and others) spanning eight countries, where high-level terrorist suspects are detained and interrogated. Some detainees, it has been reported, have been subjected to so-called "enhanced interrogation techniques" such as waterboarding, slaps, sleep deprivation, nudity, constant loud music, electric shocks, beatings, and wallings (slamming detainees against a wall). The debate surrounding the effectiveness, legality, and morality of harsh interrogation practices continues.

Chapter 14

[25] Countries with the largest proven oil reserves— "those quantities that geological and engineering information indicate with reasonable certainty can be recovered in the future from known reservoirs under existing economic and political conditions and using existing technology."

2007 – billion barrels	2013 – billion barrels
1. Saudi Arabia 264.7	1. Venezuela 300.0
2. Canada 178.6	2. Saudi Arabia 269.0
3. Iran 138.4	3. Canada 171.0
4. Iraq 115.0	4. Iran 157.8
5. Kuwait 104.0	5. Iraq 143.0
6. UAE 97.0	6. Kuwait 104.0
7. Venezuela 87.0	7. UAE 98.0
8. Russia 60.0	8. Russia 80.0
9. Libya 41.4	9. Libya 48.3

10. Nigeria 36.2	10. Nigeria 37.0
11. Kazakhstan 30.0	11. U.S. 36.5
12. U.S. 20.9	12. Kazakhstan 30.0
13. Qatar 15.2	13. Qatar 25.0
14. China 16.0	14. China 24.0

The 2007 data was reported in a 2007 Annual Report from the Energy Information Administration, Office of Oil and Gas, U.S. Department of Energy (DOE/EIA-0216 (2007)). The 2013 data is from www.ceoworld.biz, May 14, 2017. The EIA reports data obtained from other sources (*Oil and Gas Journal* and *World Oil*) and does not certify the international reserves information. The above numbers should be considered estimates. The 2007 data is from the *Oil and Gas Journal*, which differs slightly from data provided by *World Oil*, both of which were listed in the EIA report.

The above illustrates the significant concentration of oil reserves in OPEC nations (approximately 80% of the world's proven reserves) and the resulting strategic importance of the Strait of Hormuz, through which much of the world's oil traverses.

[26] Office of Naval Intelligence. "Iran's Naval Forces from Guerilla Warfare to a Modern Naval Strategy." oni.navy.mil. http://www.oni.navy.mil/Intelligence-Community/Iran Fall, 2009 (assessed August 17,2017).

[27] The State Department is the only federal cabinet-level agency with two co-equal deputy secretaries.

[28] In 2009, the headquarters was relocated to Al Udeid Air Base in Qatar.

[29] Four members of the West Point class of 1974 achieved four-star rank. General Martin E. Dempsey served as deputy commander, U.S. Central Command and briefly became its acting commander before being selected as the Chief of Staff of the U.S. Army. He then became the 18th Chairman of the Joint Chiefs of Staff from October 1, 2011 until September 25, 2015. General David H. Patraeus graduated in the top 5% of his class and, like General Dempsey (and any four-star officer), commanded numerous organizations during his career, including command of CentCom from October 31, 2008 to July 4, 2010. He later served as director of the CIA from September 6, 2011 – November 9, 2012. General Walter L. Sharp was the director of the Joint Staff from 2005 to June 2008 and then served as the Commander, United Nations Command; Commander, Republic of Korea-U.S. Combined Forces Command and Commander, U.S. Forces Korea from June 2008 to July 2011. General Keith B. Alexander held numerous positions within the intelligence community throughout his career and, in August 2005, became the 16th Director of the National Security Agency (NSA). Concurrently he became the initial Commander of the United States Cyber Command in May 2010 when that command was established. Fictitious characters General Karl W. Alexander and Lieutenant General Walter V. Townsend are included in West Point's class of 1974 solely for dramatic effect.

Chapter 15

[30] Introduced to the fleet in the early 1970s, the S-3A Viking, with a crew of four (pilot, co-pilot, tactical coordinator, and sensor operator), was designed primarily for anti-submarine warfare. In the early 1980s the navy transitioned the S-3 to a single pilot aircraft with a naval flight officer (NFO) assuming the duties of the former co-pilot. Also, in the 1980s the aircraft was modified to become an inflight refueling tanker. From 1987-1994 improved weapons system upgrades were installed, resulting in the S-3B. In 1997, the S-3 community changed its name from Air Anti-Submarine Squadrons to Sea Control Squadrons. In 1999, the navy removed the submarine sensors from all S-3s due to budgetary constraints and the diminishing submarine threat associated with the end of the Cold War. The Vikings continued their other missions of airborne refueling, over-the-horizon targeting, surface search, and sea and ground attack. On May 1, 2003, an S-3B flown by VS-35 Blue Wolves Executive Officer Commander John "Skip" Lussier, with President George W. Bush seated to his right, landed on the USS *Abraham Lincoln* (CVN-72), the only time a sitting president has trapped aboard an aircraft carrier at sea. The last S-3B squadron deployment occurred in 2007 and the aircraft was officially retired from the fleet in January 2009.

Chapter 19

[31] Means "will comply"; used in civilian and military radio exchanges; the message or order was received, understood, and will be followed or complied with.

Chapter 21

[32] CincUSNavEur: Commander-in-Chief, U.S. Naval Forces, Europe. Changed to Deputy CincUSNavEur on January 1, 1983 when CincSouth, the Commander-in-Chief, Allied Forces Southern Europe, a U.S. Navy four-star NATO command located in Naples, Italy, was dual-hatted and assumed additional duties as CincUSNavEur. The Deputy Cinc staff remained based in London. Over the years, command realignments and designations have changed. In March 2004, CincSouth was deactivated upon the activation of NATO's Joint Forces Command (JFC). CincUSNavEur became Commander, U.S. Naval Forces, Europe (ComUSNavEur) and completed its relocation to Naples in August 2005. In September 2005 Naval Forces Europe and Commander, Sixth Fleet merged. U.S. Naval Activities, United Kingdom, deactivated in September 2007. Currently, a Navy four-star admiral based in Naples heads NATO's Joint Forces Command and also the Naval Forces Europe-Naval Forces Africa command.

Chapter 24

[33] Aircraft carriers are now equipped with an Integrated Catapult Control Station, or ICCS. This bubble-like device

protrudes up from the flight deck and houses the catapult officer and firing control mechanisms and indicators.

Chapter 25

[34] http://www.thereligionofpeace.com (assessed October 10, 2018). www.discover-the-truth.com (assessed October 15, 2018). Note: single verses quoted from the Quran (and the Bible) lack context and thus are subject to differing, sometimes conflicting, and occasionally contentious, interpretations.

Chapter 27

[35] The B-52 crew is composed of a pilot, co-pilot, radar navigator, navigator, and electronic warfare officer.

[36] Navy carrier air wings often conduct air power demonstrations during visits of foreign dignitaries and occasionally include the wall of water event for its overall impact. Sailors—and visitors—standing on the flight deck of 95,000-ton vessel some 60 feet above the water's surface, over a mile away from the detonations, see, hear and feel the impact of the exploding bombs and the resulting sensory invasion.

Chapter 28

[37] Von Clausewitz, Carl. *On War*. 1832. Prussian Major General von Clausewitz (June 1, 1780 - November 16, 1831), a highly regarded military theorist, died before he finished his seminal work. His wife published it posthumously in 1832. In it he described the lack of clarity

and certainty about an adversary's capabilities and intentions and the effect of unanticipated events as the "fog of war." A real-life example is the American hostage rescue attempt discussed in note 3. The end of note 17 contains two other examples.

[38] Central Intelligence Agency. "FLASHBACK: April 18, 1983. U.S. Embassy Attack in Beirut." cia.gov. http://www.cia.gov/new-information/featured-story-archive/2014-featured-story-archive/flashback-april-18-1983-u-s-embassy-bombed-in-beirut.html (assessed September 8, 2017).

[39] Imad Mugniyah, the head of Hezbollah's security service at the time, planned the 1983 suicide car bombings of the U.S. Embassy and the U.S. Marine Corps and French paratrooper barracks in Beirut. Lawrence Wright. *The Looming Tower: Al-Qaeda and the Road to 9/11."* (New York: Vintage Books, 2007), p. 197. History. "Beirut barracks blown up." history.com. http://www.history.com/this-day-in-history/beirut-barracks-blown-up (assessed September 8, 2017). Michaels, Jim. "Recalling the deadly 1983 attack on the Marine barracks." usatoday.com. http://www.usatoday.com/story/nation/2013/10/23/marines-beirut-lebanan-hezbollah/3171593/ (assessed September 8, 2017).

[40] Martyrdom offered an alternative to young men whose pursuits of life's rewards were limited or nonexistent. A glorious death awaited the martyr, who would enjoy the conjugal pleasures of virgins, the "dark-eyed houris" who

were "chaste as hidden pearls." Quran 78:33 and 55:72-74 are among numerous verses on martyrdom. Wright, *The Looming Tower*, p. 123. The Religion of Peace. "What Does Islam Teach About … Suicide Attacks (and Islamic Paradise)." thereligionofpeace.com. http://www.thereligionofpeace.com/pages/quran/suicide -bombing.aspx (assessed March 10, 2018). Bryner, Jeanna. "The Truth About Muslims in America." livescience.com. http://livescience.com/5157-truth-muslims-america.html (assessed March 10, 2018). Caschetta, A. J. "Does Islam Have a Role in Suicide Bombings?" meforum.org. http://www.meforum.org/articles/2015/does-islam-have-a-role-in-suicide-bombings (assessed March 10, 2018).

CPSIA information can be obtained
at www.ICGtesting.com
Printed in the USA
LVHW030152251121
704426LV00001B/106